An Hidden Secret In Love

Brooke Bugnion

Contents

Chapter 1

The ladle my mom had been holding drops suddenly into the pot of sauce. Silence fills the room with the sudden news.

"Daniel, what are you talking about?"

Dad walks into the room with a smile plastered on his face. He looks as if he just won the lottery.

"Jim brought me in his office today," He stars and places his bag down. "He wants me to oversee a new department in California. This would be a huge jump for my career, Susan."

"I understand..." Mom trails and sits down. "I just don't know how we will be able to sell this house so quickly before up and moving to a brand new home in California. That is such a big decision and we have no time to really decide."

I look back and forth between both of them as they converse. I can't believe there's chance I'll be spending the rest of my senior year in a brand new school. It feels wrong to not be excited for my him but this is all I've known.

For 17 years this has been my home.

All of my friends, school, college sco-

"Olivia?"

I look back up and lock eyes with my mothers blue ones. The same pair of ocean eyes I'm blessed enough to have too.

She's my calm. She's always had a way of keeping me grounded when things change.

"Sorry... I was just thinking. I'm excited for you dad, I guess it's just a lot to take in."

Dad nods in understanding and reaches out to hold my hand. "I know this has been a big year for you, bug. I want you to know we will still make sure you have a great senior year in San Diego and get you ready for college."

He's a good man. A great man.

He really does deserve the absolute best in life.

He's worked with a small business that provides different softwares for clients to help manage and grow their own businesses better.

Lately, he has been working a lot of overtime and staying late during the week to try and prove his worth. I've seen him in tears over this job and that isn't his normal.

"I know, dad. I love you and I'm proud of you." I smile warmly and he pats my hand.

"Alright!" Mom shouts suddenly and stands up, "Who is ready for some dinner?"

The three of us laugh together as she passes out the plates.

Just a normal chilly night in New York.

Stuffed on pasta and breadsticks.

Everything perfect. The same

I never would've expected what was to come.

◇ ◇ ◇

I step off the last step and take in a deep breath of crisp air. Clear, blue skies take me in along with the blistering sun overhead.

"Olivia!"

I turn back towards my mother and notice she's struggling to get our carry on's off the plane. A few people behind her audibly groan as she waves frantically at me.

Flying had been the quickest way for us to get here considering my father's new position was starting Monday. We were going to survive the weekend sleeping on the floor and eating take-out until the rest of our items showed up.

I apologize to the people standing behind my mom and grab the bags from her. "Let me help you."

"You're too good to me, Liv," She smiles brightly and adjusts her hat.

I have to admit it. California is beautiful.

The sun was hot and beaming down brightly on my bare shoulders as if millions of little kisses were brushing against the exposed skin. It certainly was no New York City.

I pull our bags up into my arms and loop my arm with mom as we rush to find my father who had already been obnoxiously taking pictures of the scenery.

The three of us eventually made it to the front of the airport where we waited for an uber to pick us up and drop us off at our new and final destination.

The drive felt as if I was living some surreal dream. Everyone on the streets seemed to blur together as we passed by but it all looked so different, so unique.

Girls in crop tops with golden tans and rollerbladers zooming down the sidewalks on skates with funky mo-hawks.

It was almost like watching a movie.

The thought of finishing high school here brought on so many emotions I didn't know how to handle it.

Soon enough our driver came to a stop as we stepped out of the car and grabbed our belongings.

We stood before our new beginning.

The house was a cute, multi-level family home that was soft white with a variety of vines and shrub seeming to crawl up the side of the house. It looked to be modern enough and was a lot bigger than the little apartment we had in New York.

"Welcome to our new home."

Dad sighs happily and motions for us to follow him up the stairs.

The home smells of fresh paint and our footsteps echo throughout its emptiness.

The split-level home went off in two directions from the entrance land-ing. Downstairs led to the basement and garage while the first set of stairs took us up to our new living space.

The smell of fresh paint was very noticeable and the carpet was free from stains. It was certainly cozy and thankfully not big enough for me to get lost in.

Dad finally speaks, "I know it won't be fun sleeping on the floor but we will make it through."

I walk up the stairs and start flipping on switches as I go from room to room.

"That's alright, dad."

I finally make my way into a spare bedroom at the back of the hallway and push it open. The same paint smell overwhelms me immediately and I rush over to yank the window back for some fresh air.

I peer around the neighborhood sidewalk for a moment until I realize there's a girl staring up at me with a big smile.

"Hello there!" The girl shouts and waves her hand at me.

"Hey!" I reply back awkwardly.

"Sorry to bother, I just saw you all moving in and wanted to see who you guys were. I live down the block," She explained and puller her phone out. Her long black hair hanging in loose curls around her tiny waist. "Where did you all move from?"

"We actually just arrived from New York."

She nods and taps away on her phone, popping gum between her teeth. "That's pretty cool. Why did you guys move?"

Wow, twenty questions already.

I stammer," U-uh...my dad actually accepted a new job."

"Well, I hope you like it here! My name is Kimberly," She smiles widely.

"I'm Olivia."

She holds her phone up. "Do you have a cellphone? I can text you?"

"I do."

Kimberly starts yelling her cellphone number to me as I struggle to type it in quick enough.

"Got it!" I say confidently.

"Cool! What school are you going to?"

"I think Westview."

She squeals in a high pitch voice. "Oh myyy gooodd! I go there too."

"No wayyyy!" I mimic back in the same fake tone.

"Well, let's walk together Monday morning! I have to run back home and finish up some stuff." Kimberly says and blows a kiss with her glossy lips before skipping back down the road.

I sigh and close my window before any other strangers decide to find interest in the new family moving down the street.

I sit on the floor of the empty bedroom and pull my phone out. I flip through photos silently and feel a tear start to swell up when I come across the video of my best friend, Amy, and me on my 17th birthday.

The two of us laughing together and cheering after she surprised me with my favorite cheesecake and ice cream at school. She's always been my rock and biggest supporter when it comes to my dreams of Art school.

I'm going to miss them so much, but I will do anything I can to get back to New York to start college off with my real friends.

But...for now, this is home.

San Diego

Chapter 2

The past couple of days had been spent with the three of us unpacking as much as we could as everything arrived from New York. The weekend had gone by way too fast and I was not looking forward to my first day.

"OLIVIA."

I can hear her voice clearly now as her footsteps echo across the hallway and my door flings open in a haste.

"I heard you. "I groan dramatically.

She huffs and grabs the boxes by my door. "I told you to break these down, Olivia."

"I know. I'm sorry."

I can tell that she's already been hard at work. Her messy, dark hair in a sloppy bun and clinging to beads of sweat on her forehead. The woman never stops until the job is done.

I watch from the corner of my eyes as she grabs a few more boxes and storms out of the room again.

I turn my attention to the only clean and matching clothes I can find at the moment and grab my cellphone from the nightstand.

4 new text messages.

I click the newest one and scroll down.

Goood mooorrrning! It's Kimberly. Are we still walking together?

Seems you are still asleep. :(Meet me at the school entrance? 7:30

You sleep a lot! I thought I slept too much.

Well, text me soon! <3

I can already tell she'll be a handful.

I finished up doing what I could to make myself look presentable and rush down the stairs to grab my bag and head out the front door.

The California sun is already beating down on me and I am not looking forward to my morning walk.

Thankfully, my dad had picked a house close to the school and even a cute shopping outlet just 10-15 minutes down the road walking. It didn't seem like it would be so bad but I knew it would take time to adjust.

After a while, I noticed a

Westview High

sign perched at the edge of a lawn and caught several buses turning into the school parking lot.

Several students rushed from the buses and piled inside as the first warning bell rang.

It didn't look so bad and honestly took me by surprise. The grass was a bright green and kept short. Several palm trees and shrubs littered the courtyard.

"Olivia!"

I glance up towards the familiar voice and see Kimberly waving me down.

She hurries over to me and I immediately catch the scent of floral perfume. Her dark hair is braided and she's wearing a very tight maxi dress that is tie-dyed bright colors.

"Wow! You're so pretty up close. Look at those eyes." Kimberly compliments and smiles at me.

"T-thank you," I stammer out. "So are you."

"What's your first class?"

I hand her my schedule for her to read over.

"Awesome, we have first hour English and Algebra together 7th hour."

I smile a bit at her, feeling relieved to know I'd at least have someone I knew in two of my classes.

The two of us hurry down the hallway together and I feel the nerves hit me like a wave. The students around us seem to just pile up by the minute. How the hell do people move around in halls like this?!

Kimberly grabs me by the elbow and steers the both of us towards the side of the hall. "Locker?"

"302"

She laughs, "You're so lucky."

"Why?"

"I'm 315 so I can take you right to it after this class."

I nod and take a deep breath before she leads us back into the crowd. Our first hour is a lot closer than I had expected but I was just relieved to get out of the mass of people trying to not be late.

"Miss?"

Shit. Of course.

I look up towards the voice speaking from the front of the room and find a plump, middle-aged woman standing there with a nameplate that reads "Mrs.Davidson." She has kind eyes and a soft smile fills her face.

"I'm sorry,"I apologize and glance at my feet. "I'm Olivia Moore."

"Welcome, Olivia! So glad to have you. Feel free to grab an empty seat."

I hurry over to the closest empty spot I can locate and try to keep my eyes away from all of the curious stares.

Mrs. Davidson jumps right into the previous day's lecture which gives me an out to focus on my sketches.

I decide to come up with a concept on how I'm feeling. A silhouette of a girl who is living between two worlds.

One is familiar. That world makes her happy and safe. Her friends are there and so are her dreams.

The second is new and terrifying. She feels alone and impatient for it to end. Each day is unpredictable and she's starting over at such a weird time in her life.

I watch my hand as I begin to trace out the image skillfully. Within minutes I can feel myself becoming wrapped up in the drawing before I feel a presence looming before me.

"Olivia?"

I look up to see Mrs. Davidson beaming down at me.

"We'd love to learn about you while we have a free moment. Do you mind introducing yourself to the class?"

I fight back the annoyance building up in my throat and stand up so I can face the others. Kimberly gives me a thumbs up for encouragement.

I glance around the room briefly to take in all of the new faces before I prepare my introduction. Lots of faces stare back at me but there is one that catches me off guard.

Who is that...

He's beautiful and I swear he has been sculpted by Michelangelo himself.

His skin is a beautiful olive tone and almost seems to have a glow to it. I can't help but notice the sharpness of his cheekbones and the curve of his sculpted jaw.

He's staring back at me in the most intense way. His nearly pitch-black eyes seem to be drilling into me. Trying to figure out who I am.

His black hair falls loosely in front of his eyes and bushy brows. I watch for a moment as he leans into his desk and sees the edges of his muscular arms straining against the plain tee he has on.

After what feels like an eternity, I finally come back to reality and tear my eyes away from the beautiful stranger.

"My name is Olivia Moore. I'm from New York, but we made the big move here recently since my dad accepted a new job."

The class mutters back some half-assed greeting before Mrs. Davidson thanks me for my introduction and allows me to sit back down. I glance back over my shoulder and notice the boy from before focused on carving something into his desk with a pencil.

He doesn't look back up which to that I'm grateful. I use the rest of the class to try and focus on my art before the next bell finally rings.

The rest of the school day felt no different from English. I would give some dumb introduction and then bury my head in whatever lecture was going on or my artwork.

When the 7th bell finally sounded, Kimberly was eager to drag me out of the room and right into the hallway.

"Want to meet some friends?" She asks me.

"Sure," I responded awkwardly.

She smiles reassuringly and starts waving down some people walking towards us.

"Austin! Sierra!"

I watch as the boy and girl push through the crowd and make their way up to the two of us.

The blonde boy smiles first, "I'm Austin. Nice to meet you, Olivia. Kim has said great things."

I shook his hand and grin back. He's super cute.

His hair is a golden blonde and in loose curls. He has a bit of a boyish appearance to him and the most gorgeous hazel eyes.

The girl next to him introduces herself as Sierra. She's super petite with a dark pixie cut and rainbow bands on her braces. Her voice comes out small and almost timid.

"It's so nice to meet you both!" I tell them and look up to catch a pair of familiar eyes watching me.

The boy from English class.

His long, tall body is leaning against a set of metal lockers and he has his arms crossed over his chest. An unlit cigarette hangs from in between his lips.

Kimberly catches my gaze and laughs.

"Alessio Romano."

"What?" I ask and look at her.

She rolls her eyes at me. "Alessio Romano. I see you undressing him with your eyes. He's gorgeous but from the rumors that fly around here, I wouldn't waste your time."

"What do you mean?"

Austin starts up," His family is known for being trouble. The Romano's are a really wealthy family and have a history of being dangerous."

I frown and look back towards Alessio again. He is still standing in the same spot but now conversing with a dark-haired girl and a man who looks like a moving brick wall he's so large.

I can't seem to pull myself away from his burning gaze. He watches me carefully as he pulls a lighter from his pocket and lights the cigarette right in the hallway.

Kimberly's voice chirps up and saves me from his pull.

"We should probably get going. My parents get cranky when I don't show up on time to help with my sister and I know you got a lot to do." She nudges me playfully.

"Of course." I grin at her and glance back to where Alessio was.

The spot against the metal locker now empty and lacking his presence along with the others with him.

I don't know his story, but a big part of me is eager to find out.

Chapter 3

F uck! I'm late.

Twenty missed calls already from Beto.

My cousin really knows how to drive me up a wall.

He has been living with us since both of his parents died some years back. I was grateful though to have him so close, especially knowing what a great asset he is to the family.

Though my dad taking him in certainly was not an act of kindness.

He's ruthless and a piece of shit. He only cares about himself.

He is your typical gangster. Mob boss. Don.

All of us were born into this life for a reason and we will die in this life. There will never be a chance at normal.

And once I graduate from school, I will have my shot.

I'll become boss. The don.

I have always wanted to the boss more than anything. I have spent years since the age of thirteen proving myself to this family.

"Ciao" (Translation: Hello)

"Where the fuck are you?" Beto snaps.

"Overslept."

"Well, I'm not waiting all day. I still have Anna and Giovanni with me."

I hang up and grab my cigarettes before heading out the door. I spot my step-siblings standing near the back of the Cadillac with Beto.

Giovanni and Anna are fraternal twins and both a couple of years older than me. They are the product of my father's second marriage.

Anna is a lot like her mother which really makes her a scary person.

Her mother had been known to be a very ruthless and mean woman. She was hateful and not one to fuck with.

She even made my dad scared, even as she died from her cancer.

Anna has always said she would walk in her mother's footsteps. So she decided to travel through Italy for a few years with an alley of ours.

She fell in love and is now engaged to marry a Fubini son by the name of Alonzo. Once they tie the knot, our families will unify together.

This will give us access to a percentage of their ports and profits. In turn, it will strengthen our control of Sicily.

Now aside from Anna's terror, our brother Giovanni is a monster. He stands roughly at six feet and is about 260 pounds of pure muscle.

He is one of my best friends and I rely on him for many things. Especially, his muscle and lack of emotion when it comes to killing others.

Once the time comes, he'll be my second in command.

I walk up to the three of them and we all start to climb into the car together. Looking back at the manor, I can feel the dread build knowing I have months left of my senior year when I could be here fulfilling duties.

We live in one of the wealthiest places up in the hills of California. Our mansion is large enough to provide sanctuary for our family, including several guards and housekeepers.

We top the current 1% of billionaires in the state.

"Took you long enough!" Beto glares and takes my cigarette.

I hand him a lighter. "Get over it."

Out of all of us, Beto is the smallest and youngest.

His signature Oakley sunglasses pushed onto his head to keep his dark hair back. Even with him being the baby of the family, Beto is known for his mind.

He can get us out of any situation and is an absolute mastermind when it comes to technology.

The car pulls away from the driveway and onto the side road. We make our way into the city and to Westview High.

First-period English sucks. Mrs. Davidson sucks. The entire school sucks.

I slump back into my seat at the back of the room and let my fingertips play with the edge of my switchblade.

I hate high school and loathe my father even more for making it a condition of my leadership.

He didn't have a normal teenage life so he expected Beto and me to be the ones to fulfill that weird fantasy for him since Giovanni and Anna both were homeschooled up until eighteen.

At the age of 17, my dad had his first marriage to a girl from Italy for a few years. It didn't work out at all and actually ended with her death for the betrayal of the family.

He met Giovanni and Anna's mother shortly after and they married within three months of knowing each other. She was the daughter of another family in Italy and her mean spirit was a huge turn-on for him apparently.

My dad though is not a loyal man when it comes to women and while she was battling cancer he was starting a new relationship with my mother.

She was his last wife and according to the stories, he did love her more than anything.

I don't remember my mother but I do keep pictures of her with me. She was beautiful and had the same black hair and brown eyes.

I was just four years old when she was murdered in the middle of the night. My dad had been away handling business and was on his way home when it happened.

That night has haunted me for years.

I could hear her screaming down the hallway when she was killed and the whole house erupted into chaos. Nobody understood how anyone got to her.

My uncle, Michele, had drug me back into my room and locked the door.

I had screamed for her over and over again. Hours felt so long that night.

"We'd love to learn a little more about our new friend. Would you mind sharing?" Mrs. Davidson's voice rings out in the room, pulling me from my mind.

I glance up and spot a girl I haven't seen before.

She has thick, chocolate brown hair that tumbles down to the edge of her waist. Her hand stops moving across a sketchbook and she looks up.

She seems to be struggling with the thought of having to introduce herself. I don't blame her though.

It is such a corny and silly part of starting a new school.

She stands and turns around to face the class. I feel my breath catch in my throat as she locks her eyes with me.

She's beautiful.

Her chocolate hair seems to frame her angelic, soft features and highlights the most stunning part about her.

Ocean blue eyes pop against the contrast of her dark hair and fair skin.

She seems so innocent. Fragile.

She starts to speak, "My name is Olivia Moore. I'm from New York, but we made the big move here recently since my dad accepted a new job."

I watch her lips as she parts them with each word.

Full and pink. Pearly white teeth and a bit of sparkle as the light hits them.

Her blue eyes land on me again and my chest tightens from her intense gaze.

I feel myself lean into the desk as I study her again and again. I want to know her.

I need to know her.

Snap out of it! Stop it!

I shake my head again and try to pull myself away from her hypnotization. I pulled out a pencil from the bag at my feet and went to work on my own artwork on the desktop.

Praying the time passed by quickly.

◇ ◇ ◇

The last bell rings and I hurry out into the crowded halls.

Students are rushing around trying their hardest to get out of the school as quickly as they can.

"Watch it fucker."

I stop and turn to find the biggest asshole of Westview High.

Beloved quarterback, Nelson Tucker, is your typical "my dad is rich" driving around in his sports car and spending too much on his drugs. Despite how much I hate this kid I do love selling him marijuana at an outrageous price.

He curls his lip into a snarl and pushes his glasses back on his head.

"I'd watch yourself, Nelson." I laugh darkly.

He looks back at his football buddies and tries to take another step forward towards me.

"Stay out of my way or I won't help fund your shitty ass cigarettes anymore. Everyone knows you are only good for your drugs, bitch." He smacks the pack of cigarettes from my hand and they hit the floor.

I feel my body tense immediately and without thinking I pull him by the collar. My free hand edges my shirt up to expose my gun.

"Leave now. "I spit out and he catches the weapon at my waistband.

He takes a few steps back from me and flips me off before heading off with his little football gang.

I snatch my cigarettes from the ground and shove them back in my pocket just as Beto walks up.

"What was that all about?" He asks me.

"Just some punk bitch shit. Don't worry about it."

Beto laughs and we both look over as Giovanni and Anna make their daily entrance into the school.

Several students seem to back up against the lockers in fear as Giovanni passes them. The scary, mysterious Giovanni Romano always had a way to make men piss themselves and women swoon over his bad boy look.

Anna is hot on his trail and seems to be yelling at someone on her phone in Italian.

"Hai 24 ore o ti tagliamo le palle!" (Translation: You've got 24 hours or we're going to cut your balls off!)

"What's going on?" I ask.

"Alejandro is fucking around, Alessio. I really hope he is legit like you said."

"He has always come through for me on time" I reply.

"He told me he'd have the money by tonight. Now I'm finding out that he only has half of our cut."

"Are you fucking serious?" I snap.

She sighs loudly, "Unfortunately."

"Well...I think your threat was justified then."

She chuckles and pulls out a cigarette.

"I'll talk to Alejandro tonight as well," Giovanni snickers and pulls his switchblade out, "Just so he really gets the message."

I laugh at him and look up towards a familiar face that appears in the crowd.

The beautiful girl from English.

Olivia Moore.

She's with three other kids from the school who I had seen around before. The Kimberly girl was known for being a bit of a flirt. She had thrown herself at me a few times but I just wasn't interested.

The short girl next to her was one I had seen before but knew nothing about. The boy with them, Austin, I knew plenty about.

His dad worked for the San Diego police department and Austin himself was a bit of a bitch.

I could only really focus on Olivia though.

My eyes traveled up and down her womanly figure tight in her jeans and dark tank top. I watch as she tosses her head back and laughs at something before glancing over and finding me staring at her.

Her cheeks blush a bright pink and she looks down nervously.

"Alessio?" Beto snaps out.

Yes?"

"Ready to go?" He asks and follows my gaze towards Olivia.

I nod and light the cigarette that had been hanging between my lips.

"Piccolo uomo." Giovanni teases as he walks behind Beto. (Translation: little man)

Beto mocks him and pushes his Oakley's down onto his face as the four of us climb into the car and head out onto the street.

After a few moments of driving in silence, I decided to get some detail on today's business.

"How did the shipment go today?"

Anna responds from the back, "Shockingly well. No trouble from the 12 or the San Diablo's this time."

The San Diablo's are notorious for sticking their noses where they don't belong.

They are just some random, bullshit excuse of a street gang that immediately tried to start trouble with us when they caught wind of the Sicilian mafia being in California.

Of course, they have never been a match for us.

We have several ports we control here and still back in Italy. We tend to only move quantities of guns and drugs that turn a significant profit.

If it is small, there's no point in the risk.

We move only large quantities of drugs and guns.

If it doesn't turn a significant profit, there's no point.

Our top priority tends to lie in the businesses we currently own.

We try to put our money in places where cleaning the money will be the easiest, such as clubs and casinos. We own a few restaurants around the area as well.

The more we have control of means our income will be higher and we can put our money into several different places if needed.

I knew exactly how the process worked and had perfected it as my art.

My father, Adolfo, had stepped back from the inner workings of the organization due to his old age. He would be turning 83 later this year and he knew it was time to slow down.

I was ready to take over the family. I was ready to make a real name for myself.

I have to stay focused.

I have to keep the end goal in sight.

I just couldn't get Olivia Moore out of my fucking head.

Chapter 4

The sun is especially bright this morning and I can already feel myself dreading the day. I reach over and snatch my phone from my bed.

7:02 am

The only good thing about today was that it is finally Friday. I had completed my first week at Westview.

It wouldn't have been so easy without Kimberly, Austin, and Sierra. The three of them had made my first week here a total blast.

Each morning I would go through my morning routine and walk to school with Kimberly. She shared with me recently the latest rumor mill gossip about her ex who had been sleeping with some cheerleaders.

I assume she's pissed because it had been the morning topic for three days.

I climbed out of my bed and slid my dress Kimberly had gifted me on. It was black and strappy with an open back.

Even though she has a much larger chest it seemed to fit me nicely.

I had been so used to wearing the same school uniform back in New York, it still felt strange to have to really think about my appearance every day.

I hurried down the stairs and into the kitchen where my bag was and my mother who looked like she was ready to explode.

"If I find another chipped dish," She growls under her breath, "I'm going to kill that man."

I clear my throat and she glances over at me with a smile.

"Good morning, Liv."

"Hi mama."

"You hungry?" She asks and hands me a plate of food.

I nod and grab two pieces of bacon from it before getting my water bottle from the fridge.

"I'm probably going to be late tonight, "I tell her as I shut the fridge door, "I'm taking a resume to school and printing out a few more. Kim said she'd walk with me a few blocks down from the school so I could apply to a few places near there."

"Oh, wonderful!" She cheers. "I'm so glad you found such a good friend here."

I laugh at her, "She has helped me quite a bit so far. She said she'd even put in a good word for me at the coffee bar she works at down the street from the school."

She smiles again and wraps her arms around my shoulders.

"I'm so proud of you."

"Thanks," I tell her and kiss her cheek.

I yell a quick goodbye as I step out onto the front porch and spot Kimberly near the sidewalk waiting for me.

She looked up and smiled. I notice her glossy lips and big gold hoops she had added for the day.

Possibly looking to make some men swoon or girls jealous.

"Mornin' gorgeous." She smiles and pops her gum.

She hands me a gloss from her purse. "Add this."

I grimace but swipe a bit of the goopy lip gloss to my lips.

Kimberly looks me up and down, "No bra?"

I look down and my cheeks flush. "Fuck!"

"You look hot! Don't worry about it."

I roll my eyes and give her a playful bounce before the two of us start down the sidewalk. Before long, I notice there's a car that is creeping up on us and turn back to the sound of a loud engine roaring nearby.

Alessio Romano.

He slows down a bit in his sleek silver Porsche and comes to a steady crawl near the curb.

I watch in awe as he leans out a bit and smiles. His dark eyes hidden behind his sunglasses.

"Good morning, ladies."

"Hey, handsome!" Kimberly beams at him.

Alessio nods towards her but his eyes never leave mine.

"Olivia Moore, right?"

I stammer, "Y-yeah."

"I just wanted to properly introduce myself...I'm Alessio Romano," He says and I notice he has a heavy Italian accent. "I hope you are enjoying San Diego so far."

"It's been great so far." I smile sheepishly.

He chuckles. The sound rough and deep. "Well have a good day, girls. See you around, Olivia."

Kimberly and I watch in silence as he pulls away and continues to drive off down the road.

"Oh...my...god! I can't believe he stopped and talked to us. He is SO hot it just blows my mind." She gushes in her girly voice.

"Yeah, real crazy," I mutter out. "So...do you know a lot about him?"

"Not really," she shrugs as we start walking. "I guess his family is really rich and really crazy. Lot's of illegal things they are apparently involved in.

"What kind of things?"

"Well...I guess you could say...drugs? guns? Just a rumor though."

I frown and look back towards the sidewalk in front of us.

Everyone seemed so sure that Alessio Romano was just bad news.

I had to find out for myself.

◇ ◇ ◇

"Olivia! Hey!"

I smile and turn towards Austin as he wraps me up in a tight hug. My feet leave the ground as he spins us around.

"How are you today?" He asks and releases me from the unexpected embrace.

I look into his pretty hazel eyes and get a flutter of butterflies in the pit of my stomach.

Austin had been really great so far. He would always go out of his way to talk to me during school and even spent hours with me just texting after school.

He had shared a bit about his family and how he was majoring in Computer Science. All around he was just such a nice guy.

"I got you something," He says randomly and his cheeks redden. "That's not weird right?"

"Of course not!"

He grins and puts a little box in my hand with a red ribbon on the top.

I pull it open and reveal a charm bracelet with two charms on it. One for New York with the city skyline and the other a palm tree and sun showing CA at the top for California.

"Oh, Austin. You didn't have to get me anything! This is so pretty." I tell him and he takes my wrist in his hands.

He laughs nervously and turns it over to clasp the jewelry on me.

"Where did you get this?" I ask.

"My family owns a tiny shop not far from here." He shrugs and holds onto my wrist. "I figured you deserved a welcoming gift."

"You're the best. Thank you!" I beam at him and pull him in for a hug.

Austin squeezes me back and stares down at me almost as if he has something else to say. I wait for a few moments but stop as Kimberly and Sierra hurry up to us.

"You ready?" Kimberly asks and eyes us both suspiciously.

I nod, "As I'll ever be."

"You have nothing to worry about. I looked it over and your resume is solid." Sierra reassures me.

I thank her for the review and the four of us head out into the bright sunlight. My nerves were already a damn trainwreck so when I caught those dark eyes, I was about ready to pass out.

Alessio looks up from the canopy pole he's leaning against and lets his eyes travel up and down my body.

I watch for a moment in silence before he glances over at the girl next to him and nods to whatever she said. She's the girl who had been with him the other day.

As they continue to converse, I watch as Beto comes up to them. Kimberly had mentioned he was Alessio's cousin and apparently a major flirt.

He looked like a smaller version of the others but with more of an Abercrombie and Fitch look.

You never would've known the king of khaki pants and polo shirts would be related to the gorgeous, dark-haired Italian always wearing leather and motorcycle boots.

Suddenly, the big man next to them started yelling something at Alessio before storming off with the girl.

"Come on, Liv." Kim says and tugs my arm.

I start to follow her down the sidewalk. She starts up some small talk about some guy she was flirting with today.

I try to focus on her but stop when a Green truck comes flying into the parking lot nearly taking down several students.

Three men pop up from the bed of it and start waving guns around in the air.

Everything seems to slow down at the sound of the first gunshot.

I feel Kimberly pull me to the side and throw us into a bush. My face smashes to the dirty ground as several more gunshots fire out loudly followed by several screams of terror.

Two more shots ring out from behind us. I keep my face smashed to the ground, trying hard not to eat dirt and twigs.

I hear voices getting closer and peek up from my hiding spot to find a bald man with several tattoos on his skull staring at someone behind me.

He starts to say something in Spanish before looking down and catching me watching him.

"STOP!"

A deep voice booms from behind. I'm frozen in terror and can't bring myself to look back. I can hear Kimberly crying next to me.

The tattooed man leans towards me a little. A gun in his hand.

"Hermosa." (Translation: Beautiful)

My stomach turns as he addresses me and I close my eyes. I wait for the moment the gun will rest against my head.

Seconds pass. Minutes pass.

He is taking way too long.

The pain never comes. I look down at myself and I'm free of any blood or wounds.

I look up and notice the tattooed man had taken several steps back and his eyes were locked on someone else.

"Watch your fucking back!" He spits and looks down at me again.

"Hermosa."

A shaky breath escapes me as the guy runs back to the same truck that had been waiting at the entrance. I watch in shock as they peel out quickly.

The sound of police sirens coming closer. Students still panicking and teachers running around to make sure nobody has been injured.

Kimberly pulls me to her side and starts to hyperventilate.

"I'm so sorry!"

"It's okay, Kim. It isn't your fault." I rub her shoulders.

"I don't want this to be your impression of this school," She says with a sob. "I swear that was not normal."

I give her a tight squeeze again and pull both of us up to our feet.

"A-are you okay?" A breathless voice asks from behind the two of us. I turn around and find Alessio staring down at me.

He's unharmed but looks angry.

"Uh...I think so." I whisper out.

He nods a little and looks around at the chaos still unfolding before us.

"Did...did anyone get killed?" I ask him.

He looks back down at me and his expression softens. "No."

"That's good."

He takes a step forward and wordlessly reaches out to brush some twigs out from my hair. I hold my breath as his fingertips move across my cheek.

"Be careful..." He whispers.

Alessio takes a few steps back and looks over his shoulder at the sound of others running towards us.

"Kimberly! Olivia!"

Sierra and Austin shout loudly as they reach us. Their arms wrap around the two of us and begin looking us over to make sure we were unharmed.

"I'm glad you are both okay! That was fucking insane." Sierra says and holds Kimberly close.

Austin looks down at me with a look of concern. "Me too."

He releases the girls and pulls me in for a hug. His mouth and nose nuzzling my neck.

"I was so worried about you." He whispers into my ear.

I stand there silently and let myself melt into him. I turn my head to the side a bit and notice Alessio stepping into his car.

He doesn't look thrilled.

ALESSIO

"Te l'ho detto! cazzo!" (Translation: I told you! Fuck!)

Anna is standing next to me and shouting loudly as she reads off texts from Alejandro. Before they arrived at the school she had discovered that he had been keeping our entire cut from us and lied about the money that was made.

He was really trying to fuck us over.

"What do you want to do?" I ask her.

"Sai cosa dobbiamo fare." (Translation: You know what we have to do.)

I nod a bit and look around as the crowd of kids continues to pour out of the building to enjoy their sunshine-filled weekend. It doesn't take long for me to find the one that stands out.

She looks amazing.

Olivia walks out of the doors followed by her new best friends. Her womanly body dressed in a black sundress.

No bra. Her skin soft and exposed.

I just can't stop staring at her. I kept imagining having her in every way I possibly could.

I want her so bad. I need her.

She finally looks up as if she heard my thoughts. Her bright, blue eyes burning me.

"Che stai facendo?" Anna yells angrily and I look down.

I roll my eyes, "niente di calmo". (Translation: Nothing calm down)

Suddenly Beto walks up to us with Giovanni following close behind. Without hesitation, I'm having his cellphone screen shoved in my face.

"This is fucking bullshit!"

Alejandro had declared an attack on our club. The news had been intercepted by our guards.

"I'll kill him tonight," I announce to them.

"Fuck that," Giovanni snaps and points his finger at me. "You shouldn't of let him in this. I'll clean your mess up, Alessio. You better start acting like a fucking boss if you are going to live up to Adolfo."

Giovanni motions for Anna to follow as they storm off back towards their car. I sigh loudly and look over at Beto.

"What a fucking day."He hands me a cigarette.

I light the end of it and look back over at her. Olivia's cheeks flush with pink as she watches me studying her every move.

I let the flame of the lighter flick in the wind for a moment before the end lights up. Smoke blows out in one strong cloud.

"Alejandro! Pezzo di merda!" (Translation: Alejandro! You piece of shit!)

My head snaps up and I look over where Anna's voice came from.

They are both already across the parking lot and moving towards a green Truck. I spot Alejandro standing at the front of it.

Guns were drawn and ready to go. They were ready to start a turf war here.

"This can't happen here," I tell Beto urgently.

Before either of us have time to process anything we start moving just as Alejandro yells something in Spanish at the two of them before several warning shots are fired into the air.

Screams of panic and terror erupt around us and chaos breaks out.

"This is not the place!" Anna shouts at him.

Alejandro is barely paying her any attention. His gun pointing right at Giovanni's head.

He's a small guy with a lot of shitty tattoos all over his body and bald skull. I had hoped he would've been a good alley for us considering his gang ran a large part of San Diego.

Beto and I move closer to them but I stop in my tracks when I hear the sound of Kimberly's voice nearby.

I look over and see her tucked behind some shrubs with Olivia.

I tell Beto to continue and start to move towards them. Hopefully, I can get them out of here before this gets any worse.

I get a little closer to her and realize Alejandro had spotted me. He had his gun on me now and was smiling widely.

His eyes following my gaze to where Olivia was hidden.

He's closer and it makes my stomach turn. I watch as he reaches out towards her and she catches him in the act. Her eyes are full of terror as he leans towards her.

"Hermosa" He purrs out.

"STOP!" I shout and pull my gun out on him.

Alejandro cocks his eyebrow and looks down at her. His smile shows he has pinpointed my exact weakness.

I don't know why I felt like I had so much care for this random girl. I can't get her out of my head.

Would I really risk myself for this girl? My family?

He starts to make a move towards her but stops when he hears shouts from his men back where Giovanni is.

The two of us look back and notice Giovanni has them all on the ground. Each one a gun pointed at their hands.

Alejandro flares his nostrils and looks over at me.

"Watch your fucking back! "Alejandro growls out and looks back towards Olivia.

"Hermosa..."

I keep my gun locked on him as he runs back to his boys and they get back into their truck. The car roaring loudly as they disappear.

I sigh and take a few steps towards Olivia. She's now standing with Kimberly as they both cry out of shock and confusion.

"A-are you okay?"

"Uh...I think so." Olivia whispers. Her blue eyes are wide.

She looks me over. Almost as if she wants to know I'm not harmed.

"Did...did anyone get killed?"

"No," I reply robotically and scan the lot.

Teachers were moving fast and checking on students. I could already hear the police sirens coming to the school.

I need to make my exit fast.

"That's good." She says slowly.

I catch sight of something sparkling and silver on her wrist. A new charm bracelet.

That wasn't there this morning...

I take a step towards her and reach out to remove some twigs and dirt from her. It seems as if she is holding her breath.

Her skin is soft to the touch. Just as I had imagined.

She gazes up at me nervously. Her cheeks pink.

"Be careful."

She swallows and tries to nod a little. I stare down at her a little longer and want to freeze time.

"Kimberly! Olivia!"

I groan internally at the sound of her friends coming over. I regretfully pull away and start to walk off just as they ambush the girls with hugs.

I make my way over to my car just as the police start to show up. I glance back and see Austin holding Olivia close to him.

I struggle to break my eyes from hers and get into the driver's side.

If I don't leave now, I know I'll do something I regret.

Chapter 5

"How are you feeling today?"

I look up from my plate towards my father. His eyes were full of concern this morning.

I sigh and push my plate away. "I'm fine."

I had broken the news to my parents right after they got the call. Kimberly had tried to suggest putting the resume day off but I was not wanting to go home right away.

They freaked out big time.

My mom thought I was dead and threatened a new school. Dad was even wanting to go down there and raise hell over it.

"We just want you to be safe," Mom says from the other side of the kitchen. "We worry about you, Liv. This is a big change for you and I can't even imagine how scary this was."

I sigh, "I've been through worse."

They glance at one another for a moment but don't push the conversation.

I get up from the table and head upstairs. I just can't be around them when all it's going to be is concern and fear.

I curl up on my bed and stare down blankly at my phone. All I can think about is Alessio.

He had moved into my mind for good. I kept replaying him so close to me.

His fingers against my skin. The smell of his cologne. He was s-

My phone starts buzzing wildly and pulls me from my thoughts.

"H-hello?"

Kimberly's voice echoes on the other line. "You okay?"

"Yeah sorry about that. I guess I wasn't prepared for your morning call today."

I can practically hear her eyes roll.

"Do you want to hang out today with Austin, Sierra, and I?" She asks.

"Sure. What's the plan?"

"Not sure but I'll be over in an hour to get you."

"Okay. See you in a few." I tell her and the line hangs up.

I hurry through getting ready and rush out the front door. I can hear my mom calling after me but I need some time to myself.

Kimberly looks up and pops her bubblegum.

"Did you hear anything about the job?"

I shake my head in disappointment. I didn't have any call backs yet, but I'm not going to get too upset yet knowing it hasn't even been a full 24 hours.

She smiles again and holds her phone screen up showing the message from the owner. Edgar had told her he loves me and thinks I'd make a great addition.

I start Monday!

We both cheer for a couple of minutes over the thought of working together before heading down the road towards the shopping outlet.

The morning sun beats down on the both of us and it feels good against my exposed legs. The two of us walk swiftly, discussing the latest Westview drama Kimberly had to spill.

Once we met up with Sierra and Austin, the four of us decided to go into a few shops down the strip.

"What do you think?"

I turn around and find Austin's warm smile.

We decided to stop inside of a super cute mom and pop shop with handmade jewelry and adorable antiques.

Austin looks so cute today. His blonde curls under a ball cap and light blue shirt bringing out the colors in his hazel eyes.

"What do you mean?" I ask him.

He waves his hand around the shop. "My family owns this place."

I glance around at the little shop again and smile at him.

"I see you get your good taste from your parents."

He laughs at me and pulls a charm off a nearby stand before placing it in my hands.

"What do you think? Reminds me of your eyes."

I turn it over, admiring it as it glitters in the light. A tiny silver charm in the shape of a heart with a brilliant blue gem.

"It is really pretty. " I say softly.

"It's yours."

"Are you sure?"

He nods, "Absolutely."

Sierra's voice chirps from behind, startling us both.

"Are you done flirting yet?" She barks out. Her voice sounded very annoyed.

My face reddens and I catch Austin looking away shyly. I was grateful when Kimberly rushed inside and pulled me out to see some dress she found next door.

We start heading down the sidewalk after a bit and set our minds on pizza and frozen yogurt.

I'm trying to listen to some joke Kimberly is telling everyone when my phone starts to buzz.

"Hello?"

"How are you gorgeous?"

The voice immediately sends a chill down my spine. His voice so rough and deep over the phone.

"I-I'm okay. How about you?" I stammer.

"I'd be a lot better if I could see you, "Alessio replies, "Are you busy right now?"

"I'm actually with some friends,"I respond and look towards Kimberly. She's staring back at me with a confused look. "I'm sorry."

Alessio laughs, "No need, beautiful. I'll see you later."

"W-wait how did you get my nu-"

Before I can get my question out, Alessio ends the call. I stare at the phone dumbfounded before I realize they are walking back towards me.

"What was that about?" Sierra asks.

"Nothing,"I lie. "Some spam call."

She nods but doesn't push on the topic. We continue on to a little place called "Dom's Pizzeria" and engorge on slices bigger than our heads.

We decide to swing by a local frozen yogurt stand and head down to the beach until it starts getting dark.

I had spent an entire day with my new friends and I honestly didn't miss New York as much anymore.

I did miss my friends, but days like this made it easier.

"I should probably get going. I didn't realize it was already getting so late," I tell all of them. "We've been out here all day."

"Sure. If you want I can walk back with you but I will just have to let my friend know." Kimberly says as she stares at her phone.

"Friend?" I tease.

She rolls her eyes, "Yes, Olivia. He's a friend...with benefits."

We all laugh together before Austin pipes up. "I can take her home, don't worry about it."

"Are you sure?"

"Yeah, go have fun." He smiles at her.

Austin and I sit on the beach in silence for a moment and watch Sierra and Kimberly head in the opposite direction. The wind has a bit of a chill to it as it rushes over the two of us.

"You ready?" Austin asks when he notices me shiver.

"Yeah." I smile nervously and stand up.

My stomach was in so many knots. I had only ever had one boyfriend when I was a freshman and it ended quickly.

I was always focused on school and art. I just didn't have time for a boyfriend, plus I wasn't really interested in boys...ever.

Or...people in general.

This is the first time I had actually been alone with another boy. Especially one as cute as Austin.

The fifteen minute walk feels endless with the two of us walking in awkward silence. Our shoulders barely brush one another.

I notice my house coming up at the top of the street as we turn onto my poorly lit street.

"I had fun," Austin says and looks over at me, "It was a really nice day. I'm glad I got to see you."

"Yeah," I reply and brush my hair behind my ear, "Thank you again for the charm. It's really pretty and I can't wait to add it on."

Austin grabs my wrist without a warning and looks down at the bracelet. I feel my heartbeat pick up as he holds it in his hand and looks at me.

"Olivia..."

"W-what?" I stammer out.

"I think I have feelings for you."

My heart flutters. "Austin... I-"

He cuts me off and puts a finger against my parted lips.

"Please,"He shakes his head."I haven't felt like this in awhile. I can tell there is something here."

I nod a bit, knowing I shouldn't deny the feelings I feel for him as well. I try to focus on the pulse in his neck as he continues to stare at me.

"I should go..."

Austin says nothing else but his grip doesn't loosen. Without a warning, his mouth is on mine in a flash.

It has so much aggression behind.

"N-n," I say against him.

I feel my feet move as Austin guides both of us to a nearby dividing wall and pushes my back painfully against the jagged brick there.

His tongue hungrily explores the inside of my mouth as I struggle to breath against him.

I feel his hands start to explore my body through my clothes and my stomach drops immediately.

"Austin," I beg as he pulls back. "Please stop. I'm not ready for this."

He isn't listening and continues to kiss a trail down my neck before wrapping a free hand tightly around my waist.

"Don't push me away, Olivia. We are so good with each other."

I feel myself growing weaker under his hold. I try to look around us in the dark and see nothing.

Dark houses, shitty street lamps, and no people.

I'm alone with him.

I whimper against his lips but he takes my cry as a sign of lust. "Don't be too loud now."

A lump forms in my throat as his hands continue to move all over me. His mouth on mine feels sloppy and wet now.

I can feel his hardness against my thigh and realize he has his pants pushed down off his waist. He grabs my hand and I-

"Get the fuck back."

My eyes open at the familiar voice and I look over to the side.

Alessio is only a few feet away from the two of us.

With a gun.

My jaw drops in horror as I realize he has the gun aimed right at Austin's head.

"I said get the fuck back." He snaps again and kocks Austin's skull with it.

Austin releases me quickly and stumbles backwards, nearly tripping over his own feet.

"I want you to leave and if I ever catch you around her again I will fucking blow your brains out."

I watch in fear as Austin fixes his jeans and starts running as fast as he can down the road. I can feel Alessio's eyes on me but am completely frozen to where I stand.

"Alessio..."I whisper out.

He stands in the same spot with his hand still curled tightly around the gun. His breathing is heavy and fast.

"Come with me."He demands and puts the weapon away.

"I c-can't,"I stammer but he interjects.

"You can... tell your parents Kimberly asked you to sleep over. "He says and hands me my cell phone. I had no idea I had even dropped it.

I stare at him for a moment and contemplate if I should actually call my mom and lie.

It felt so wrong to lie, especially after I had ran out of the house this morning without a word.

I look down at my phone and dial her cell. Alessio watches me in silence as he listens to her scolding from the other end before finally giving into the idea of me spending the night with Kimberly.

Alessio speaks lowly, "Let's go."

I walk quickly behind him as we approach the Porsche I had seen him driving before. He reaches out and opens my door for me before walking around to the driver side.

The engine roars to life within a couple of minutes. I watch his knuckles turn white against the steering wheel as we both sit in silence.

A couple of minutes pass before he does something that catches me off guard.

He rests his arm on the console and turns it palm up. I stare at him for a couple of moments before resting my own hand in his.

He immediately intertwined our fingers together. I can feel the both of us start to relax.

Soon enough we are driving through the dark city streets towards some unfamiliar destination. Yet, I don't feel scared.

Part of me knows I should after seeing him with that gun.

I just feel...safe.

The car soon approaches a bronze gate and I watch as he leans out towards a speaker.

"Aprire i cancelli." (Translation:open the gates)

They groan loudly as they pull apart from one another. We drive through the entrance and up the long winding driveway towards the biggest house I've ever seen in my life.

Well, to be fair, it's a fucking massive mansion.

A stunning olympic size pool beams under the moonlight. There are several ancient looking statues scattered across the yard. I take notice of the large yard and trees wrapped around the estate.

In the middle of the driveway sits a massive fountain that looked to be at least a couple hundred years old.

It didn't look like any mansion I've seen before on TV. It was more of a modern day castle with a bit of an Italian touch.

Alessio brings the car to a stop and looks over.

"How are you?"

"Okay."

He says nothing else as he steps out of the car. I start to reach for the handle but he is already there.

Without another word, he pulls me into a tight embrace.

I melt into his hard chest and I do the last thing I wanted this perfect human to see.

I cry. I cry really hard.

It is a really ugly, annoying cry. I'm pretty sure I stained his shirt with a lot of tears.

"Let me take you inside." Alessio says softly as my sobs turn into small hiccups.

His hand finds my own again before he leads me through the glass entrance sitting at the top of the staircase.

A man dressed in complete black and armed with a rifle gives Alessio a nod before opening the door for the two of us.

We step into a dim lit room with glorious marble floors and the most elegant decor. It's an open floor plan so you can see every room displayed right out in the open.

Crystal Chandeliers hang gracefully from the ceilings above us. Inside you can really see the age and elegance of the home.

"T-this is..."I say in awe.

"You'll get used to it,"He says and winks. "Would you like a drink?"

I nod and wait for him to return from the kitchen with a glass of water. I drink it a little too fast and feel my stomach tighten from the liquid.

I gulp it down, drinking it a little too fast and giving myself a stomach ache.

"Are you tired?" He asks.

I stare at him. "Kind of."

"Olivia... I won't hurt you, "He says softly. "You need your rest."

"Okay."

He sighs and rakes his fingers through his hair. "I'm sorry I wasn't there earlier."

"How did you know?"

"Good timing."

He's lying.

"And the truth?" I challenge him.

He looks down at me and seems amused with my sudden change of attitude.

"I just have a way of knowing things."

He gives me a little grin and takes my hand in his again before leading us both up a staircase closest to the kitchen.

We turn into a long and dark hallway with lowlights and beautiful red rugs with accents of gold running down the length of it. A collection of what appears to be family photos hang along the interior wall leading to a set of double wooden doors.

The room inside is freaking massive. More bedroom than any normal person would ever need.

The floors are the same marble as the lower level and something about it just feels so dark and gloomy with it's lack of unique decor. I look up and notice a few photos of what I assume is a young Alessio with his parents.

The woman in the photo is beautiful. Her skin the same olive tone as his with dark hair and green eyes.

"Who is that?"

Alessio glances up at it for a long time. "My mother."

"She's beautiful."

He nods and moves around me to enter the room. I look around nervously at the most private parts of his life.

I look around nervously at his most private part of his life.

Alessio takes notice of my expression,"What are you thinking?"

"This place is just...amazing." I tell him. Not a total lie.

He smirks and reaches over the bed to grab a nightgown that looks silky and pink. Certainly not something I would opt to wear and I'm a little shocked he is even offering it to me.

He tosses it to me and I look at it as if it's going to explode.

"Girlfriend of yours?" I joke.

He rolls his eyes, "Step sister... she knew you'd be coming tonight and wanted you to be comfortable."

Apparently, a little too comfortable.

Alessio walks across the floor and enters what looks to be his bathroom.

"I'll be waiting. Take your time." He tells me and disappears behind it.

Once he is gone, I hurry through the motions of tossing my dirty clothes to a chair in the corner and pull the nightgown onto my body. It clings to my curves and makes me realize how much of me he will be able to see.

There is a small sound from the bathroom and I look up to see Alessio waiting to make sure it is safe for him to come out.

"I'm done."

I watch as he exits the room and stands before me.

Dear god...he's shirtless.

His chiseled stomach is completely exposed. I notice the line of hair plunging beneath a pair of dark sweats that hang dangerously low on his hips. A deep v hidden just beneath the fabric.

Up around his side and back I spot several dark tattoos. They look to be written in Italian or some kind of scripture.

"What's wrong?" Alessio smirks.

I blush a little and look down at the floor beneath my feet. I hear the sound of him walking closer and suddenly his hands are cradling my face.

I try to focus on my breathing as he leans towards me. The smell of his intoxicating cologne hitting me. His dark eyes study my face for a long time before he trails his finger slowly up the length of my jaw.

"Olivia,"He says softly. "Let's go to sleep."

I nod and try to swallow the lump in my throat. He's so close.

I can make out every stubble of hair and even the hidden gold specks in his black eyes.

"Ok." I whisper.

He releases me and climbs into the bed on the opposite side. I wait for a moment before he lays comfortably on his back and exposes a spot on his chest for me to curl into.

I follow his lead and let my body mold into his curves. He sighs and lets his head falls onto my own.

The both of us lay there in silence for what feels like forever before sleep takes over.

It was the best sleep I've ever had.

Chapter 6

This morning is different from any before.

Olivia Moore is in my bed. She's in my arms.

I turn over onto my side and look at her petite frame dressed in the pink nightgown.

Her soft and pink lips are parted slightly. Small snores are coming from her as she slumbers soundly.

Looking at her I'm just grateful she's here. She is safe.

If I didn't show up when I did who knows what that fuck Austin would've tried with her. I should've known he was bad news.

He's a walking dead man. I'll kill him.

When the time is right.

I already had so much going on with Alejandro's gang and then this just happens to pop up at the perfect time.

After Alejandro had declared a turf war and tried to attack our club, we decided to make a move of our own.

Let's just say he shouldn't have been drunk and without his buddies after a night of partying.

It was a quick death for him and his head ended up in a box delivered to his brother.

After our fun with sending out a message to his boy scouts, I had a chance to talk to Olivia. Hearing her voice was everything I needed at that moment.

It also helped locate her phone.

I wanted to see her so bad and I know it is creepy as fuck to stalk women. I just had a weird feeling and after getting word back from uncle Mateo that Austinw as walking her home, I felt like I needed to be there.

I had been at a local club of ours that night with the boys. The three of us were handling some business, cutting lines of coke up on the table.

My phone rang and I answered it immediately. "Talk."

"Ms. Moore is being escorted by the boy."

My body tensed up quickly. I wasn't in my right mind at all.

I'm not really into partying, but there are days where I need the drugs and alcohol to function. A girl next to me had leaned over and tried to kiss my neck.

I put my hand against her and told her to move away.

"Austin?" I said into the phone.

Mateo started listing off his identifying descriptions which only confirmed what I had feared.

Austin and his family seemed normal for the most part, until I decided to have Beto help me with some research.

I discovered Austin was a sexual deviant and had two attempted sexual assault cases that were dropped against him back when he was fifteen years old.

He also had several charges against him as young as twelve years old when he attended a school in another state and had been involved in several fist fights with men and women alike.

Apparently, his police officer daddy had a way of getting his drug addict son out of trouble when he decided to pop too many pills and attack women.

The case was dismissed before the trial even happened. According to what we found, the families were paid to shut their mouths.

Austin was free to walk and would continue to prey on the girls he wanted.

"Thanks for helping, Maeo," I told him on the phone and waved Beto over. "I'll take it from here."

The phone call ends and Beto sits down next to me. "What's going on?"

"I have some things I need to take care of," I told him and slipped my jacket on. "I need you and Giovanni to finish here. Make sure the deal is done before you leave."

He nods and leans down to finish cutting the coke that was laid out on the scale. I looked around the dim room over to where Giovanni was chatting it up with our potential business partner and hollering at the strippers performing for them.

I trusted him with the business and right now, Olivia is what matters the most.

The drive to her house had felt too long even with me speeding and nearing at least 95 mph the entire drive. I had pulled up close to a curb where her phone had pinged her and tried to make out whatever was in the dark.

I could faintly make out movement against a dividing wall between two homes. There was a male voice followed by what sounded like a woman in distress.

I hurried out of the car and had my gun already in my hand. My vision was a blur of red and I was ready to blow his brains out.

Austin had Olivia pinned against the wall there and his pants were down. I could see she had her eyes closed as he continued to feel her up and kiss her.

My stomach turned at the sight and without hesitation my gun was aimed at his head.

"Get the fuck back."

He froze and looked back to where I was. I watched for a moment as he eyed the weapon and looked back at me.

Olivia had finally opened her eyes as well. She was scared.

Scared of me.

"I said get the fuck back!" I snapped again and knocked his temple with the barrel.

Austin stumbled back several feet and pulled his pants up.

"I want you to leave and if I ever catch you around her again I will blow your fucking brains out." I told him sternly. He nodded quickly and without another word was running down the street.

My head was spinning and the rage felt uncontrollable. I was half debating hunting him down to finish the job and also calling Giovanni to kill him tonight.

At some point, during my mental fight I could hear Olivia whispering my name.

She needed me. Austin had to wait.

I dropped my shoulders and put the gun away. I looked over at her and studied her carefully to make sure she wasn't hurt.

"Come with me." I told her.

"I c-can't-" She started but I stopped her.

"You can… tell your parents Kimberly asked you to sleep over." I said and handed over her phone.

Once everything had been settled with her parents, I took her back to the manor.

It felt right having her with me. I knew she was safe and sleeping with her in my arms was a dream.

She was perfect in every single way.

I notice Olivia starting to stir in her sleep and look over at her. Two bright, blue eyes open slightly and she smiles.

"Good morning."

"Morning," I smile back and notice the bracelet on her arm again. "Who gave you this?"

"Austin." She frowns and tries to unclasp it.

I take her hand in my own and silently break the chains apart from one another. She watches without a word as it scurries across the floor.

"There are some things I need to take care of today," I continue on. "There's also a party my family is hosting tonight. I'd love if you attended."

Her mouth falls open. "I don't know if that's a good idea, plus my pare-"

I place a finger against her soft lips. "I just want to make sure you are safe and I would feel a lot better if you were here. I can help you come up with something to tell them. You are also welcome to use my sister, Anna, as an excuse for staying."

"What if they don't believe it? I've never mentioned anyone before aside from Kim."

"Anna can join you later and meet them first." I reassure her.

"I'm sorry...I just...I really don't think I can." She starts again and moves off the bed. "I really appreciate what you did though."

I watch silently as she gathers her stuff up in her arms and tries to head towards the door. She reaches out and pulls against the handle unsuccessfully.

"Please...unlock it." She demands and huffs loudly.

I move off the bed and muse at her attitude. "One day, Olivia. Please?"

Olivia just laughs at me and rolls her eyes.

"Did you just roll your eyes at me?" I ask, annoyed.

Her mouth opens and instead of giving in she proceeds to continue with her taunts. "If I did?"

I don't say anything else. Within seconds I have her over my shoulder in one swift motion. She lets out a girly scream and laugh as she lands onto my back.

"Let me down!"

I toss her onto the bed and pin her there. The two of us staring at one another for what feels like forever.

The temptation to kiss her all too real.

"Please...one day. Just spend today with me."

She thinks for a moment before finally nodding a little. I look down under me and can't help but let my fingers trail up the length of the silk sticking to her curves.

A moan slips from her with my touch and I feel myself harden at the sound.

Fuck...I want to take her right now. So bad.

I pull back a little and her cheeks redden. "Do you like that?"

She doesn't reply but bites down on her lower lip softly. I don't need her response to know how much she wants me to fuck her right now with those eyes.

I pin her wrists down to her sides and lean in closer to her. Our lips inches from touching each other.

"You have no idea what you are doing to me," I tell her quietly. "I want you in every way you can imagine."

Her breathing starts to come out harder and fast. She looks up at me and waits. Her blue eyes are wide and eager with lust.

I debate with the idea of fucking her now for a long time before I decide now is not the time.

With a sigh, I pull myself up from the bed and pull her up with me.

"We'll play later."

Chapter 7

OLIVIA

What the fuck just happened...

Alessio had left his room and left me alone in a complete daze.

He had left me with so much to think about and I had no idea how to feel. He wanted to spend the day with ME and he wanted me to attend a party with HIS family.

Why would Alessio Romano want his family to see him with a girl like me? I'm not anything like the Romano family.

Surely, I'd stick out like a sore thumb.

After a while of sitting on his bed and fighting with the thought of what to do, I decide to get up and go through the motions of showering.

I slipped into my clothes he had cleaned overnight and hurried down the stairs to find him waiting for me.

He looked fucking amazing.

A pair of dark sunglasses holding his black hair back. He had changed into a leather jacket and his favorite black boots with faded jeans.

How did a human this perfect exist?

A smile crawls over his face as he sees me enter the room and he reaches out to take my hand.

"You look so beautiful."

"Thank you." I smile up at him. "You look good yourself."

I let him lead me out of the house and to the Porsche waiting outside. The weather is beautiful today which makes our drive even better. The windows are down and we keep our hands intertwined tightly with one another.

I catch Alessio throwing me little glances here and there as he speeds a little too quickly for comfort through the hills.

Eventually, he comes to a stop in front of an unfamiliar building with boarded up windows.

"I will be back," He says and steps out. "Please do not leave the car."

Part of me wanted to protest because I was so curious to see what he does, but I decided against it.

I watched him disappear through a set of doors and then did the best I could to keep myself preoccupied for the next 45 minutes.

I was grateful to see him step back out of the doors after some time and climb back into the car. He smelled like weed.

"Few more stops."He tells me and slides his sunglasses back on.

The next few stops were almost the same as before. He would go inside some weird warehouse before coming back. I was a little confused as to why he wanted me to come if he was going to be so busy, but also grateful it meant I could have a peak at his daily life.

Eventually, he had pulled up to a really cute retail store. The front was very classy and cute. Beautiful dresses and modern teenage clothes displayed neatly in the storefront window.

I look over at him for an explanation but he says nothing as he comes to my door and helps me out from the car.

Inside the building we are greeted by a girl wearing a ruffled blouse and black pencil skirt. She rushes up to us with a wide smile.

"Welcome! It's so good to see you again Mr. Romano."

Alessio nods, "Likewise. How's business?"

"Amazing as ever! You know we'd do anything for you," She says flirtatiously.

I raise a brow. "For you?"

He laughs, "We own this business. Well, it is mostly one of Anna's projects."

He pulls me along gently and guides me some clothing racks. I let my fingers feel through the different fabrics until I find something that feels silky and smooth.

I pull it off the rack and my cheeks blush a bit. It is very classy...and daring.

"Would you like to try it on?"Alessio asks from behind.

Before I have time to answer the blonde girl from before is guiding me excitedly over to a dressing room.

She hands me the dress and tells me to take my time before the door shuts behind her.

I stare at my own reflection in the mirror and hold the black dress against my stomach. My eyes were bright and wide but I looked...happy?

I stare down at the dress in my hands and take a deep breath. "Just do it."

I turn my back to the mirror and strip down to my underwear before sliding into the dress. It's a beautiful black with hints of blue. Two slits cut on both sides to expose each thigh with a plunging neckline.

I turn around to study the dress and admire the way the material glitters with the hints of blue and purple under the store lights. Everything about it screams class and wealth.

And expensive.

After a few minutes, I start to feel stupid. Someone like me would never be caught dead in this.

This isn't me. Olivia Moore isn't rich and classy.

I wear paint covered overalls for crying out loud.

I'm ready to take it off and start to pull the strap down just as the door behind me opens and someone steps inside.

"Hey!" I shout and turn around to cover my chest.

Alessio leans back against the door of the dressing room and lets his eyes roam over me.

"How did you get in?" I ask stupidly.

He doesn't respond, instead he takes a step towards me and rests his hands against my hips.

My breath catches in my throat as his leg easily slips in between my thighs and my back pushes against the mirror.

His mouth leans towards my collarbone and brushes the skin there. "You have no idea what this does to me."

I freeze in place as the skin of his lips continue to tease me there. Little goosebumps form and spread out over my body.

"We're purchasing it." He mutters softly and releases me.

I watch in silence as he disappears from the dressing room and push my back against the mirror.

My chest feels heavy and my head starts to spiral out of control.

I finally convince myself to change before Alessio comes to see why I'm taking so long.

When I exit the room, I find him waiting at the counter. The same store associate now leaning over the counter with her manicured claws brushing his arm.

He nods politely as she speaks but his eyes are on me. I gasp a little at the sight of him and hurry up to his side with the dress.

The blonde girl looks at me and smiles a little before scanning the tag.

"Ten thousand even."

My jaw falls open and Alessio just pulls his card out.

"Alessio, I can't ac-"

"I like it and I want to purchase it for you," He argues and hands the card to her.

I bite my tongue to keep myself from saying anything else. I watch her bag up the items and reach out for his hand as we head out towards the car.

I realize there are three people standing by the Porsche.

"Olivia," Alessio starts as we approach them. "I'd like you to meet Beto, Anna, and Giovanni."

All three of them are insanely attractive. They all have the same model features and Italian skin with dark hair.

"Good to see you, Olivia." Beto smiles at me.

At Westview, I see Beto in one of my classes but he tends to spend most of his time flirting with every single girl who looks at him.

I don't blame the girls though, he is a very attractive kid. Plus, who wouldn't go after the cousin of the mysterious Alessio Romano when he doesn't give anyone the time of day.

Except...for me, I guess.

"You as well." I grin back and look over at the siblings.

The big man I'd seen at the school before speaks up, "I'm Giovanni. Nice to meet you."

His voice matches him perfectly. It is low and extremely rugged.

He is the kind of guy you would expect to see competing in bodybuilding competitions or pushing the limits in the gym.

Aside from the similar features to his relatives, I notice he has a variety of scars all over his arms.

Knife wounds?

I nod a little in acknowledgement and look at the girl who doesn't even look up from her cellphone at me.

"I'm Anna."

She is beautiful. Her dark hair frames her face in wind blown curls and she has more of a honey brown eye color compared to the others. She's pretty tall like her brother and has the body of a damn Victoria Secret model.

Something about her makes me feel so uneasy right away.

"It is nice to meet you all," I say politely and feel Alessio squeeze my hand.

Anna looks up from her phone finally and looks at me with a bit of a glare.

"Alessio, mentioned something about meeting your family so they knew who you'd be with tonight."

I look at Alessio and wait for him to speak. He turns towards his sister, "Yes, please. I just want them to trust who Olivia is with."

"Sure, let's go." She mutters and walks towards a black Cadillac.

I start to move towards the car but stop when Alessio pulls me towards him. His hands finding my face again as he cradles me under my chin.

"Will you stay til Monday?"

"I don't think my parents would like that." I frown.

"I'll take you to school and work."

"How do you know about my j-"

Anna cuts me off, "Ready?"

I look at her apologetically before looking back at him. "I'll see you later."

He smirks a little and plants a sweet kiss on my forehead before letting me go. I watch as he climbs into the Porsche with the other two boys.

I turn and climb into the passenger seat next to Anna. The tension starts to build between the two of us and I look over at her shyly.

"D-do you need my a-address?"

She shakes her head and turns the car on. "Alessio gave me the address."

I turn to look out of the window in silence as she starts driving. I didn't know what to say to her.

Something about her just felt so intimidating and I could tell she was not my biggest fan.

After a few minutes, I decide I have to say something.

"I'm sorry you were dragged into...whatever this is."

She laughs a little, "My brother can be a handful. He is compulsive, I just don't want anyone to get hurt."

"I get it," I nod a little. "I just don't want to be the reason I cause issues."

"It's nothing personal," She says and turns left. "My brother has a lot of obligations in our family and I just want to make sure he says focused."

"You sound like a good big sister."

"He would probably disagree, but I try my best." She smirks a little.

The conversation tapers off a bit and I feel myself relax. Anna makes little small talk here and there about the plan with what we are telling my parents and even how I feel about San Diego so far.

After a little bit, I noticed she's really not as bad as I thought. Maybe I shouldn't have judged her for being cold so quickly.

"Don't stress out. I'm good with parents." She announces as we pull up to my house.

The two of us walk up the stairs together and I push open the front door.

"Mom? Dad?"

"Come up to the kitchen, dear!" My mom yells from the upper level.

Anna follows me quietly up the stairs as the two of us enter the kitchen together. I notice my mom has been preparing what looks to be a four course meal.

"What are you cooking?"

"I'm preparing a business dinner for your father tonight," She says and pulls a pan out. "Very important men coming."

I smile a little at Anna and look back at my mom. "I want you to meet, Anna. She's been helping me catch up with stuff at school and we are working on a presentation this weekend together."

Anna extends her hand, "Nice to meet you, Mrs. Moore."

Mom beams at her. "You as well, dear." She looks at me and smiles. "I didn't know you made another friend. She's beautiful!"

Anna blushes a little. "Thank you, ma'am."

"Who is coming for dinner?" I ask and change the topic.

"Potential business partner and investor," She says and starts setting plates. "I guess this was a long time process before we made the big move."

"So...what does that mean for dad? If they say no?"

She frowns a little, "I'm not too sure, Liv. We're just staying positive."

"Has dad met this potential buyer before?"

"This will be the first time. I think his name is Mr. Romano."

I look over at Anna but she seems unbothered by the news.

"Do you know his first name? Is he older or younger?"I ask and start to wonder if Alessio would keep something like this from me.

" Uh...I don't think he's a younger man. Why?"

Anna intervenes. "Romano is my family's name. I'm sure it's with my dad."

"Oh, how lovely. I can't wait to meet him!" Mom cheers. "I think Olivia's father had mentioned his name being Abe? Angelo?

"Adolfo Romano," Anna corrects. "That's my father"

"How wonderful! I'll have to mention how lovely his daughter is."

Anna thanks her for the kind words and the two of us decide to help her with setting the table up for her meal.

Mom looks over as she puts down the last fork. "Are you sure you don't want to stay? I made way too much food."

"I wish, but we actually have some dinner plans set up before our project." Anna explains.

"No worries, dear! It was so nice meeting you."

After we finish helping, I let mom know the full plan again before running upstairs to grab a bag of my items before heading out the door again.

The drive back to the manor, Anna is pretty quiet. She seems to be focused on some conversation she is having with someone by text.

We pull through the same entrance gates as before and come to a stop in front of the home. I start to step out of the car just as someone opens the door for me.

An older man with a patchy dark beard and kind eyes smiles at me. "Miss Moore?"

"Yes?"

"My name is Mateo, Alessio's uncle, I'd be happy to hand your bags off to the maids."

"O-oh. Thank you so much." I stammer and hand them to him.

I wait for Anna and the two of us head up the stairs and inside together.

"Do you know if Alessio is back?" I ask her and follow her up the stairs.

"Not yet. He had some business with Giovanni and Beto."

Disappointment starts to settle in a bit but I try to not let his absence upset me too much.

Anna looks over at me, "Would you like to go swimming? It is beautiful today."

I think back to the massive swimming pool they have outside with the infinity edge. I hadn't been swimming much before since New York was usually not the spot for it. I used to stick to inside swimming facilities as a kid.

"I don't have a swimsuit..."

She rolls her eyes, "Olivia, you think we don't have extra swimsuits."

She motions for me to follow her down the hallway and leads me through a set of doors I haven't been by before.

Inside is a room a lot like Alessio's but with a girly flare. Her bed is decorated in rich rose gold silks and fluffy pillows.

"Check the bottom drawers of the armoire." She tells me and heads over to her vanity.

I don't seem to have much luck there except for fingering through several pairs of bras and underwear.

Anna points over her shoulder towards a door next to the bed and goes back to fixing her mascara.

I step inside and my jaw drops. "Fuck."

It's dripping with wealth and class. A stunning chandelier hangs from above, white shelves line each wall along with hundreds of high end fabrics and diamond necklaces displayed on stands.

I pick up a gorgeous red Gucci bag that still has a price tag on it.

$34,000

I feel my vision cross and put it down in shock.

"Need some help?"Anna asks coming in.

"T-this is i-insane."

"Let me know if you like anything," She grins and waves her hand around. "I have a bit of a thing for fashion.

She stops and pulls something off a shelf. "Try this one."

I wait for her to exit the room before pulling the one piece suit on.

It's white with gold hooks holding together the pieces of the fabric down the sides. The neckline creates a sharp v which basically leaves almost nothing to the imagination.

Anna walks in as soon as I pull the last strap up and hands me a pair of chunky sandals and a cover up.

Anna had opted for a tiny black swimsuit top and bottoms with a large brim hat and sunglasses. I couldn't help but gawk at her curves and perky breasts beneath the fabric.

The entire family was just perfect.

The two of us head out to the pool and carefully dip our feet in first.

"It's heated and salt water." She tells me before plunging right in.

I gasp and laugh as the water splashes all over me before following her lead.

We float around for a while letting the hot sun beat down on our exposed skin.

After some time splashing one another we noticed a maid walking out with a bottle of champagne on ice and a platter of crackers and cheese.

"Let's lay out."

I pull myself up out of the pool and pick a spot next to her on a nearby lounge chair. She rolls onto her stomach and pours us both a bottle of champagne.

Anna snorts loudly with laughter and drinks her first glass way too quickly before reaching for the bottle again.

"Will you untie the back?" She asks and points at her top.

I reach over and untie the back for her and try not to look as she tosses it away. She settles comfortably into her chair on her stomach and shields her face from the sun.

I look around awkwardly for a moment before deciding I might as well join. I use my free arm to cover my bare breasts as I move the top down a bit and roll onto my stomach like her.

The two of us spend some time chatting and drinking for a while before the little kisses from the sun and soft breeze take me away into a deep sleep.

Chapter 8

"Hey, beautiful."

My eyes flutter at the sound of Alessio's voice and I wake up to the brightness of the sun glaring in my eyes. Something soft strokes up and down the skin of my arm.

It feels good...

There's something else though.

The soft breeze against my skin. Exposed skin.

Exposed. Bare.

I immediately sit forward and cover my chest. I realize Alessio is sitting next to me on the lounge chair and staring out towards the setting sun.

"You're beautiful, Olivia. I wish you wouldn't hide.

I ignore his compliment and pull my straps back up over my chest. He waits until I'm finished and looks back at me. The sun casts shadows against his high cheekbones.

He silently leans forward and rests his forehead against mine. "It's time to get ready, love. Anna is waiting."

I nod a little and let him lead me upstairs back to Anna's room. She's sitting in the middle of her bed with several black boxes

"Here you go." She says and impatiently tosses me a box.

Inside I found a pair of black stiletto shoes with red bottoms. Tiny diamonds decorate the surface.

"Love those!" Anna grins and tosses me another with no warning.

There's a gorgeous teardrop diamond necklace inside with matching earrings.

"Wow!" She nods in approval, "Alessio really does have good taste."

"Anna..."I start. "What kind of party is this?"

She doesn't respond. Instead, the last box lands in my hands.

Inside there is a cute and dainty black mask with intricate details through the matte mask that seems to expand out like little butterfly wings with silver glitter. It is stunning but the sight of it makes my stomach hurt.

She chuckles when she notices my expression. "Did he not mention that it's a masquerade ball?"

"A ball!? You have to be kidding!" I drop the mask.

She rolls her eyes. "Stop being so dramatic. You'll be fine and you'll look gorgeous."

I start to pipe up and argue with her when a pair of unfamiliar girls walk in with two portable chairs and what looks to be salon equipment.

"Makeup and hair time!" Anna winks.

The two girls set up shop in the bathroom. Anna decides to pop open a bottle of wine and pours out two glasses for us both.

"How many people will be there?" I ask and look down at my shaky hands.

"Maybe fifty...maybe two hundred."

"Two hundred," I repeat robotically.

"What's the problem?" She laughs.

I look over at her. "I'm the problem, Anna! I'm not masquerading material."

She sighs and takes a drink. "It's really no big deal. We host these parties every year."

I nod and decide to change the subject. "Can I ask you something?"

"Sure."

I try to swallow the lump in my throat. "People tend to talk a lot...about things...with your family."

"Things?" Anna raises her brow.

"Things that are not necessarily legal."

My skin is burning hot. I'm so worried I will say the wrong thing.

"What are you asking?" Her voice hardens.

I don't reply.

She grows annoyed. "Olivia."

I panic. "Anna, I'm sorry! Don't feel like you need to answer that. I know I'm invading your privacy."

She laughs and sets her glass down, "Just know we do what we need to for our family, alright. We'll also keep you safe. We're smart, especially Alessio."

I nod and look back towards the mirror as the girl behind me starts to curl my hair.

Finding out the truth isn't going to be easy.

"You look so beautiful!"

I smile down at Alessio as I finish descending the stairs. I'm grateful that my ankles don't snap like I thought they would.

He looks so good. His suit black and hair neatly slicked back with gel. Looking at him makes me feel so small just being at his side.

"Where is everyone?" I ask.

He takes my hand. "Just down the hall and through the doors."

I nod nervously and a shaky breath comes down. I feel his lips at my ear.

"Are you ready, love?"

"If I said yes, I would be a liar." I admit and feel my heart pound in my chest.

Alessio gives my hand a little squeeze and leads the both of us through the doors together.

Inside is a magnificent ballroom full of people in gorgeous gowns and suits. All of them seem to move with one another in sync as the harps and violins play at the front of the room.

Several silks hang above us from the ceiling as people in full body silver suits wrap themselves in the silk as they plunge towards the floor.

I look out towards the dance floor and find Anna. She looks incredible.

A man with blonde hair dips her back playfully and kisses the exposed neck. Alessio and I watch them for a moment as he spins her out and back in towards his chest. They laugh together loudly and kiss.

"That is Anna's fiance from Sicily," Alessio whispers. "They'll be married early next year."

I smile and continue to watch them move together gracefully. Alessio's arm snakes around my waist and he pulls me closer.

"Would you like to dance?"

I look up at him terrified. "I've never danced before."

He smiles a little and positions his hands on my waist. I wrap my arms around his neck and stare at him before I realize we are already moving.

Our feet step side to side as we sway back and forth.

"What are we doing?" I giggle.

He laughs and kisses my nose. "Dancing."

"I'm not a good dancer."

"You're doing just fine."

I laugh a little too loud as he spins me away from him and dips me low. His mouth finds my neck and I feel his breath tickle me there. "What do you want, love?"

He pulls me up to him again and we stand before one another. Our lips just centimeters away.

Without even thinking about it I feel the pull between us. I feel as if I'll explode at any moment.

"Alessio?"

The electricity between us dies down as a new voice rings out. I realize Alessio is staring someone down and he doesn't look happy.

The voice had come from a beautiful girl with caramel locks in a stunning green dress. The material clung to the curves of her body and she moved with confidence.

Everything about her screamed elegance. She looked like a real life angel. Something about her seemed so surreal.

She approached the both of us slowly and glanced over at me with a pair of poison green eyes.

"Monica." Alessio spit out.

She smiled warmly at him. "I was hoping I'd see you tonight."

"You did." He states blandly and looks away. "Did you need something?"

"Not really," She purrs out in a heavy Italian accent. Her hand plays with the edge of his suit. "I've missed seeing you."

"We'll see about that." She taunts.

"Alessio?"

"Take Olivia to my room." He demands.

I look over at his uncle Mateo. "Do you know what is wrong?"

I nod a little and follow Mateo out of the ball and back up towards where Alessio's room is. Once I'm inside I take no time undressing and climbing into the massive bed.

It was as if all the progress we had seemed to make today was just gone. I didn't understand Alessio and I felt so lost.

◇ ◇ ◇

"Olivia."

The sound of his voice in the morning causes me to jump and I push up in the bed and rub at my eyes.

He's facing away from me and staring blankly out the window. His voice seems strained...almost as if he is upset.

"Are you okay?" I ask softly and my fingers itch to touch him.

He continues to stare out of the window as he speaks.

"Mateo will be taking you home this morning."

I stare at him as hurt and confusion cover my features.

"Alessio...what's going on? Why won't you talk to me? Why wo-"

Time seems to stand still as he takes me in. His mouth is warm and hot as we embrace one another for the first time.

I moan against his lips as his mouth hungrily kisses me. His hands snake down my curves and hook onto my waist tightly.

I can feel my core tighten as my nails dig into his back through his shirt.

"P-please."

His grip loosens and he's standing up running his fingers through his hair. I can see his breath coming in hard as he tries to compose himself.

I struggle to sit up and push my hair away from my face. My skin is still red hot from our touch.

My lips part and I stare blankly at him. His words rang continuously through my ears.

I stare after him as he crosses the floor and disappears. Once more...I'm alone.

I don't try to stop the tears from falling.

Chapter 9

ALESSIO

"It has been decided. The Rossi and Romano family WILL become one."

My fingers curl around the edge of my father's desk. I can't even see straight.

Red takes over my vision and all I can picture is my fist going through the damn wall.

"Did you even think to mention this to me before you agreed to this?" I snap. He laughs and leans back in his chair.

"Why ever would I need to do that, Alessio?"

My eyes narrow. "What the fuck is that supposed to mean?"

He groans and pushes himself up from his chair. Shadows cast across his aged face. Silver tinged hair and dark eyes.

"I still make the decisions, Alessio. I make decisions that I know are best for you and the family."

My anger flares and my fists come down against the desk without warning. He doesn't even flinch.

"I will not marry that, bitch."

He laughs and lights a cigar. "You will because I ordered it. The contract has been signed."

The urge to punch him right now is so fucking unreal.

He continues, "I'm sure you are worried about the pretty little vixen you've had around here. You're welcome to keep doing as you wish but keep your focus on your soon-to-be bride."

"What are you talking about?" I lie. I don't want him to even think about Olivia. The thought of him looking at her made me sick knowing his past.

"The pretty little girl with the blue eyes that has been running around here. Is she just another whore from the club?"

"Don't talk about her like that. She's not a whore."

He snickers, "Have your fun, son. I was your age once, don't forget it."

"What do we even get out of this, Adolfo? What is the point? This has never even been a thought for us with the Rossi family."

"More than half profit and several ports we have never had access to before. The Rossi family has expanded and have even moved into France and a few places in Russia. We need to grow, Alessio. It's important for the family to have enough security."

I sit there and sigh. Defeat settling in fast.

I stand up from the chair and turn my back to him.

"Fine. I'll do it."

OLIVIA

The engine turns off and I look over at Mateo. His dark eyes soft as he stares at me silently.

My heart was aching and the lump in my throat hadn't gone away. I didn't understand what was going on with Alessio.

We didn't even really know each other. Why would he say he's falling in love?

Was...Was I falling in love with him too? Can it really happen so quickly?

"Miss Moore?" Mateo's voice breaks the silence.

I look over sadly, "Can I ask you something?"

"Yes?"

"Should I worry about him? About Alessio?" I ask nervously.

He smiles and reaches out with a reassuring hand on my forearm. "He knows what he's doing. Give him some credit."

I nod but the hurt is still very clear on my face. I climb out from the passenger side and take my bags from Mateo. He waits patiently as I walk into my home and find mom moving around in the kitchen.

"Olivia?" She calls out.

"Yeah!" I yell up to her. "It's me. I'm home a little early."

I carry my bags towards my room and notice the smell of cigarettes. Mom only smokes when something is going on.

"Everything alright?" I ask and walk out to meet her.

She tries to smile but it doesn't meet the eyes. "Of course, dear. Just figuring out things with your father's job."

"What's going on?" I worry.

She motions for me to sit next to her and wraps her arms around me on the sofa.

"The deal with the Romano family may be a bust. Daniel doesn't think Mr. Romano was feeling confident in the investment."

I completely forgot my dad was having a business meeting with him.

"Did something go wrong during the dinner?"

"It went really well," She nods and rubs my shoulder. "He was a very nice man, a lot older than I expected, but he was very kind and seemed intrigued by the business but just left a lot of questions on everyone's minds before he left."

"What will happen now? If it falls through?"

She sighs a little. "I can always pick up a job. I know it's been awhile for me but I have no problem even working at the supermarket."

"No, mom. I can help out," I smile at her. "I start my new job at the coffee shop."

"We'd never expect you to pay bills."

"I'd be happy to still help." I snuggled into her side.

She pulls back and looks at me. Her eyes suddenly full of excitement. "I think you should save your money for college."

My brows furrow. "What do you mean?"

She passes me an envelope and waits patiently as I scan the blank ink scrawled across.

Cornell University

A gasp escapes me as I look up at her in shock. I tear into it and start reading immediately.

Mom grows impatient. "Well?"

"I got in!"

She gives me a tight squeeze and the two of us joyously laugh together as we read it over again. I can't believe this is my first acceptance letter and from my first choice!

"Baby! I'm so so proud of you," She says proudly and kisses my cheek. "You're going to be amazing! My artist."

I roll my eyes and stare at it. As excited as I should be, I can't stop thinking about Alessio.

I hadn't been in San Diego very long but it was already growing on me.

The front door suddenly opens and I hear my dad kick off his shoes against the hard floor as he comes up the stairs. "How are my girls?"

Mom looks over at me. "Olivia has some big news."

I hand him the letter, "I got accepted!"

"That is so great, Liv. I knew you could do it!" He gives me a tight hug and looks at the both of us. "Pizza for dinner?"

Mom applauds that idea and pulls her phone out to place the order.

"How was your day, dear? Any updates?" She asks as she types.

"Really great actually," He starts and removes his suit jacket. "Romano accepted and we came to an agreement."

My interest peaks. "He did? Mom had mentioned he was having cold feet."

"A few doubts, sure." Dad acknowledges. "Mr. Romano brought his youngest son with him to this meeting and he was actually the one who was very persistent that we close the deal. He even doubled what they wanted to put in."

"What was his name?"

"Something Italian like his father. Started with an 'A'."

"Alessio." I say robotically.

"That's it! Alessio. I'll need to give him a call tomorrow to thank him for his contribution."

The thought of Alessio and his father technically owning my dad's business made my stomach sick.

I tried to focus on anything but him though for the rest of the night. We ate way too much pizza and spent some time watching bad horror movies from the 70's and 80's. I realized my parents had eventually passed out on the catch and headed upstairs.

As I reached my room, I looked down and spotted a text message from Kimberly.

Do you know what's up with Austin? He won't respond to anyone.

Seeing his name made my stomach hurt all over again. I typed out my lie and hit send.

I'm not sure. He walked me home and that was it.

I frown and toss the phone to the bed. I just wanted this damn day to be over.

The next morning I felt like I was in a complete daze as I walked with Kimberly to school. It was almost as if a dark cloud was hanging over my head with all the lies I had conjured up regarding my interaction with Austin.

If I had it my way, Austin would never come near me again.

"Are you excited for tonight?" Kimberly smiles at me.

"Yeah!" I reply and try to focus on the thought of working my first shift. "Any tips?"

"Nope! Just be you and don't stress. It's super easy and you get free drinks every shift." She winked and bumped her hip against mine.

"Hey! Hey! "

We both turn around at the sound of Sierra's cheerful voice. She's shockingly wearing a girly sundress and has makeup on.

I don't think I've seen her in anything aside from leggings or oversized shirts.

"You look so cute!"

She curtsies and perks up. "I have big news!"

"What news?" Kimberly asks, almost sounding annoyed.

"I have a boyfriend! It happened last night."

Kimberly narrows her eyes. "Why didn't you call me? Who is it? When did you start actually liking BOYS?"

"Calm down!" Sierra playfully punches Sierra's shoulder. "It was a long night and I was tired but I am actually with A-"

Just as she is about to finish, Austin pops up next to her and wraps his arm around her waist.

"Hey cutie!" She cheers and kisses him.

I want to fucking puke.

Kimberly laughs, "Wow! I guess I can't say I am shocked."

Sierra blushes a deep red and Austin kisses her cheek.

"Congratulations," I mutter out to the two of them.

Austin looks up at me and smiles. It makes me feel ill. "Thank you, Olivia."

My head starts to play the scene all over again. His hot breath on me, mouth against mine, hands all over. The aggression and pain.

My stomach turns. I am going to puke.

"I'm not feeling so good. I'll see you later."

I dash down the hall without another word and am grateful when I find the bathroom empty. I hurl myself into the closest stall and puke violently into the toilet.

My head starts to pound and I rest it against the cool of the metal. I sit there on the floor for a minute as several girls come and go from the bathroom.

I eventually muster enough strength to stand and walk towards the sink.

"Olivia...can I talk to you?"

I glance up from the sink and look over to where Sierra is standing. She looks concerned.

"What's up?" I ask weakly.

She leans against the wall and looks at the floor. "I just wanted to check on you. I wasn't sure if you were mad at me or something after I told you about Austin."

"No. You've done nothing."

"Alright, I just wanted to make sure because Austin told me you liked him and got upset when he turned you down the other night."

Now I'm fucking pissed. "I do NOT like Austin. That's a bullshit lie and it never happened."

Sierra cringes from my reaction. "I'm sorry! I don't want to start any problems. I'm just relaying what he told me."

I sigh deeply and run my fingers through my hair. "I don't like Austin at all, Sierra. Be with him and be happy."

I look up at her and suddenly she's wrapping her arms around me and squeezing my body against her. "You're a good friend, Olivia."

I smile a bit and let myself hug her back. My heart is squeezing with the need to tell her the truth.

I'm not as good as you think.

The rest of the day moves in slow motion. Each class is long and boring. I try to stay buried in my art as the teachers discuss final prep for tests coming up as we enter the last few months of the school year.

To make things worse... Alessio hasn't shown up at all. I haven't even seen Beto today.

"You ready?" Kimberly asks as we exit the school.

Nerves start to take over as I think about starting my new job. I need the distraction though, something to keep my mind off of everything.

"Let's do this!"

The two of us take our time enjoying the weather and chatting as we make the walk to the cute little coffee shop a few blocks away. We round the corner and I hear the faint sound of indie music drifting from inside.

"Hey Tucker!" Kimberly shouts out.

She tosses me an apron and I slip it on. I look around and try to finally admire it's pleasing aesthetic.

It is a small cafe which really brings on the personal and intimate feel. Lots of tiny twinkling lights hang from the ceiling.

Most of the customers seem to be your on-the-go business type or hipsters in their twenties that come to blog about their feelings or strum a tiny ukulele with their friends in the corner of the store.

The back door to the kitchen swings open and Tucker steps through. He smiles brightly at the both of us.

He's very attractive, I won't lie, he has gorgeous ginger curls and big brown eyes. Not to mention, the cutest smile that is just a little too cocky.

"Hey ladies!" He greets and hands us our name tags. "How are you feeling about your first day, Olivia?"

"Pretty good! A little nervous though."

"You'll do great," He promises and slide onto the counter. "Today is a slow one so Kim here will just show you the ropes."

I smile at him a little and feel butterflies flutter around in my stomach.

"I'm going to handle some stuff in the back. Let me know if you need anything

Kim waits until he leaves and bumps my hip. "You like him!"

"Shut up! I do not!"

The two of us laugh together and continue our childish game of bumping into one another just as a voice interrupts us.

"Excuse me"

My heart flutters when I hear his familiar Italian accent. I look up and find Alessio leaning against the counter. His dark hair perfectly brushed from his eyes and a smirk on his face.

H-hi...."I say awkwardly and glance at Kim.

She ignores me and leans over the counter towards him. "How can we help you, sir?"

"Nothing, thank you. Can I borrow Olivia?" He asks and keeps his eyes locked on me.

Kim gives me a mischievous smile but waves her hand for me to follow him. I can practically feel her eyes burning holes into my back as I follow him around the counter and towards a sofa nestled in the back of the cafe near the bookcases.

"Are you okay?" I ask him

He sighs and pulls me onto his laugh without a warning. His mouth nuzzles into my neck as he wraps his arms tightly around me.

"I missed you."

Frustration flares through me and I push back. "I don't think so, Alessio. You need to explain what happened the other night."

His jaw flexes and he looks away. "I'm sorry...I had some unexpected business to tend to. I shouldn't have left you in the dark."

"That's not all...you said...you said you love me?"

He smiles and looks back up at me with his black eyes. "I did, yes."

"That was a joke? Right?"

"No, it wasn't." He says sternly. Almost seeming offended by my assumption.

" How do you know? We barely know each other, Alessio."

He picks my hand up and kisses each finger. "Are you saying you deny feelings you have for me?"

My breath comes out shaky. "No...I just...I-"

He continues to kiss my hand and looks back up at me patiently.

What the fuck did I feel? I couldn't deny what was there.

He was my every thought. Since the day I saw Alessio he had consumed my mind...my dreams...everything was him.

Was this what love is for some people? Love at first sight?

"You don't have to tell me right now," He interjected. "Just know I meant it."

"You confuse me,"I groan out and pull my hand back. "You are so damn frustrating."

He grabs my face in his hands and presses his mouth to mine in a heated kiss. I feel myself getting wrapped up in the moment before realizing where we were.

"I can't do that here. I'm at work."

He smiles against my mouth and pulls back. "I'll see you later, love. Enjoy the rest of your first day."

I watch silently as he stands up and makes his exit. My heart pounding in my chest and a thousand thoughts running through my head.

How the fuck was I going to focus on training now?

"Done making out?"

"Ahh!" I shout and clutch at my chest as Kimberly comes into view. "I'm sorry! He's gone."

"Good!" She tosses me a rag. "Get to work, bitch."

My first shift at the cafe goes a lot quicker than expected but I actually had a lot of fun.

Kimberly wasn't a bad trainer and to my surprise Tucker had mentioned I was already picking up on quite a bit.

By the time the last customer had left for the day, Kimberly and I were just about done wiping down the tables and chairs.

"Great first day!" Tucker praises.

I smile at him, "Thank you!"

Kimberly anxiously looks down at her phone. "Do you mind if I leave a few minutes early? I have some crap going on at home."

"Sure. You okay with that, Olivia?" Tucker looks over at me.

"Of course. I'll see you later, Kim."

She gives me a thankful smile and a quick kiss on the cheek before tossing her apron to the counter and running out the door. I go back to scrubbing down the sticky coffee stains on the counter as Tucker walks up to my side.

"How are you liking it so far?"

"I honestly really like it."

"You did a great job," He smiles and gives me that fluttery feeling again. "Want to continue the week working with Kimberly on her shift?"

"I'd love that."

He grins at me and walks away for a moment to grab the store keys. I take my time to admire him and his appeal.

He kind of had that bad boy look to him but a baby face. He had slipped into a leather motorcycle jacket that looked faded and had a pair of tattered jeans on with his combat boots.

Despite the Sons of Anarchy look he was trying to go for he seemed like a really nice, genuine guy.

"I'm glad the old man hired you on," Tucker says randomly and starts flipping lights off. "I think you are going to be a great addition to the team."

My cheeks blush. "Me too."

I toss my apron and name tag to the bin by the counter and grab my items as the two of us walk to the door. He pulls it open and I wait patiently as the wind blows around wildly in the night.

He puts the keys in his pockets and just stares at me awkwardly for a moment.

"What's up?"

He looks away, "Nothing...it's nothing."

I nude his shoulder, "You can tell me! I know I'm new and all, but I swear I am a good listener and I don't judge."

"I don't want to sound unprofessional, but I was just admiring how beautiful you are."

I can feel my cheeks heat up immediately. I open my mouth to say something but he speaks before I can.

"I'm sorry! That was completely out of line. I just... I shouldn't have-"

I put my hand on his shoulder, "Tucker, it's fine. I would be a liar if I didn't admit I find you attractive as well."

He relaxes a bit under my touch and nods. "Well, have a good night, Olivia."

Tucker turns and heads down the sidewalk towards a beat up looking focus parked against the curb.

I look back at the cafe and towards the walk ahead. I couldn't help but wear a smile the entire walk home.

I was so happy. So, so happy!

I felt like I was on top of the world and I never wanted this to end. Everything finally felt right.

Chapter 10

Two months had come and gone.

Things were going great and I was in love with my life. I was excelling at Westview, my art was being noticed and I even got to participate in a local art show, I was growing closer to Kimberly, and I even started up a new relationship.

Tucker had asked me out about 3 weeks after my first day. I spent most of my shifts with him and Kim.

It just felt right. Tucker was sweet and he was always going out of his way to do things for me.

We would go on little dates to a local diner to stuff ourselves on burgers and spend our weekends at his apartment watching shitty movies.

Plus, he respected me. I didn't feel any overwhelming pressure to have sex with him.

We were taking it slow and I was so grateful for that. I worked up the courage for my parents to meet him and they were sold.

I had a good boyfriend, great friends, and I finally was finding my way. I had a plan for the rest of my life after Westview and the thought of Tucker possibly moving with me to New York when I started in the Summer was fueling me even more.

I needed this. I needed a normal, happy life for a very normal and average girl.

I'd be lying though if I denied that I didn't think about Alessio anymore.

The last day I saw him was when he came to the cafe that first shift. The next day he still wasn't at school and my calls and texts were never returned.

I even tried Anna but that never got me anywhere.

I didn't know where he was and I sure as hell didn't know how to find him. The feeling that Alessio had used me and blown me off for something else tore me apart.

I really had just been a game for him and the others. I was the sweet, average girl that he played like a violin and tossed to the side like garbage.

I shouldn't have been surprised. Alessio Romano isn't the kind of person to have relationships with quirky, art school girls from New York.

He is with girls like Monica from the masquerade. Beautiful, Italian women with supermodel bodies and lots of money and class.

The only time I felt any hope was about a week after I had seen Alessio when Beto finally showed up at the high school and I caught him going into the office.

He had several envelopes in his hands and tried to act like he hadn't heard me when I called out his name.

When Beto did turn around, he didn't react like I hoped he would. He was dismissive and very cold.

"Beto, what is going on? Where's Alessio?" I begged him.

He sighed and tucked the envelopes under his arm. "Olivia, it just didn't work out, alright? There's nothing else to it."

"Don't lie to me, please. I know something is going on. Where is he? Why haven't you guys been in school?"

He sighed and brushed his hair back. "We aren't coming to school anymore. We finished early and we are moving on."

"Just moving on? I don't under-"

"Olivia," Beto snapped at me. "Stop asking questions! Alessio doesn't want you. You need to move on and forget him and the rest of us. Do you understand?"

My mouth fell open and I felt the tears burn my eyes. "No...I don't."

"That's not my problem."

With that, Beto turned around and stormed out of the school. I stood there in the hallway by myself as the tears fell. I was so sick to my stomach and confused.

Why would he do this to me? What did I do wrong?

As those weeks went by, I was constantly thinking about him. I only felt normal when I was with Kim and Tucker.

I was struggling to focus on school and spent night after night in my room. I was just so hurt and so lost.

I had no answers and it killed me.

As the days went by, it eventually got easier.

I opened up to Kimberly about it and she had been doing her best to keep me happy. Alessio never left my mind, but it started to hurt a little less.

I was now preoccupied with my 18th birthday coming up and prom. School would be ending within just a few months.

I was so ready to go back home to New York. Kimberly knew I'd come see her on breaks, but I missed my friends. Finishing my senior year without them had been really hard.

Plus, I needed to spill myself to someone who knew me since the diaper days.

"So what are you wearing for prom?" She asks and turns on MTV.

Kim and I had been curled up on her bed and flipping through old fashion magazines her mom had.

She decided to go with her friend who turned more into a boyfriend. Joe was on the football team at Westview and from what I've seen he was a sweet kid.

He put up with Kimberly's mood swings and kept her in line. They had been practically attached to the hip at school and I was just grateful she had someone when I was with Tucker.

I missed our daily girl time though.

"Not sure," I muttered and scrolled through my phone. "I haven't thought about it much."

I wasn't exactly thrilled about prom.

I didn't really have anyone aside from Kim and I knew I would have to play third wheel since she'd have Joe and of course, Sierra and Austin would be there together.

Unfortunately, with Tucker being twenty-one and the school not allowing outside attendees, I was basically destined to go solo.

"Well, get on it," Kimberly groans and rolls onto her back. "How are things with Tucker?"

I grin at her, "Really good."

"Oh yeah," She teases and pokes me. "Have you done the dirty?"

"Kimberly!" I smack her arm. "We're taking things slow."

She nods,"I admire that, but it could NEVER be me."

I roll my eyes at her and watch as she stands up from her bed and goes to her closet.

"What are you doing?" I shake my head as she starts tossing clothes.

"Aha!" She exclaims and pulls out a very tight fitting, glittery gold dress with no straps. It is very Kimberly.

"Is that the one?" I ask.

She nods and holds it to her body. "Yes, ma'am. I probably have something for you too."

"Or...or...I could just hang out...with Tucker?" I say quietly.

"Olivia, you promised! You know Joe and I aren't going to ditch you and I WISH Tuck could come but the school is never going to let that happen." She whines out.

"I know, I know! I'll go for you." I laugh and hold my hands up in surrender.

She smiles at me and bats her eyes before a dress is thrown right at my face.

I pull it off my head and hold it up. It's a beautiful deep purple shade with tiny specks of silver glitter. The skirt of the dress had wire beneath it to give it more of that puffy, formal look.

"The school is going to allow us to wear dresses..." I start and turn it around, "This short?"

She rolls her eyes, "It is not that short, Olivia."

I bite my tongue from arguing with her anymore and decide to let her play barbie with me. I slip into the dress and look at myself in the mirror hanging on her closet door.

The hem of it barely reaches the top of my thighs and it is completely strapless.

Again...very, very Kimberly.

"We look so hot!" Kimberly cheers and spins around. "Let's take pictures."

I try to keep my best smile on for her as she sets up a mini photoshoot for the both of us.

I couldn't help but feel a wave of sadness wash over me with the realization that I wouldn't be with Alessio.

Our time together was so short but part of me had really hoped that there would be more dancing. I hated dancing, but for him, I would do it until my legs fell off.

I wanted this to be our moment together.

◇ ◇ ◇

"Excited for your birthday dinner, cutie?" Tucker asks and wraps his arm around my waist.

I wrap my arms around his neck. "Are you ever going to spill where we are going?"

"Why would I ruin it?"

"Fine!" I laugh and roll my eyes. "Let me finish up here."

I feel his eyes on me as I lean over and clean off the last few tables and carry the bucket of dirty water and rags back into the kitchen.

"You're so cute when you have your work face on." He teases.

I roll my eyes and playfully hit at him as we head out of the cafe together and lock up. He leads the way to his car and opens my door.

"Should I change?" I ask and look down at my black shirt and slacks.

"You look great."

I smile and climb into the passenger side. Tucker walks over to the driver's side and his hand finds mine almost immediately.

We had a good routine going. It was almost like we moved as one unit.

Before long we are pulling up to some unfamiliar Italian restaurant in the city. The outside already looked packed with cars and I could tell I was definitely not dressed right for a place this nice.

"In the mood for Italian?" Tucker asks and turns the car off.

My cheeks blush but I don't say another word as he leads us up to the front of the entrance where a young male greets the both of us.

We're led back towards the south end of the restaurant where a cute little booth is set up with piping hot breadsticks and adorable tea lights.

"Thank you for this," I tell Tucker as we sit across from one another. "This looks so nice."

"Anything for you." He smiles and kisses my hand.

I smile back at him and look up just as a waitress comes to take our drink order. The restaurant is getting crowded fast with hungry customers but I realize not all of them are waiting for tables.

A line has formed in front of a guy who looks to be working as security for a section located upstairs.

I let my eyes wander over the people standing there and realize one of them sticks out like a sore thumb.

"Excuse me," I say politely to Tucker. "I see an old friend. I'll be right back."

He nods a little and watches me curiously as I hurry from the table and rush over to the crowd standing there.

"Anna!"

She turns around and her eyes widen. "Olivia! What are you doing here?"

"I guess I should ask the same," I smile awkwardly. "I'm out eating for my birthday."

"Ah, that's right." She smiles and looks past me to where Tucker is sitting. "Who is that?"

"He's the assistant manager where I work. We're...we're dating."

She stares at him a little longer before smiling back at me. "Well, congratulations, Olivia. Also, happy birthday. You look so beautiful."

I try to force a smile back at her but my heart strains and I can't stop myself from wrapping my arms around her without warning. She laughs a little at my sudden embrace and pulls the two of us down towards a nearby bench

Her eyes flick back towards a blonde man who had been standing with her. I realize immediately it's her fiance Alonzo from the dance.

"Continua. Ci vediamo presto." (Translation: Go ahead. I'll see you soon)

She sighs and holds my hands in hers.

"I know you want to talk to me about, Alessio."

"Where is he Anna? I just want to know he's okay."

"He's in Italy."

My brows pull together. "Italy? Why?"

"We have a lot of family and close friends. He's handling some stuff with them regarding business matters for a couple of months there."

I breathe out heavily. "Anna...why did he just leave? Why did he not say anything to me?"

"Olivia," She squeezes my hands. "Alessio really does love you. He cares so much about you but he is doing this...to protect you."

"Protect me?" I ask a little too harshly.

"Yes, Olivia. I know you had a lot of questions about us and what we do," She says and glances over my shoulder towards Tucker. "Let's just say being with Alessio isn't safe."

I frown at her vague response and follow her gaze towards Tucker. He gives me a little wave and points to our breadsticks.

"Go ahead." Anna reassures me.

I look back at her and frown. I so badly wanted to ask her everything, but there was just no time.

I knew I wouldn't get the answers I wanted.

"Oh, Olivia!" She says as I start to stand. "Happy birthday. Alessio wanted you to have this."

I look down at the tiny black box in my hands and pull the top off to reveal a gorgeous silver necklace with a heart.

On the inside is the word Amore sprawled out in beautiful scripture against the velvet lining.

My heart squeezes and I brush my fingertips against the lockett.

I look back up at Anna one more time before slipping the necklace into my pocket and heading back towards our table.

ALESSIO

The sun was rising quick this morning in Venice. This was my favorite part of every morning.

Watching the sun rise and having my morning cigarette.

I loved Venice. It's beautiful and the environment here is like no other.

It didn't stop me from thinking about her though. Two months had gone by and she was still my waking thought.

I was a piece of shit for leaving Olivia without a word. I knew my absence was going to ruin her that day, I went to see her in the cafe.

I don't know why I even went to see her. Why I even made it sound like there was hope.

I just needed to kiss her. Feel her before I left.

After my meeting that evening with Adolfo, I knew I couldn't continue my pursuit with Olivia.

I was falling for her fast. I barely knew the girl and I wanted her in every way imaginable.

The contract was already signed. I would marry Monica Rossi within months and my duty was now to help handle business with Giovanni in Venice while planning my wedding with my soon-to-be bride.

After the masquerade ball, my father had invited the Rossi family to return the next day for a small party.

I got down on one knee and asked Monica to be my bride in front of all of them. She sure put on a hell of a show.

Almost looked like we actually loved each other.

"Fidanzato." (Translation: Fiance)

I tense at the sound of Monica's voice and feel her arms wrap around my waist. She walks around to stand in front of me. Strands of her chestnut colored hair blow against her face and mask her green eyes.

I stare down at her with no emotion.

"Last night was wonderful." She purrs and trails her manicured claws down my bare stomach.

I nod in response and take another drag.

Monica and I were doing everything as a normal engaged couple was. We were shopping together, planning our future, and having sex.

It was just that though. Sex with her was simply a way to keep me from wanting to strangle her every second.

I had no desire to be with Monica Rossi. She was a pest.

The only good she could do for me was make me cum and shut her mouth at this point if I was to spend my life with her.

Despite her efforts, I knew Monica didn't like me either. She was just trying to please her father.

This marriage was nothing but a business arrangement. My heart and soul would stay with Olivia.

I couldn't keep myself completely away from her though. Even in Italy, I was still having my men keep their eyes on her.

I knew she was dating Tucker and things were going okay. His background came up clean and he seemed like a safe choice for her.

"Qual è il tuo problema?" Monica snaps out, clearly annoyed with my lack of response. (Translation: What is your problem?)

I continue to ignore her and shrug.

"You are thinking of that girl," She spits out. "She's old news, Alessio. Let it go."

"Monica, leave it alone."

She smiles up at me seductively. "Can Olivia make you cum like I can?"

My jaw flexes a bit as her fingers trail against the hem of my jeans. I flick my cigarette out over the balcony and pull her towards the house.

OLIVIA

"Hurry!"

Kimberly laughs loudly as the two of us rush towards the school gym. Running in heels is the hardest thing ever. I suck at being a girl.

The two of us enter through the handmade arch the prom committee put together and walk up towards a table with snacks and punch.

"Joe!" Kimberly shouts and starts waving.

He walks up to the two of us wearing a dark suit with a matching corsage to coordinate with the colors in her dress.

He's a cute guy and certainly Kimberly's type.

Tall, athletic, dark shaggy hair and muscular.

"How are you?" He asks as she kisses him

"Great." She swoons.

The two of them go back to sucking face so I decide to scan the room a bit and see what's going on.

The entire gym was decorated for a "beach/sea" theme but it really reminded me of The Little Mermaid a lot more.

I noticed Austin and Sierra curled up with one another at a table across the room. The two of them both match with a violet dress and tie.

My stomach turned watching the two of them playfully kiss and hold each other. The thought of Austin possibly hurting her in the way he was with me that night didn't sit well.

He finally caught my gaze and a creepy smile crawled across his face. I watched as he nudged Sierra and pointed to us.

"Hey guys!" She shouts and sprints across the room.

I tear my eyes from Austin and smile back at her. "You look great!"

"Thank you! You too!"

Kimberly slides up between us with Joe, "Anyone want some punch?"

"Sure."

We all stock up on drinks and head back out to the floor.

"Wow...remind me to thank the prom committee," Kimberly snorts loudly. "This is bad."

I laugh and roll my eyes at her. All of us move out onto the dance floor and start dancing with one another to the Chris Brown song playing on the speakers.

I step back a bit and watch them all dancing together with one another. Austin was back to making out with Sierra and Kimberly was just a few pieces of fabric away from basically having sex with Joe.

So much for being included.

I groan and look down at my throbbing feet. I slip the painful heels off and toss them onto a table so I can get a good rub on my sole.

"You okay, miss?"

I glance up to find an unfamiliar man in a trench coat with a grey fedora looking down at me. He didn't look like any teacher I've ever seen.

"I'm fine."

"Just checking, beautiful."

My heart stops as I hear him say those words. It's such a common phrase but something about his voice sounds so familiar.

I feel like I should know him.

"Wa-" I look back up and he's gone.

My stomach starts to hurt as the memory hits me and I suddenly have the urge to puke. I rush out the back door and spill my guts all over the ground. Several people nearby groan in disgust.

I hadn't thought about that night in what felt like forever now.

It was just rushing back...

I was 12 years old and it was a week before Christmas. I decided to walk down to the local shop to pick up a gift for my parents with the chore money I had earned along with some snacks.

That night the weather was especially harsh and cold. The snow covered the ground and there had been flurries in the air.

I had my headphones in like I always did and kept my coat close to my body.

I looked down at the sidewalk as I walked and watched my feet create little streaks in the snow as I moved.

I was only a block away from my townhome and knew if I didn't get back soon my mom would flip out.

"Hello, beautiful."

I stopped walking and looked up towards the alley to my right. I couldn't make out who was there but I could tell there was a figure looming in the darkness.

"Do I know you?" I asked, my voice breaking.

"No, princess," He said back and took a step forward. "I'm not someone you'd want to know."

My heart had quickened in my chest and I felt nauseous. He took another step towards me and I caught the glimpse of his coat blowing in the wind.

"I have to go."

I turned to walk away when he suddenly reached out and grabbed my wrist.

"Hey!" I shouted and pulled against him. "Let me go."

I felt my body move backwards as he pulled me into the dark alleyway with him and pushed me up against a nearby wall. Something cool touched the edge of my neck and I realized quickly he had a knife.

"Don't be rude." He snapped.

"What do you want?" I cried out. My body shook with terror.

His hand clamped over my mouth and he leaned down to say something but stopped when a new voice spoke up from behind.

"I want her back, darling. I'm sorry it has to be this way." The voice said from the shadows.

I looked at the dark figures of both of them in terror. "I don't know what you mean!"

A laugh escaped the man holding the knife against me and I felt the edge of the blade dig a little deeper.

I closed my eyes and waited for it to end.

"What's going on back there?"

My eyes popped open at the sound of a female voice. I tried to look to the side so I could move my mouth from under his hand.

"Let her go." The man standing the furthest away spoke.

I felt the knife disappear from my neck as he released me and fell to the ground. I could feel a trickle of blood there from where the edge of it had cut me just slightly.

"We'll meet again." The man said before turning around and disappearing with the other behind a corner.

The both of them had vanished and I couldn't stop crying.

"Sweetheart! Are you okay?"

I looked up at the woman rushing over to me with several others and couldn't say a word. I just kept staring back in the direction of where they ran off too.

Chapter 11

*"F*uck."

I groan and wipe at my mouth. The taste of vomit is still fresh in my mouth.

I stand up from the hard ground and run my fingers through my hair. "You got this."

I turn and walk back inside the gymnasium and before I have time to react Kimberly is standing before me smelling strongly of alcohol.

"Olivia!" She gushes and hugs me, "Joe is going to have a party. Let's go!"

"I really don't think my parents would like that."

"I'm begging you!" She pouts and bats her big, dark eyes. "Tell them you are sleeping over."

I laugh and throw my hands up,"Okay, okay! Just for a little."

After all the shit I've been dealing with, I could certainly use a night to relax. Plus, I've never been to a high school party before.

Kimberly decides to go on a spree of making sure the word is spread before we exit the gym together and head towards Joe's mustang.

The three of us climb into the car and I look down at my puffy, prom dress. "There's no way I can wear this all night."

Kim rolls her eyes at me from the front seat and holds up a bag for me to see. "I got you, bitch."

"This is why you are the love of my life." I sigh happily.

Thankfully, Joe only lives about ten minutes down the road from the school so before long we are pulling up to a gorgeous house that looked to be a million dollar home. I knew he had mentioned his parents were lawyers but I wasn't expecting this.

I follow Kimberly into the house and back through the kitchen towards a guest room. She tosses the bag on the bed and hands me a tank top with some black shorts.

"Nothing...less revealing?" I ask desperately.

"You look hot."

I fight the urge to argue but figure it will be better than having to wear this damn dress all night. The two of us finish up with changing and head out to the front to find Joe high fiving a group of football buddies as they pass by us with beer in tow.

"Need any...help?" I ask as more people enter.

He laughs and highfives another. "I guess not!"

Within the next hour the house is over capacity and it is a freaking mad house. The music is blasting and shaking the walls. I could barely even move through the livingroom to find an open seat on the couch.

I plop down on it quickly and look over at a girl who is passed out next to me. I think she's the same girl from my math class.

I pull my phone out and send Tucker a text.

I miss you. Everything is going okay but I am at a party at Joe's house.

I look down at the table in front of me and see a tray of jello shots. I pick up two and slurp them back before the alcohol taste can talk me out of it.

My phone buzzes.

Send me the address just in case. Let me know if you need me to get you.

I smile at his text and stand back up from the couch. If I'm going to deal with this party, I need something strong.

I make my way into the kitchen and locate two shots of whiskey. I knock them back without hesitation but feel my head spin.

"Woo!" I say cheerfully and grab onto the island.

"You okay?"

I look up and see Austin staring at me. He had a beer in his hand and no Sierra attached to his bicep.

"Y-yeah."

I push away from the edge of the counter and am a little shocked with how fucked up I already feel.

Would they have spiked it?

I feel a hand catch my elbow before I have a chance to face plant on the kitchen floor.

"You need to lay down."

I don't really fight whoever is pulling me with them and am grateful when I feel the softness of the bed under me.

"I'm okay." I mutter against it.

A few moments pass of silence before I feel the bed shift. I try to roll onto my side and realize Austin is still in the room with me.

"Did you tell anyone about that night?" He says randomly.

I scowl at him, "No, Austin."

He chuckles and the sound makes my stomach hurt. "Good, I didn't think you would."

"Alessio knows." I remind him.

"Where is he then, Olivia?"

"He's still around." I lie and he rolls his eyes at me.

"I'm not worried about, Alessio. I just want to make sure you and I have an understanding about that night, considering I'm in a committed relationship with one of your best friends."

My vision blurs and I'm suddenly seeing red. "You forced yourself on me, dick!"

"Don't fucking fool yourself, Olivia." He snaps back and I flinch from the harshness. "I did no such thing. You are a fucking whore and a liar."

"No, I'm not."

He pushes up from the bed and runs his hands through his hair. "Everyone knows it, Olivia. You couldn't get the Italian to stay with you so you are running to everyone else. You obviously liked me before him."

I shake my head and look away. "You're drunk, Austin. Please leave."

He laughs darkly and leans against the wall, "You're so dumb, Olivia. Why even waste your time on someone that doesn't give you the time of day. You could've had a good relationship with me."

I stare silently back at him and feel my heart squeeze. He's right about Alessio at least.

I was dumb for wasting my time with him.

He continues on, "All of you women are the same! It's fucking insane."

"Where's Sierra?" I ask, changing the subject.

"She's at home. She didn't want to come."

I push up from the bed and start moving towards the door with whatever strength I could muster up. "Focus on your girlfriend and leave me alone."

I pull the door back and it slams shut again. Austin slaps his hand against the wood and blocks me from leaving.

"Move!"

He laughs in my face and shoves me backwards until I hit the back with a thump. I feel my head spiral from the alcohol and try to roll over.

"Let me show you what you missed out on." Austin purrs out and grabs onto my thighs.

"Get off of me!"

I try to swing my leg around and aim for his balls. He catches my legs and his grip only tightens as he shifts his weight onto me.

"I can be your prince charming, Olivia."

I grind my teeth together as I feel his hot breath on me again. His mouth starts to kiss down my neck and I try to force my body from under him yet again.

I try to shove my knee upwards again but before I can connect with his stomach the weight of him is suddenly gone.

"What the fuck!" Austin shouts and there's a loud thud.

I push up from the bed and realize someone else entered the room. Alessio.

Seeing him made every part of me feel alive again. He was actually here. Here in front of me.

His dark eyes full of rage and staring down at Austin now. A silver glock resting against his temple.

Austin holds his hands up and trembles. "Don't do anything stupid,dude."

"Get up and exit the room without a word. My brother Giovanni is waiting outside the door. Do not say a word or even look at, Olivia. You got that? Dude?" Alessio taunts, his voice ice cold.

The safety switches off and Austin shakes. "P-please. I'm going."

Alessio straightens up and flexes his jaw a bit before the gun strikes down painfully against the back of Austin's head. I stifle a scream as he hits the floor hard.

"Go now."

Austin stands up and grabs the back of his head, dark red blood oozes between his fingers. He looks back at Alessio one more time before the door opens and he disappears through it.

I stare back up at Alessio in silence. My head is still swarming from a mix of tonight's events and the alcohol.

It feels like forever passes by before he finally looks down at me. His features seem to almost soften immediately.

"Alessio..."I start out and feel tears spring to my eyes.

Without another word he closes the distance between us. His mouth crushes against mine and our bodies mold together. I feel myself gasping for air as we embrace one another tightly.

I felt like I needed his touch like I do air or water.

I needed every part of him. Without him it was like a missing puzzle piece.

There seemed to be so many invisible forces against us. I knew there was so much I didn't know yet.

I just wanted him in every way.

But...Tucker.

The thought stopped me immediately. My heart skipped a little and I pushed him back.

He paid me no mind and crushed me against him again. "I missed you so much, Olivia."

"Alessio, wait."

His mouth and hands continued to move. My head was so light.

"No, please! Alessio, stop."

He pulls back a little and stares at me silently. Both of us were breathing hard and his dark eyes scanning every inch of my face. Almost as if he was memorizing it.

He reaches out and brushes my lip with his thumb. "Olivia."

I stand up from the bed and run my hands through my hair. "You can't just show back up two months later and expect it to be okay."

"Let me-"

"No!" I yell at him, anger fueling me. "You left without a word, Alessio! You tell me you are falling in love with me and disappear again.

All I could feel was pain. Every emotion I had been trying to suppress for weeks was just boiling over. I was so pissed off at him.

He looks down at me and narrows his eyes. "Olivia, I had important matters I had to take care of."

"It's always something, Alessio! Always an excuse!" I snap and reach for the door.

Without hesitation, his body slides in between me and the door and blocks me. His hand finds my neck and he cradles my head back so our lips are barely touching.

"Stop with the attitude. You need to calm down and let me explain."

I stare back at his face silently. My eyes wander from his black eyes to the hint of stubble on his face now tickling the edge of my cheek. His full, warm lips just inches from mine.

"You shouldn't be drinking this much,"He whispers and brushes his nose with mine. "It's dangerous."

"I'm allowed to do what I want."

Alessio sighs, "I know you are."

"So stop acting like you can control me, Alessio. Always showing up when it's convenient, but not being there when I needed you."

"Let me take you back with me and we can talk. I promise."

I push back against him and he releases me. "I have a boyfriend now, Alessio. I don't think that is a good idea."

He laughs, "You think I care what Tucker thinks?"

"Have you been spying on me?" I accuse.

"Protecting you."

"That's an invasion of my privacy!" I snap and hit my fists against his solid chest. "I'm not just some helpless doll."

He catches my fists in his hands and pins me to the door. His mouth comes down just inches from my ear. His breath tickled my lobe.

"I won't leave you again. Ever"

I say nothing and his mouth moves to my mouth again. The tip of his tongue tracing the edge.

"Do you want this?"

My breath quickens and he moves down to kiss my collarbone.

"Answer the question, Olivia."

"Y-yes,"I stutter out.

"I need you, Olivia. I can't move on without you in my life."

A small moan escapes me as he playfully bites at my neck.

"Come with me." He says against my skin.

I look up at him and nod a little. Alessio releases all of me but my hand as we exit the room and make our way together out of the house.

Part of me knows I should inform Kim but we don't stop moving to his Porsche.

He opens my door. "How did you find me?" I ask him.

"Mateo."

"Where is he now?"

"Probably back at the estate."

I climb inside and wait for him to climb into the driver's side.

He starts the car and I look back over at him, "What will happen to Austin?"

No answer.

"What will happen to Austin?" I demand again as he pulls from the curb.

His grip tightens against the wheel and I see his knuckles go white.

"Please tell me," I say softer.

"He'll never hurt you again." He answers. His eyes are still on the road.

I look back out towards the dark road ahead and try to swallow the lump in my throat.

"Alessio, please."

No answer. Silence.

My stomach turns and I feel bile move upwards.

Yep. Going to puke.

"I'm going to be sick," I tell him and reach for the handle.

I hear him mutter something that sounds like a string of curse words in Italian as the car pulls up to the curb. I shove the door out of my way and vomit all the alcohol I had onto the street.

Within seconds I can feel Alessio trying to clear my hair from my face so I can breathe and see.

"Are you alright?" He asks after a moment.

"He's dead," I state randomly and sit up, wiping my mouth.

"I can't let anyone hurt you like that again, Olivia."

I look over at him. His dark eyes are full of worry.

"Who are you?"

He lets go of me and settles back into his seat. Something inaudible slips from him and he sighs.

"I'm in the Italian mafia."

Chapter 12

I wake up and look up at the tall ceiling above me. I can feel my head already pounding and now I am about to have a massive hangover.

I turn onto my side and pick up the comforter beneath my hands. Alessio is nowhere to be found.

His confession from last night was still very fresh in my mind but I couldn't remember much after since I apparently passed out from being so drunk.

The thought of Alessio being in the mafia was too much. Even worse was knowing he had been the one to kill Austin.

What would happen now? People would be looking for him.

His friends...his family.

My stomach started to ache and I knew I was going to puke again. I sprint across the marble floors and throw up in his bathroom. My head resting against the cool of the toilet.

My mind was spiraling with every thought. I didn't know what to do.

I was in the house of the Italian mafia.

Alessio kills people. He's a monster.

I can't be here.

My throat constricts and I dry heave once more. My head pounds against my skull again and I try to pick myself up from the floor.

"I have to get out of here." I whisper to myself.

I couldn't just not tell someone. Wouldn't it be morally wrong for me to do nothing?

Murder is still murder.

I walked out from the bathroom and noticed I had been changed into a nightgown. I picked up the satin fabric between my fingers and rubbed it with my thumb.

I looked over the nightstand and noticed the clothes Kimberly leant me the night before were there and vomit free.

I slipped out of the little dress and back into them before grabbing my shoes and hurrying out the door.

It was so silent.

Nobody was rushing down the halls with baskets of laundry. I didn't see any guards and not a single Romano.

I walked as slowly as I could on the tips of my feet as I walked down the dim lit and narrow hall. I could see the steps coming into view and let fingers glide along the cool of the metal banister.

My heart was beating so loud I swear someone could hear me.

"Please don't!"

I froze as soon as I heard the scream. It didn't sound too far away.

I carefully descended down the stairs and down onto the first level. Still no sign of anyone.

It was so strange to see such a big house so empty. It felt creepy.

"Please someone help!"

My head snaps towards the sound of the voice crying out in pain from the hall to my left. I look back towards the double glass doors.

I should go. I should call the police. Why am I not running?

"Help!"

"Fuck!" I whisper under my breath and tiptoe down the hall. The hall seemed to go on forever as I approached the door at the end. I could hear what sounded like metal music coming from behind it almost to mask out the cries.

"Shut the fuck up!" A new voice shouts. I jump at the sound and stop in my tracks.

"Please! Someone!"

"Se non chiudi il cazzo!" (Translation: If you don't shut the fuck up)

The voice didn't sound like Alessio. Maybe a guard or even Giovanni.

"Listen! I'm sorry."

I reach the door and lean forward to press my ear against it. The music below has been turned down and I can hear someone else speaking.

"Oh, I'll make sure of it. Don't you worry."

I could pick his voice out of a hundred people. Alessio was down there.

"My dad will find me you piece of shit!"

"I'm not worried about your dad," Alessio laughs harshly.

It's Austin. He's still alive.

Alessio didn't kill him...yet.

"She's not fucking worth it, dude! Olivia is just some bitch."

I push against the door and it groans lowly. I take a step into the darkness and stand as still as I can at the top of the stairs.

There's a loud clank from what sounds like a pipe hitting something hard. "Don't fucking say her name ever again."

"You aren't going to kill me!" Austin taunts and laughs. "Bunch of fake fucking gangsters. You are no different from the street gangs here in LA."

There's a pop from a gun firing and Austin bellows out in pain from the cellar below. I cover my mouth as the sound echoes through the stone walls and stifle my scream.

"Finish it," Alessio commands and the music starts up again.

My legs don't move. I am completely stuck to where I stand. I know if I don't run down there, Austin will be killed within minutes.

If I do, would Alessio kill me? Maybe Giovanni would?

Get to the police! Get to the police!

I shout in my head.

I try to focus on my new mantra as I spin around and grab the old iron door handle. I see a bit of light as the heavy door starts to pull open.

I try to keep my footing on the stair as I fumble around through the door but within seconds I feel something pulling me backwards as the door slams shut again.

"What the fuck are you doing here, Olivia?" Alessio snaps out and pushes me against the wall. His hands like a vice on my waist.

"P-please, stop!" I beg as his hand clamps over my mouth.

"You need to calm down, Olivia." He whispers fiercely.

"I won't tell anyone! I swear to-"

Alessio lets out a weird laugh that seems to be a mix of frustration and amusement. Before I have time to process what is going on he pulls me forward through the door and tosses me over his shoulder like I weigh nothing.

I try to kick against him as he walks swiftly up the stairs and towards his room. It is not worth it though.

He is too strong for me to even break an inch of his hold.

"Please! Stop it!" I slam my fists against his back.

He pays me no mind and kicks open his bedroom door with his foot. We enter the bedroom and I feel my body hit the bed as he tosses me onto it.

I start to panic as soon as I land and start looking for something to hit him with.

"Olivia," Alessio starts and raises his hands. "You need to listen to me."

"Stay back!" I warn him.

I look down and grab a shoe from the floor.

Good ol trusty shoe.

He stares at me with a bit of a smirk on his face and keeps his hands where they are. "Baby, 1-"

"Fuck off!" I shout and toss the shoe right at his dumb head.

Of course, Alessio knocks it away but I make my daring escape to the bathroom and lock it just in time.

"Olivia..." Alessio bangs on the door. "Let me talk to you."

"You're a murderer! Stay the fuck away."

"Olivia."

I press my back against the door and pull my cell phone out. "I'm going to call the police. You aren't getting away with this."

I try to press the 9 but my damn fingers are shaking so bad that the phone scatters across the floor.

"Shit!" I curse and lunge after it.

Before I even have my hand on the phone I hear a horrible cracking sound and look back to see Alessio has actually kicked through the damn wood of the door and broken in.

"No! Stay the fuck away!"

I try to rush past

him but he scoops me up with one arm around my waist and drags me back towards the bed.

He pins me with his weight and I struggle beneath him.

"Are you going to listen?" Alessio says in a soft tone.

I close my eyes shut tight and wait. "Just kill me! I know you have to kill me now like you did with Austin."

The room grows silent and I brace myself. I know it's coming.

Yet, it never does.

Instead, Alessio starts laughing. I mean really fucking laughing.

He rolls off of me and starts laughing so hard he clutches his stomach and starts to turn red in his face.

I feel my body stiffen with anger from his reaction and have the urge to hit him.

"It isn't funny, Alessio! You killed someone!"

He nods and grows silent. His dark eyes stare back at me as he tries to compose himself.

"I would never kill you."

"You're going to kill Austin though."

He sighs heavily. "We discussed this last night."

"You mean you stayed silent each time I asked you and then admitted to being in the mafia."

"I know."

"You expect me to be okay with this? I'm supposed to just forgive you for this?" I snap.

"Of course not," He groans and tucks his head under his arms. "I just didn't expect you to come downstairs so early."

"Well, waking up and realizing you are in the home of a mafia family isn't very comforting."

"Olivia," He starts and rolls over to touch my cheek. "Take a shower, eat breakfast with me, and I will tell you everything. We can go explore the city for a bit together so you don't have to feel trapped."

"Why would I want to hear you out?"

He narrows his eyes," Shower and breakfast. Now."

I stare after him in silence as he pushes up from the bed and pulls his dirty t-shirt over his head. I try to not let myself stare at his naked, muscular chest for too long as he opens the door.

"Don't even think about trying to figure out a new escape plan. I'll be waiting for you." He says and winks over his shoulder.

I sit on the bed for several minutes after he is gone. I wanted to try escape plan number two but I didn't even have a clue of how I would work that one out.

Alessio and his family have to be monsters. The mafia are bad people.

I can't possibly be considering this, right?

Yet...I knew I was.

I wanted to hear his story. Since I first saw him and heard about him, I wanted to know more about the mysterious Alessio Romano.

I had my chance.

I get up from the bed and head to his oversized bathroom to stand under the heat of the hot water for what feels like forever.

The steam starts to burn me after too long and I grab a towel and wrap it tightly around my body.

I wipe away some condensation from the mirror and stare at my reflection.

I look like shit.

My eyes were dark with circles and entirely too big for my face which was so pale I'm sure I could pass as a ghost.

How could anyone find this attractive right now?

I try to focus on brushing my hair out when I realize something feels off. Something moves behind me.

"Ahhh!"

Alessio leans against the frame where the door used to be to his bathroom and smiles at me.

"Do you knock?" I sneer out.

He looks up at the broken door, "What would I knock on?"

"Well, you are the one who broke it."

"I just wanted to make sure you were okay." He says simply.

"You mean you wanted to make sure I didn't jump out the window or magically escape without you knowing."

He chuckles, "Right."

"I need to get dressed."

"I know," He says and puts a basket down on the counter. "I have some stuff for you. Toiletries and other items I know girls like."

I look up at him and feel my heart squeeze. "You didn't have to get me anything."

"I wanted to." He shrugs and turns back towards the door. "I'll see you soon."

I look back towards the little basket once he disappears and pick up a few items from it.

Bottles of my favorite perfume, toothpaste, toothbrush,hair bands, even a few tampons.

Surely, he had help from Anna.

I finish up in the restroom and walk out to find a super cute pale yellow sundress with sandals that was laid out on the bed. I try to dress as quick as I can before Alessio decides to get curious again and hurry downstairs.

I find him sitting in the dining room at the obnoxiously long table. Food for miles laid out along the top.

Pancakes, eggs, bacon, waffles, fruit. My stomach growled immediately at the sight of it.

"You look beautiful." Alessio compliments and pushes his hair back with his sunglasses.

He looks amazing. His face was freshly shaven and he had changed into a plain black shirt and jeans.

I was so obsessed with his bad boy look. I won't lie.

"You have good taste."

"I had some help from Anna," He admits. "Have a seat."

I nod and take a seat at the end from him. I wait as a maid hurries up to my side and helps pile my plate full of food before handing me a container of syrup.

I pour it all over the top of my pancakes and feel my mouth drool.

"So," Alessio says after I have my mouth full of food. "Would you like to talk?"

"Yes."

"Go ahead."

I swallow my eggs. "You're in the mafia."

"I am."

"Why?"

He sighs and stands up from the table. "Let's continue in private, shall we?"

I stare down at my plate and take a few more bites. I was already more than stuffed.

The realization that I hadn't checked on my parents or my friends was starting to settle in. I wanted my phone back.

I knew they would be freaking out soon.

I look up at the sound of footsteps just as Giovanni enters the room. His massive muscles rippled with every move.

"Olivia." He says and picks up a piece of bacon.

Up so close I realize how deep his scars really are. I wonder what they are all from.

"How are you?" I ask.

"Doing well. It's nice to see you again."

I force a smile. Knowing he had probably killed Austin just a couple of hours ago made me want to puke for the fourth time. "You as well."

Alessio steps back into view and they stare at one another. He shakes his head at Giovanni and looks over at me.

"You ready?"

"Where are we going?" I ask hesitantly.

He smiles and puts his hand out. "Let's see where the day takes us."

The two of us climb into his car and he starts our drive. The weather is beautiful and really makes the whole situation feel more innocent than it really is.

I tried to fight the urge to look at him the whole drive but I kept finding myself looking back in his direction. The curve of his sharp jaw flexed slightly as he inhaled on his cigarette. The hints of his tattoos under the collar of his shirt.

Everything about him was just so perfect. I didn't understand it but I guess they did say even the devil was beautiful.

Alessio catches my gaze. "See something you like?"

"When do I get my phone back?"

"I need to make sure we are on the same page first," He explains and blows out smoke. "I'm sure you can understand that."

"So you don't trust me then?"

He sighs, "Not yet."

I nod and look forward through the windshield. I guess I should've expected that response.

"Ready to ask your questions?" He asks.

"Yes," I say confidently. "You told me you are in the mafia. How does that work? Why would you want to be part of something so violent?"

"It wasn't by choice," He explains and his tone seems to grow weary. "All of us were born into the family. The Romano family has been around for a very, very long time. All I've ever known is this life, Olivia."

"Can you ever leave?"

He shakes his head, "No, you don't leave. You are in it forever especially because if anyone finds out or if you try to break your loyalty to the family it is a death sentence."

My body stiffens. "You told me."

"I know," He nods. "That is why I need you to hear me out and swear to me that you won't tell a soul."

"If I do?"

He looks over at me and pushes his sunglasses back from his eyes. "They'll kill you and then they will kill me."

My stomach tightens from his words. "Tell me about your family?"

"My father is Adolfo, he's the don, you have met my siblings and cousin, of course. There are a lot of Romano's, including my uncles, some of them don't live here in America. We try to keep it pretty spread out."

"Your mother?"

"She died."

I frown and suddenly feel bad for even asking. "I'm so sorry."

"It's okay."

"Can I ask what happened?"

"I was only four years old when she was killed. My dad does a lot of traveling for business, as you can understand, well he was not around and there was an ambush. It was chaos and I was taken away before I could be found but my mother was murdered in her room."

"Oh, Alessio...I'm sorry."

"It was a family from Russia. They had once had an alliance with the Romano's before things got tense and greedy between the two of them. My father had shot and killed the second-in-command and they fired back."

"I can't even imagine."

He shrugs, "Horrible things happen all the time. I've grown used to it."

"So what happens...if your father passes? Will you take over?"

"Yes," He replies and turns into town. "Giovanni will be my second-in-command and I will take over as don soon."

I grow silent. Being in the mafia is terrifying but the idea of Alessio having to lead it was a lot to take in.

"Olivia?"

"It's just a lot to take in." I admit. "Can I ask you about Austin now?"

His hands grip the wheel. "Okay."

"He's dead?" I ask."Did Giovanni kill him?"

"Giovanni did as he was told."

"I don't understand how you can get away with this. He was only 18 years old, I understand he was a shitty person but-"

"Olivia," He interrupts and looks at me. "You need to understand that there was more to him than what he presented at the surface. Austin's father is a chief in San Diego with the police department. His son has been involved in several assault cases involving women since he was a freshman. He never learned and was constantly bailed out."

I scoff at him, "There's no way! I've met his parents, how could they afford such large payoffs for him?"

"His dad has connections to some local street gangs. The police ignore them in exchange for a cut of the profit. It's just a few bad cops involved and he happens to be one of them."

I open my mouth to say something else but he continues on, "I don't want to make up your mind about me, Olivia. I just need you to understand that I do what I have to do."

"I'm trying," I say quietly. "I just don't understand how you can just avoid people finding out you did this."

"We're the mafia, Olivia. We have our ways."

"I feel like there's more to this."

"Give me time." He mutters and reaches out to hold my hand.

I squeeze it in response and feel my body relax a little, "Okay."

I decided to change the topic to something else. "Why did you go to Italy?"

"I went with Giovanni."

"For what?"

"Business."

"What kind of b-" he cuts me off quickly.

"What did I say about time," He reminds me gently. "Let's take it slow."

"Let's go back to before you left for Italy."

"Sure."

"Do you still feel the same way?" I ask, my voice barely a whisper.

He looks over at me and his expression softens up. "I'm in love with you,Olivia Moore. I've never been so sure of something."

"How are you so sure? This is so...new."

"I'm a simple person. I've never wasted my time with love and everything else in between has just been so trivial." He explains, "I do know that I have never felt this way about anyone and I need to have you in my life."

Millions of emotions flood over me and I stare back at him. He seems so genuine.

Alessio Romano...loves me?

The car suddenly comes to a stop and I look up at a store front sitting before us.

"What's this?"

"This is Boutique di Anna."

Alessio walks around to my side of the car and extends his hand.

"Anna?" I ask him.

"Yeah. It's her store," He grins and looks up at it.

"I like the idea of Anna wearing normal teenager clothes."

"It keeps her feeling fulfilled and

normal

." He chuckled and took my hand.

The two of us enter together and start to browse the cute little store. It reminded me a lot of the one he had taken me to before, except it was more modern and not as expensive compared to a 10,000 dollar dress.

"I brought you here for a reason," Alessio explains. "Come here."

I walk with him over to the counter where a perky, brunette greets us with a smile and hands us a little black box.

Alessio thanks her and puts it in my hands. "For you."

I stare up at him for a moment before pulling the lid back. I found a cute gold charm bracelet inside with real diamonds. There's a palm tree, paint brush, skyscraper, and a gorgeous heart dangling from it.

It was almost like the one Austin gave me but obviously very real and probably expensive.

"What do you think?" He asks by my side.

"It's so beautiful."

"I wanted to make up for breaking the other one, plus this will have good memories attached."

I look up to his dark eyes and smile. We start to bend towards one another and I feel my heart skip a beat as our lips touch.

"Olivia?"

I freeze mid kiss and pull away from Alessio like he had shocked me. My stomach turns as soon as I hear his voice.

"T-tucker?"

Chapter 13

My breath catches in my throat and suddenly I feel ashamed.

Tucker looks between Alessio and I, "What's going on?"

"Uh," I look over at Alessio and freeze. "He's..."

"Alessio Romano. We ran into each other." Alessio extends his hand.

"I'm Tucker, Olivia's boyfriend," Tucker doesn't shake his hand. "Can you meet me later?" He asks and looks at me.

"Yes." I nod and my throat constricts.

Without a warning, Tucker swoops me up for a kiss and crushes his lips against mine. He sets me down and I feel unsteady.

I could feel Alessio staring at my back and it made me want to curl up and hide.

"See you later."

"Bye..."I whisper out breathless. I felt Alessio's hand touch the small of my back as he stepped closer behind me.

I turn to him and the tears spill. "I'm sorry."

"Don't apologize."

I pull back a little and stare up at his eyes. He looks down at me with a soft smile and kisses my forehead. "I have some things to take care of."

"Okay..."

"I'll take you home and you can think things through."

"No, wait-" He cuts me off with a kiss.

It feels urgent and almost like he's worried. I feel myself melt immediately into it and wish we could just stay like this forever.

"Olivia, I love you," He begins and strokes my cheek, "I would do anything for you, but I also want you to be happy. Take your time, love. I'll be waiting."

I fight the urge to force him to tell me to pick him. Every part of my being screams for Alessio.

Why did it feel like he didn't want to fight?

After Alessio had dropped me off home I immediately went to my room and sat there forever in silence.

The drive home was too quiet and Alessio said nothing but kissed me on the cheek as I went inside.

It almost felt like a goodbye and it hurt.

My mom had been hot on my trail when I rushed to my room but stopped as soon as she saw the tears pouring down my face.

I was almost grateful when my phone rang and I saw it was Kim.

"BITCH!"

"Nice to talk to you as well."

"Do you realize how scared I've been!" She shouts on the other end. "I thought you got kidnapped. I had to call your MOTHER, Olivia!"

"My mother?" I snorted.

"Obviously! I couldn't just not inform her that her daughter went M. I.A."

I sigh, "I'm okay, Kimberly. I got sick and went home."

"Someone saw Austin go in there with you," Kimberly starts. "What happened, Olivia?"

My chest tightens. "Y-yeah, he helped me lay down and left. I got sick from the alcohol."

"He didn't take you home though."

"No, Tucker did."

She's not buying it. "Bullshit! Tucker called me."

Shit. Shit. Shit.

"Ok! Ok! Fine...Alessio picked me up and I stayed the night with him."

"Ahhhh," She coos out. "Does Tucker know about the two of you?"

"No, Kim. Let's keep it that way." I lie. I wasn't in the mood to drop all the drama on her.

"Did you get down and dirty?" She moans into the receiver.

"Kimberly!"

I try to change the discussion to her. "I know you did with Joe though!"

She laughs loudly, "Girl, that is nothing new. Joe and I have been getting freaky for weeks."

"Well, I hope senior prom was everything you hoped for."

"The alcohol and sex made it bearable, but those decorations were ass."

The two of us bust up laughing and go into a full blown conversation about the dance and the fight that had apparently broken out at Joe's house.

Apparently, this is huge Westview High gossip now.

I felt so relieved talking to Kim. Hearing her ramble about random, high school things made me feel so much better about my crazy issues.

I envied her. I envied her normal life.

I wanted to tell her everything. I wanted to tell her about Alessio being in the mafia. I wanted to tell her about Austin being murdered.

I wanted to tell her that I'm in love with Alessio Romano.

"Listen, I have to run, I have a date but let's catch up tomorrow."

I smile sadly, "Of course, have fun!"

The line goes dead and I fall back on the bed.

What was I supposed to do?

The right answer would obviously be to pick Tucker. He was the safe option right?

Did I love Tucker though?

No, I didn't. I knew that right away.

I did love Alessio though.

I just wanted someone to slap me and tell me to choose Tucker. I should be with the normal boy who isn't in a mafia family.

Tucker doesn't kill people. Tucker doesn't have to take over a high-profile Italian mob.

Tucker is safe.

Yet, there's so much he doesn't do for me like Alessio can.

Alessio ignites something in me I've never known before. He keeps me on my toes and I'm constantly wanting more with him.

He's dangerous and exciting.

He could give me a life of my dreams.

I should hate him for what he is, but I don't.

Not even a little bit.

"Olivia?"

I pick my head up and see my door push open a tad. "Yes?"

My mom peeks in, "Can I come in?"

I move to the edge of my bed and she walks in. Her blue eyes are comforting and soft.

"You really scared me, Liv."

I sigh, "I'm sorry. I just had a crazy night."

"Are things going okay at school? Kimberly? Tucker?"

I groan," Let's not do the whole lecture thing."

She shakes her head and holds my hands. "I'm just trying to be here for you, bug."

I roll my eyes but can't help but smile at her.

"Things are just...confusing."

"I'm here to talk," She pats my hand.

"I just have a big decision to make."

"Want me to help?"

"I think it's something I need to figure out alone this time."

She nods and stands up to leave.

"Wait!" I call out and she looks back. "How...how did you know dad was the one?"

She smiles a little and sits next to me again.

"I met your father when I was about your age. I was working as a waitress in a little diner and I had been waiting on him and his friends."

She looks up and her stare tells me she is getting lost in previous years.

"He was so kind to me and gave me his full attention. He's always been such a gentleman and so handsome."

She winks at me and I jokingly gag.

"After my shift, I had finished cleaning up and he waited for me. He walked me home and gave me his number. We went on some dates and a year later he proposed to me on my 18th birthday."

I study her face and see how in love she is with him. She talked about him with no hesitation.

No doubt at all for their love.

She looks over at me. "Does that help at all?"

"Yes, mom."

"Whatever it is, Olivia. Just know...I think you should go with who makes you happy. Don't settle for anything."

She gives me a kiss on the forehead and leaves the room again.

Once she's gone, I pick up my phone and stare down blankly at the screen to see Tucker is calling.

"Hey!"

"I'm sorry! I haven't even had a chance to get ready."

"Take your time! I'll see you in an hour." He replies and I smile sadly at the phone.

"See you soon."

ALESSIO

"How are you?"

I look up from the cigarette in my fingers and see Anna step out onto the balcony.

"I'm alright. Why?"

She pops up onto the ledge. "You seem sad. Olivia?"

"Just things I'm figuring out."

"I'm here to help," She offers gently. "I know it's weird to take advice from your big sister, but I'm pretty wise."

I roll my eyes at her smug expression.

"I'm aware, sis."

"So..."She pushes. "Want to talk about it?"

"I'll humor you," I ash the end of the cigarette. "I told Olivia I'm letting her make her decision."

"A decision?"

"Between Tucker and I."

She starts to laugh uncontrollably and I glare at her.

"Don't tell me you are worried she'll pick him."

I shrug and look at the sun casting shadows across the garden. "Maybe, I am. She deserves a happy and safe life."

"She loves you, Alessio."

I stare at her for a moment. "You think so?"

"Yes, Alessio. She's madly in love with you. Don't let that go."

"You know," I start and take a drag. "I told her about the family."

Anna's jaw drops, "Why would you be-"

I cut her off. "Calm down, Anna. She's not going to say a thing."

"You have to be careful, Alessio. If Adolfo finds out he's going to literally kill you both."

"She won't be of any trouble," I mutter. "That's also one of the reasons I know Tucker is her safest option."

Anna nods and looks out at the scenery with me. "What about Monica?"

"I'll handle it."

"Tell Adolfo you refuse?" She offers.

I scoff at her ludacris idea, "You know that's not possible. You are in an arranged marriage."

"I love Alonzo though."

"I'm glad," I tell her and a strand of hair blocks my view. "Let Giovanni know we need to wrap up some stuff. You can join us."

She hops up from the banister with excitement. "Give me like ten minutes!"

I laugh a little at her reaction and look back out towards the sky.

Seeing Tucker with Olivia today had really fucked me up. They seemed so normal together.

She deserved to have that. A normal, easy-going life.

I couldn't give Olivia those things.

What if she ended up wanting kids?

Would she really want to bring kids into this kind of life. I know she'd resent me.

She'd always be in constant fear like Anna. She'd spend her nights wide awake terrified of what is to come.

She would constantly be at risk just being with me.

I can't give Olivia the world. I wouldn't always be there on Christmas. I would be away for months at a time handling business.

She'd be so alone.

I might miss important milestones if we were to have children. I might miss important memories with her.

What if I could have those things though? Did it really hurt to try?

We come from two different worlds. It just feels so impossible.

"Alessio!"

I turn around and find Anna back on the patio. Her eyes are wide and she has blood covering her hands.

I immediately start checking for wounds, "What the fuck happened?"

She says nothing and stares at me blankly. She's in shock.

"Speak to me!" I snap and slap her cheek.

"Giovanni...and..."

"What about Giovanni?" I ask, panicked.

"He...he's been shot."

I let go of her and move past while pulling my gun from the waistband of my jeans.

"Alessio...wait."

I turn around at her. Rage and fury fueling me. "What now?!"

"Beto was shot too."

My body stiffens and I feel sick. "What are you saying to me?"

"I could be wrong...I don't know, Alessio. I couldn't find his pulse."

Chapter 14

"Thank you for coming tonight."

I smile up at Tucker and pick the crust from my pizza. We had decided on the little shop that was only a block from the cafe.

I was grateful he had decided on this place. It was always empty and the pizza was some of the best in the area.

It has been twenty minutes already and we haven't even touched on the topic of Alessio. I knew it would be coming soon and I was just getting queasy thinking about it.

"Want some ice cream?" Tucker says randomly. I nod and stand up from the booth.

He tosses some money down on the table and the two of us walk awkwardly down the sidewalk to the little shop on the corner.

The seriousness of the situation was really starting to weigh down on me. I knew it would be getting late soon and after what I pulled, my mom would not let me off tonight.

Tucker smiles at me and nods to the menu. "What are you thinking?"

The both of us decide on plain vanilla cones with sprinkles and hot fudge. I'm typically not a huge sweets fan but I needed something packed full of calories and carbs right now.

I'm a huge stress eater.

"I'm paying."

He rolls his eyes, "In your dreams!"

"You already paid for dinner."

Tucker raises his hands in surrender as I pass the employee a twenty and wait for my change. We take the cones and head over to a window seat facing out towards the beach.

"So..."Tucker says and licks at the dripping ice cream, "We should talk?"

I stare down at the ice cream in my hands and nod. "I know."

"Who is he to you?"

I press my lips tight and think for a moment. There really was no point in not telling Tucker the truth.

If I sugar coated anything, I would just feel horrible about it later.

Tucker had been a "bandaid"

"We have history."

He stares at his cone. "So...you aren't just friends?"

"No, we aren't just friends." I sigh and look at him. "I promise while he was gone...it was just you and I."

Tucker nods and a few ginger curls fall from place, "I understand, Olivia."

"I'm sorry," I reach out and touch his hand. "I never meant to hurt you."

"I know, Olivia. I know."

He gives my hand a squeeze and I sigh a little. "What now?"

"Be happy, Olivia. You clearly have a lot of feelings for him and I don't want you to stay with me out of pity. I understand why you would want to pick him."

Maybe in another world I would've picked Tucker. We would still have our ice cream dates and crappy movie nights.

I'd never have to worry about the things I'll be concerned about with Alessio. In another world, I would have picked him.

"Thank you for always being so nice, Tucker."

He grins back and finishes his cone up. A bit of ice cream gets stuck on his lip and he dabs at it. I decide to chuck the rest of mine away and pull my cell out.

"I should probably head back soon. My mom is already pissed at me." I tell him.

Tucker nods and the two of us scoot out from the booth and head outside. The street lights are starting to turn on and it seems the traffic in the area had disappeared.

"Thank you, Tucker," I tell him as we walk back to his car. "I had a nice time and I appreciate our chat."

He gives me a little smile but doesn't respond. For the rest of the walk we kind of just walk next to one another in silence.

I notice he has his hands shoved in his pockets and he almost looks extremely uncomfortable or worried.

"Are you alright?" I ask him.

He looks at me a little but doesn't seem to relax. "I'm alright."

Every possible scenario goes through my head and I wonder if Tucker is considering firing me from the cafe.

I knew that could be a possibility since I'm sure it would make him feel better to know we weren't working around one another.

I walk inside the cafe with him and gather my stuff in my hands. Tucker heads back towards the office and I assume he's probably changed his mind about giving me a ride home.

I pull my phone from my pocket and figure I'd just give Alessio a call to get me.

"Tucker, I'm heading out."

I turn around and smack into something solid and wide. I stumble back a little and nearly fall over the table behind me.

"Hello, darling."

I stare blankly at the man before me and watch as he pulls his hood down. Several tattoos cover his bald head and face. He has a variety of gold and silver caps on his yellowing teeth.

"W-who are you?" I stammer and look around for Tucker.

Tucker exits from the back kitchen and I realize he has a gun tucked in his hand.

I look between the both of them, "What the fuck is happening?"

Tucker doesn't say a word and clicks the safety off the gun. He continues to stare past me at the man standing behind me.

"Jesús", Tucker nods in acknowledgement. "Nice to see you."

"Who is this?" I beg and try to grip at Tucker's jacket. He pushes me away harshly and smooths out the crinkles.

"Don't act like you need me now, Olivia."

"What are you doing? Who is this?"

Tucker laughs darkly, "Meet Alejandro's big brother. I'm sure you remember him."

My brows pull together and I try to rack my brain for whoever the hell they were talking about.

"Your precious little boyfriend murdered him," He spat at me. "He killed him and dropped his fucking head off in a damn box."

I thought back to the day when those men arrived at the school. The guy that approached me looked a lot like him. He had the same gang tattoos and Spanish accent.

"I-I have nothing to do with what happened."

"It doesn't matter, princess," He laughs loudly. "You are involved and you obviously mean something to the Italian little shit head."

"There's no way Alessio could..."I trail off.

Would he really do that to someone? I know what he is, but would he really do something so horrifying.

"Don't be fucking dense. You know damn well who he is and what he does."

"I don't know what you are talking about." I lie and turn my attention to Tucker. "Why are you even involved with these people?"

"They paid me."

"For what?"

Tucker laughs and the sound sends a chill down my spine. I watch as he turns into someone I don't recognize.

His features look almost devil-like and he leans down close enough so his breath tickles my ear as he speaks.

"For you, baby."

I start to scream out as his words echo through my head.

Within seconds I'm being consumed by the dark.

Chapter 15

I open my eyes and realize I'm not in the cafe anymore.

The room around me has no windows at all and looks to be some kind of dirty basement under a building.

There's a horrible stench that seems to be a mix of mold and something decaying.

I was tied to a chair and placed in the middle of the room under the only light that was positioned right above my head.

As I adjust to the surroundings, I feel the wave of pain hit me from whatever had hit me across the head.

I try to blink past the pain and spot something in the corner of the room.

"What the fuck is going on?"

"If I was you, I'd stay quiet." The voice speaks out.

I realize quickly Tucker is in the room with me and watch as he steps under the small pool of light that is flooding the floor. He glares down at me and a wicked smile creeps across his lips.

"I don't understand. Why would you do this to me." I say brokenly.

He spins a chair from behind him and sits on it backwards, "I told you they paid me."

"For what? What do you get out of this aside from money?"

"You are a pawn, Olivia," He laughs and shakes his head. "They need you to get to Alessio. It's more money than you can imagine and I really need to get the fuck out of this state."

"Was all of this planned? Even before you and I got together?"

"Get comfortable,"He laughs and leans forward on the back of the chair. "The day I met you, I knew I liked you. My feelings were genuine but about two weeks ago I was approached by Jesús. He knew I was with you and let me know about your little obsession with Alessio. I knew you were with him the night of prom, obviously I was just a distraction while he was gone."

I stare at him in complete shock. I couldn't believe Tucker would be so willing to help them out.

"Anyways, they offered me a beautiful sum of money to continue our little relationship. I purposely caught the two of you in the store so I could prove he was back and get you away from him so they could use you as leverage."

"This is fucking insane, Tucker. You know it is."

He rolls his eyes," Business is business, Olivia. You automatically assumed what kind of person I am. You don't even know me."

"I can't believe this."

"Believe it, doll. Alessio is no better."

I shut my eyes tight, "Shut up."

I don't want to picture Alessio doing any of this. It's all too much.

"Act oblivious, Olivia, "He says and I feel his fingers touch my chin. "You knew what this was."

"Just get it over with, Tucker, I'm sick of the taunts."

I open my eyes and see that he has moved from the chair. "I'll let Jesús take it over from here."

The door at the front of the room opens and Jesús steps through with two unfamiliar men following close behind. He takes a few steps towards me and smiles.

I silently study his face and notice the three tear drops directly under his left eye tattooed there.

"Glad to see you are awake," He comments and sits in the same chair Tucker was in, "Sorry, we had to get a little rough."

"Tell me what is going to happen and stop wasting my time." I snap and despite my best judgement, I actually spit right on his forehead.

He grimaces and wipes the saliva away. "Nice."

Before I have time to process his movements I feel a sting burn my cheek as his palm comes down against my face hard. It whips to the side and I taste the blood pool in my mouth.

"You're going to call Alessio and tell him to meet you at this address," Jesús starts and pulls a paper from his pocket. "Act normal and don't for one second think I won't kill you right now."

I watch as Tucker takes my phone out of his pocket and hands it to Jesús. He unfolds the paper for me to read the address sprawled out in black ink.

"Tell him you need a ride home and want to talk to him," Jesús continues on, "He knows you met with Tucker so this shouldn't come as a shock to him."

I watch as he pulls his gun out and carefully rests the metal against the wood of the chair. I stare up at him as he dials out Alessio's number and the ringing fills the silence around us.

"Olivia?" Alessio's voice echoes.

"Alessio," I swallow and look at the gun in Jesús' hands, "I need you to pick me up."

"I have something going on," He starts and his voice sounds strained. "I can be there in about 10 minutes. Are you okay?"

Jesús stares back at me with a dead stare and moves the gun to the edge of my jaw. "I'm okay, I just need a ride home."

"Are you sure?" Alessio asks again. I can tell he's getting suspicious and so can Jesús.

"I'm fine, I just need a ride home," I tell him and try to force some perkiness to my voice. "I met up with Tucker but he had some things to wrap up at the cafe."

A long pause goes by before Alessio says anything else.

"I'll be there soon."

The line goes dead and I watch Jesús toss the phone back to Tucker. He wastes no time shattering it against the wall.

"Not bad, recruit." Jesús laughs at him.

"I don't think so," Tucker grimaces. "I just need to get the fuck out of this shit hole."

"As you wish." Jesús mutters and tosses him what looks to be a band of money.

Tucker fingers through the bills, "This isn't all of it."

"You'll get the rest when Alessio is dead."

Tucker shoots me a glance and almost seems to hesitate as the others get up and move towards the door.

"Man, that wasn't in the description. You told me to make sure you could get to Olivia, that's it."

Jesús looks over at Tucker for a moment and laughs. "Pedro stays here. Tucker, you come with us."

His jaw flexes and he looks back at me one more time before he disappears with the others. The boy left to guard me looks to be only 16.

He's a thin, lanky kid with dark hair and dark eyes. I notice he has a gun resting on his hip.

"How old are you?"

He glares back at me and pulls a switchblade out. "Did I say you can talk?

"You're right, you didn't. I figured we could at least pass the time," I shrug and feel my hands move against the rope. "I bet you wanted to go with them, huh?"

"I guess so...Jesús is just looking out for me."

"Big brother?"

"Yeah."

"Do you not go to school or anything?" I ask and feel a weak spot in the rope under my fingertips.

"Not anymore..."Pedro begins and starts flicking the knife in and out. "I stopped going when I was 11. Alejandro wanted me to get used to this life...I jumped into the gang at 13 years old. Only been two years of me being part of any of this."

"Do your parents know you are in a gang? That your brothers are operating one?"

"Of course," He says wide eyed. "Mama doesn't dare speak a word...my daddy was killed when I was five...it's just me, my brothers, and the rest of the family. " He sneered at the word.

"I get the feeling you aren't a fan of this life, Pedro."

"Nothing I can do now," He mutters and leans back. "It's life or death now."

"Does Jesús know you're unhappy?"

"He wouldn't care and like I said I have no choice in this."

"There's always a way out of everything," I tell him and try to keep his focus on me and not what I'm doing. "Maybe he'd hear you out."

"Easy for you to say,"Pedro says frustrated. "I bet you have a wonderful life. School, friends, college. Everything you could want right."

He's right.

I do have an amazing life.

I have Alessio, Kim, and my friends. I will always have much more than a kid like Pedro would have.

Or someone like Alessio.

"I do have it easy, but I still wish you the same."

His eyes water. "I fucking hate this."

"Run for it! Get out of California then."

"I can't leave my mama," He says sadly. "She'd never do it."

"I bet she'd make an effort for you."

"She hates this for me," He sighs a little. "She's only known this though because of my papa."

"Just give it a try."

"Maybe..."

Without any warning the rope falls to the floor and I see him look up at me in shock.

"What the f-"

He's cut off immediately by the sound of rapid gunfire just outside the door. I see him look at the door before he walks around to me and pulls his gun out.

"Who'd you call?"He snaps at me.

"Do you see my cell phone?" I roll my eyes.

"Don't move from that fucking chair."

I watch as he inches closer to the door and keeps the gun at eye level. He moves slowly to the door as a series of screams and gunfire continues on.

There's suddenly a loud pop inside the room and I crouch down behind him. I'm not sure if he fired at something or possibly even me.

I look up and realize he's laying flat on the ground.

Blood oozing from his skull. Lifeless eyes staring at me.

Everything seems to slow down and I can hear myself screaming but don't even process what is really going on when I realize someone is shaking me around.

"Olivia! Stop fucking screaming! Are you okay?"

I gasp and look up to find Anna's golden eyes studying my face. Splatters of red blood decorating her cheeks.

"Anna?"

She releases me, "Alessio tracked you."

"What do you mean?"

"He's not dumb, Olivia. Your phone call was weird."She rolls her eyes. "We pinged you before it was destroyed."

"Anna...you have to hurry...Alejandro's brother is going to kill Alessio. He has several men with him."

"We're aware," Anna nods. "Alessio knows what is goin on, we'll take care of this."

"You knew about this?"

"We did, yes," She sighs and looks down at Pedro. "I'm just sorry you got involved."

"Do you know about Tucker being involved?"

"No, we didn't, but Alessio realized that today," Anna explains and looks behind her. "We need to get moving."

I look past her and realize Mateo had stepped into the room with someone else. I hadn't met him directly before but I remember Alessio had mentioned Mateo had an older brother named Michele.

"Wait..." I look between the three of them. "Why aren't Beto and Giovanni here?"

She ignores me and guides me by the elbow out of the room. I can hear people running and I'm not sure if it's towards us.

I try to keep up with their speed as we move through the dark halls. The stench of blood is very fresh in the air.

"Anna? Where are they?" I ask again.

"Later," She hisses back and stops behind a corner. "Let's move."

I try to keep on her heels but feel my body lunge forward and I trip right into a very dead body.

.I feel a hand catch me and cover my mouth to keep me from screaming. "Please don't scream." Michele begs and his dark eyes plead with me to stay quiet.

He helps steady me before we step over the bodies on the stairs and enter a dark garage. We're surrounded by a maze of crates and several SUV's parked next to the furthest wall.

Anna leads the way and the rest of us stay right behind her.

There's an opening and we see a door come into view. She motions for us to follow and we start to make a run for it.

I watch Anna start to sprint before she is smacked by something hard and her body hits the crates behind her.

A girl about the same age as Pedro steps from behind the boxes and holds up a bat. I notice she's wearing a Minnie Mouse nightgown and has a metal bat.

"Stop! Don't move or I will bash her head in!"

Mateo and Michele step forward and quickly aim their pistols at her head.

I look back at them and put myself between them and the girl.

"Let me talk to her! Please."

"Move, Olivia," Michele snaps.

"Just wait." I turn towards the girl and she stares back at me terrified. "What's your name?"

"Angelica."

"How old are you, Angelica?" I ask carefully.

"Why do you even care?" She spits out but I notice her hands tremble.

"You're right, that was stupid," I laugh a little. "My name is Olivia. I'm probably not much older than you, Angelica. We just want to leave, I promise I won't let them hurt you."

"No! You have to get downstairs!" She screams and pulls the bat back.

"Don't even think about it!" Michele growls out from behind.

"Put the bat down, Angelica," I tell her gently. "I don't want them to hurt you. You have a life outside of this."

She looks back at me and tears fill her eyes. Her lower lip shakes as she speaks. "Just go!"

I try to take another step towards her but Anna is already moving fast. She tightens her arms around the girls neck and within moments she goes limp and falls to the ground.

"I-is she dead?" I stammer out.

"She's just out for a bit."

I follow them quickly as we make our exit through the door. We put some distance between us and the warehouse.

I spotted the familiar black Cadillac parked at the edge of the lot.

"What is this place?"

"They handle their shipments through here. It's really just the family. Lots of young kids." Anna explains.

We all climb into the vehicle together and Mateo starts the car. Michele slides in next to me and immediately starts grabbing my head.

"Let me examine you."

"Are you...a doctor?" I ask awkwardly as he pulls some supplies out.

"Retired," He laughs and smiles a bit. "I'm a little rusty but it looks like you won't need stitches."

I wince as something touches the open wound and stings a little.

"Why don't I see you around as much?"

"I'm usually running things out of the country for Adolfo," Michele explains. I notice how gentle he is despite his terrifying demeanor from before.

"Are you Mateo's older brother?" I continue on and try to keep my mind off of the pain throbbing on my forehead now. "I think Alessio has mentioned that before."

"I am,"Michele snickers and I hear Mateo scoff. "I'm a few years older than he is. Adolfo is our oldest brother but we only share a father."

"You both seem a LOT younger than Alessio's father."

He nods, "Our mother had Adolfo at a very young age. She was only 15 at the time but he left her for a while and eventually returned to tear Adolfo away from the only thing he knew and force him into...a different kind of life."

"What happened after?"

Michele frowned, "Well...our father ended up marrying years later and Mateo and I were the product of that relationship. We were both pretty young when she passed away."

"I'm so sorry," I say softly. "I can't imagine."

"Life is painful,"Michele says simply. "You're all set." I watch as he puts his supplies back in the bag and leans back.

I glance up towards Anna and notice she's texting on her phone. "Anna, I didn't forget. Where are Beto and Giovanni?"

All three of them seemed to tense a bit and Anna sighed. "They are in the clinic back at the house."

"Why? Are they okay?"

"They...they were injured," Anna starts and I hear her voice break. "I thought...I thought Beto was dead."

"What happened?"

"They were handling some family matters and...they were ambushed," She says and I notice Mateo touching her hand in comfort. "I should've been there but I was at the house. Some of the guards had to drag them back into the home."

"It isn't your fault," Michele speaks up. "We would've sent more men if we knew what was going on."

"I scared everyone so bad...I should've checked before I said anything to Al-"

Mateo cuts her off, "Let's discuss it later."

My heart sinks as she pulls up to the familiar gates and pulls through to the manor.

It doesn't feel the same as it normally does. The yard is not illuminated and I can see several guards posted outside.

The car pulls to a stop and I hurry over to Anna to see if she needs any help.

"Are you okay?"

She clutches her side but pushes out of the seat. "I'm fine."

I decide not to push her on it and follow her into the house. She walks through to the livingroom and throws herself on the couch before turning the TV on.

"How can you be...so normal right now?" I ask and stand there awkwardly. I was having an internal panic attack and tv was the last thing on my mind.

"There's nothing we can do but wait."

"How do you do it?" I ask and sit next to her. "How do you not worry about your fiance?"

"I do," She sighs and looks over at me, "I'm always worried about Alonzo."

I hug my knees, "Do you think he'll be alright?"

"He knows what he's doing."

I nod against my knees and stare blankly at the screen.

After a while Anna scoots over on the couch and motions for me to lay next to her. We sit there in silence and stare at the tv mindlessly for what feels like hours before I finally fall asleep.

The morning comes a little too quickly and when I realize Alessio is not in his bed my heart sinks.

I look over at the empty spot next to me and feel my insides turn over.

Why isn't he back?

I look over at the nightstand and notice someone has left out some pain killers and water. At the end of the bed is a pile of fresh clothes.

I decide to take Anna's advice and try to go through the motions of having a "normal" day while we wait for his return.

I go through the motions of showering and changing out my bandages before drying off my hair and dressing for the day.

The bruise on my temple is a disgusting purple color and I'm sure looks worse today.

I stare at myself for a while and slowly feel myself becoming more disgusted.

I look so dead. I'm too pale and my eyes are rimmed with black.

Hot mess doesn't even begin to describe it.

I walk back out into the bedroom and realize someone is on the bed.

Alessio.

He's flat on his back and has his arms tucked under his head. I can see faint cuts on his face but he seems to be okay. His eyes are closed but I can see him breathing steadily.

He looks so perfect. Everything about him almost seemed fake as if he was made of clay and sculpted by the finest artists in Italy.

"Olivia." He speaks with his eyes still close. A smile plays on his mouth.

He looks over at me and we stare at one another. I feel my heart beating fast in my chest and within seconds I'm running across the room to him.

He wraps me in his arms and I melt into his stone hard body.

"My Olivia..." He whispers.

"I thought you were dead." I say broken.

"I'm okay, baby. I'm here now."

I pull back and look up into his dark eyes. "I'm so sorry, Alessio. I'm so sorry I let this happen."

He touches my bottom lip, "You didn't do anything, Olivia. Nobody guessed Tucker was involved." I notice his eyes land on my bandage. "Are you okay though?"

"Yes, Michele checked me out." I assure him. "How did you know to track me?"

"I knew something was wrong pretty quickly, we just pinged you with you on the phone."

I frown at the thought of my phone. I'd have to use some of my money for a car to get a new one.

"I already bought you a new phone." Alessio blurts out.

"You did?" I ask stupidly. "I c-can't accept-"

His eyes narrow and I quickly stop the protest. "Thank you."

"Anything for you," He smiles and kisses me firmly on the mouth. "So...who did you choose?"

I snort."Do you really need to ask?"

"No, but I want to hear you say it."

"You. It was always you."

He smiles and pulls me to him again. His mouth finds mine again and I melt into our kiss as we embrace one another for as long as we can.

This is where I belong. This is home for me.

"Alessio..." I say breathlessly.

"Hmm?"

I push away from him and move so I'm practically straddling him. I catch his expression change and he smirks mischievously at me.

"Feeling playful?

"I need to tell you something." I shake my head and feel myself becoming extremely nervous.

"Okay."

I smile down at him and run my fingers along the curve of his jaw.

Everything was perfect. We were perfect.

This is what my mom had been talking about.

I knew at this moment.

It was him.

He caught my hand against his cheek and I felt my cheeks burn.

Before I could waste more time I forced the words out.

"Alessio...I love you. I'm in love with you."

Chapter 16

The words were out. I could feel them still tingling on my lips.

Alessio hadn't said anything yet and my head was spiraling.

Was this the right time? Did I fuck this up?

"Olivia." He finally speaks.

I try to keep my attention focused on the window behind him. My breathing felt erratic and I couldn't seem to keep my thoughts straight.

"Olivia."

His fingertips brush against my lip and he pulls me down to look at him.

"You love me?"

My cheeks blush," I do...I love you."

He doesn't respond but wraps me up in an embrace so intense I felt my breath leave my body as he crushes his mouth my own.

His mouth starts to explore down my neck and I can feel him kissing down until he reaches the tops of my breasts exposed in the tank top.

A shaky moan escapes me and his hands tighten on my waist.

"I want you so bad." He says against my lips.

I look up at him and feel his fingers start to move across my chest until he's making little circles over the tops of my nipples hardening beneath the fabric.

My core tightens with need and I feel myself growing wet.

I pull his face to mine again and try to distract myself with his lips as he reaches down to grab the hem of my shirt.

I help him lift it off of me and within seconds I feel my bra fall away from my breasts. I lay before him completely exposed as he gazes down at me hungrily.

I can feel my cheeks burn bright red as he examines my body and try hard to fight the urge to hide myself.

His lips brush against my erect nipple buds and I feel his tongue flick out against it before he takes each breast in his mouth.

A loud moan comes from me and instinctively I arch my back to get closer to him.

"Alessio..."I say breathless.

He continues to suck and lick at my nipples and I feel his mouth start to travel down my stomach slowly.

"I want to fuck you so bad, Olivia," He says against my stomach. His voice was rough and deep. "I want to hear you scream my name."

"Please."

His hands grip with need against my hips and I feel myself being dragged towards the edge of the bed.

I watch as he slides my jean shorts from my legs and his palm cups my core. The surface of his hand rubs against me through my lacey thong.

"You're wet," He says and I blush. "Do you want me to fuck you?"

I swallow hard and try to nod as he picks up the motion against me.

"Tell me."

"I do...I do..." I breathe out.

"I want to hear you say it."

"I...I-"

What if I can't please him? I've never done this before.

"Olivia?"

"I'm...I..uh.." I stutter out.

How many women has Alessio been with? What if he realizes he doesn't love me because I'm not experienced?

"What's wrong? Do you not want to?" He asks and his hand moves away.

" I do..I do.. I just don't know if-" I try again but fumble over the words.

Alessio moves from the edge of the bed and slides next to me. He rolls onto his side and watches me for a moment.

"I'd never force you into something, Olivia."

"I just...I don't think...I would be good."

He snorts. "Olivia, you're amazing."

"No,no!" I shake my head quickly. "I mean...your experience. I don't...have that."

Alessio grins a little and leans his forehead to mine. "Olivia, I don't need experience. I just want you. Only you.

you...you...you...

"Why though?"

"Why?" He sneers out as if I've offended him. "Why'd you even ask that?

"Look at you," I wave at him and back towards myself. "Now look at me."

"I am looking at you." He grins crookedly.

"You know what I mean!" I roll my eyes and fall onto my back. "You could be with anyone. Like that girl from the party for example."

I feel him stiffen up against me and he moves a little in the opposite direction. The air in the room seems to have shifted and suddenly it seems so cold.

"What? What's wrong?"

He moves into a sitting position and leans on his knees. The muscles in his back contract with the movement and tense.

"Alessio...please." I beg and try to touch his shoulder.

He shifts away from it and stands. "I need to handle something urgently. I'll see you tonight, love."

I feel my eyes sting with tears as he walks to the door. I immediately pull the cover against my mostly naked body and feel as if I've been slapped in the face.

How did we go from almost having sex to him leaving in just 10 minutes.

He looks over his shoulder at me. "I love you."

I watch as he exits the room and feel my chest squeeze with pain.

I'm alone.

Again.

ALESSIO

My head is spiraling.

I can't seem to get control of myself and I know I just need a moment. I knew my reaction would hurt Olivia but I hated myself.

I'm not telling her the truth and she'll hate me for it.

"What's wrong?"

I glance up towards Anna as she steps onto the patio.

"Everything."

"You got Olivia...she's safe?" Anna mutters and hands me a cigarette. "Beto and Giovanni are safe, so what's up?

Just the mention of them sends me back to that moment.

The scariest moment of my life.

◇ ◇ ◇

"Hand me my phone."

I demand Anna and she hands it to me quickly.

We had been back in the clinic for hours now. Giovanni and Beto were both in beds and being monitored 24/7 while their wounds heal.

We couldn't exactly take them to a real hospital so we had our team on standby.

Beto was the worst. He had lost so much blood and after the transfusion I was just waiting for him to open his eyes.

It seemed like it never would come.

During the ambush, Xavier, a young recruit of ours had been murdered. I notified his family and his expecting girlfriend.

He had just turned nineteen years old.

When I ran down those steps and found Giovanni and Beto laying in their own blood on the floor I nearly lost it.

Giovanni was wide awake and staring at Beto the whole time. He had a hold of his hand and just kept repeating his name.

There was so much blood. I couldn't figure out who was losing the most.

Anna was still screaming in horror at the scene. Adolfo was running around and demanding we attack back.

Everyone was in action. Moving.

I just stood there though. I couldn't stop staring at them.

"Alessio! Wake the fuck up!" Anna slapped me hard.

I looked at her blankly. "We need to get them moved."

Michele had been there immediately to apply pressure to their wounds and help some of the guards with moving them to the clinic.

Tobias had shown up within minutes and was already instructing the nurses what to do.

Beto's skin was slightly blue along with his lips. He looked so pale.

His white shirt was now nearly colored red with all of the blood coming from the wound in his stomach.

"He's alive." Tobias assured us.

Anna gasped and started crying again.

"I'm so sorry...I thought he was..I-I t-th"

"Calm down." I told her and pulled her to me. "Calm down."

The clinic team had instructed us to wait in the hall. Anna and I leaned back against the wall in front of the door and waited.

The minutes felt like they lasted hours as they passed by.

"I should've been there."

I glanced over at Anna. She was staring up at the ceiling, streaks of black makeup across her face.

"I'm sure they don't wish that."

"Beto asked me to go..."She laughed. "I told him I couldn't, I had stuff to take care of...I didn't really have anything important though. I just...I didn't want to."

She looked over at me. "I'm a horrible person, Alessio."

"You can't try to save everyone all the time, Anna."

Tears filled her eyes again and her head fell forward onto her knees.

"You keep us grounded, Anna. Without you we wouldn't have any idea what the fuck to do."

"I always just wanted to feel needed," She said softly. "Mom was always so brave and she always put herself right in the middle of the action for the men. I just want to be respected like she was."

She was right.

Anna really was a lot like her mom. She was always going where Adolfo did and never took no for an answer when it came to being right in the action.

After Anna's mother passed, something really changed in her. She became so distant and just didn't seem like the same person.

She was all work and no play. It was always business first and everything else was last of the line.

Sometimes I felt as if Anna resented me because she knew my mother was the reason our father stopped caring and cheated on her mom.

He left her while she was dying of cancer to be with my mother.

"She's proud of you, Anna," I told her. "I know she would be amazed by the person you became.

She grinned at me a little and the door swung open. Michele stepped out and waved us back.

We made our way down a nearby corridor and into an open room. There was a light blue curtain between two beds where they were laying. It was almost silent aside from the soft beeping of the monitors.

Giovanni was wide awake though and he was eating some nasty green Jello.

"How are you feeling?"

He laughed and winced a bit with the pain. "I've been better."

"What happened?"

"I wish I had a better excuse..."He sighed and took another bite. "We weren't paying attention. Some of Alejandro's gang showed up threatening the supply and I lost it right there...cost Xavier's life...and almost," he swallowed and looked towards Beto on the other bed. "Yeah..."

"I'm just glad you're okay. We'll find them, don't worry. We have the upper-hand."

Someone entered the room and we all looked up. Tobias stepped in and greeted us all with a smile.

He's an older man around his mid sixties with peppery black hair and a greying beard. For his age though he's unbelievably fit and has been one of our largest assets.

"Nice to see you all. I wish it was under better circumstances."

"Likewise," I told him. "Thank you for coming so quickly."

"I did want to discuss how they are doing with the both of you. Also, wonderful to see you up and moving."Tobias told Giovanni who was too busy slurping down his second cup of jello to do much aside from grunt in acknowledgement.

He continued. "Giovanni was lucky enough to not have the bullet penetrate anything major. We removed the bullet fully so he should have a quick recovery. It seems it had hit him in the bicep and left hip."

Giovanni flashed a grin full of lime green jello in his teeth.

"Beto..."Tobias began. "He'll be okay, but he does need to take it easy. We had to do a blood transfusion since he was bleeding profusely. Nothing was punctured but you can expect him to be in here for observation for at least a few weeks. Depending on how recovery goes we may need to explore physical therapy if he needs any support."

He continued. "There was a third wound we found in his leg. It didn't exit, so we did have to remove fragments of the bullet from there. As long as he handles the transfusions and medication, he'll be okay but don't expect him to be adventuring any time soon."

Anna nodded slowly and her eyes never left Beto's face. "We'll make sure he's looked after, thank you again."

Tobias gave us all another kind smile before leaving the room again.

Over the next few hours we decided to hang out for a while to see if Beto woke up. Giovanni ate about five containers of jello and decided to play some GTA.

I was watching Giovanni try to outrun the cops on the game when my phone started buzzing on the stand next to the bed.

"Hand me my phone." Anna snatched it and passed it over.

" Olivia?"

"Alessio," She said and I heard her voice shake. "I need you to pick me up.

"I have something going on,"I began and glanced at Anna. "I can be there in about 10 minutes. Are you okay?"

"I'm okay, I just need a ride home." She said and I could hear her echoing. Almost as if she was in an empty room.

I motioned for Anna to come closer as Olivia read off an address.

Something was wrong. This was close to where Alejandro's gang handles business.

"Track her" I mouthed to Anna.

"Okay. Are you sure everything is ok?" I continued and watched as Anna started clicking around to ping a location.

"I'm fine, I just need a ride home," She says and her voice almost sounds like she's forcing herself to sound perky."I met up with Tucker but he had some things to wrap up at the cafe."

I paused and looked back up as Anna came in showing me a flashing red dot on her phone.

Got you, baby.

"I'll be there soon."

Olivia's line goes dead and I shove the phone back into my pocket.

"Grab Mateo and Michele,"I demand and stand up. "I'm rounding up a team and going after him. Kill anyone who tries to keep you from getting to Olivia."

"How do you know it's him?"

"Alejandro was close with his brother. I'm sure Jesús is behind all of this."

"They could kill you, Alessio," Anna snapped. "You can't just run into this blindly."

"I can for Olivia."

◇ ◇ ◇

Within minutes I had rounded up my team and we pulled up a few blocks away from the address Olivia had given me on the phone.

It was near a pawn shop but I knew this was a hot spot for all kinds of drug dealers and gang activity.

We had piled everyone into three of our SUV's and kept spread out. Robin, our lead guard, was with me in the front. I watched as he moved to the back and started moving out weapons.

"I'm going in alone...give me 10 minutes."

"Not a good idea, boss." Robin said as he handed me two semi automatics. "We move as a team. There are 10 of us...if we outnumber hi-"

"If Olivia is with him I don't want to risk her anymore. Let me go in alone. 10 minutes."

Robin nodded reluctantly. I knew this was out of routine for how we directed the teams but if I let them go with me we wouldn't have the upperhand.

I tucked my pistols into my jacket and laid the other guns on the front seat. Robin moved to the driver seat and we pulled up to a parking lot just a few minutes from the shop. I could see the business just at the end of the street and stepped from the car.

"Good luck," Robin nodded.

"I got this."

I moved quickly towards the shop and took a cigar from my jacket. I let it hang loosely on my lips as the smoke obstructed my view.

I kept my pace steady as I reached the front of the store and quickly realized somebody was following me.

"And look who shows up!"

"Tucker?" I laughed as he came into view.

He had a gun in his hand and was waving it around like a child. He looked fucking crazy. As he moved his hand around I noticed something shining on his wrist.

"Why do you have Olivia's bracelet?" I asked harshly.

"She doesn't even know it's gone yet." He chuckled darkly. "She wouldn't need it anyways."

"If you hurt her, I'll kill you."

He rolled his eyes. "She's just some average skank, dude. I don't want anything to do with her. She's all yours, bro."

"You know Olivia isn't like that."

"I've already been down there," He began nonchalantly."Nothing special."

"I don't believe you."

"Fine," He shrugged. "I don't need you to believe anything. Your clock is ticking away and your time here is almost up."

"What are you even doing here?" I asked. I was already growing annoyed with him.

Tucker pushed a red curl from his face. "Good question, Alessio...I th ink...I'm here to watch you die and then watch your dumb little girlfriend die."

"Why?"

"Jesús pays good money. I barely had to do anything to get Olivia to him and now I can get the fuck out of this shitty ass state."

"So you are involving yourself with a gang and risking your own life? Just for some money?" I shook my head. "I could give you double what he did for nothing extra."

"No need," He waved his hand. "Your money isn't worth it."

"Smart man."

Tucker and I both looked up at the new voice. Jesús came into view under the streetlamp and flashed his capped teeth.

Looked like he had added some new shitty tattoos to his head.

"Jesús," I smiled widely. "Been a long time, friend. I can see your hair hasn't come back."

"Let's go have a chat, Alessio."

"We both know why I'm here."

"Come with me or I'll have my boys go fuck your girl and kill her right now?" He shrugged and Tucker laughed. "Your choice."

"Don't you fucking touch her."

Jesús smiled again and reached out for his phone as a few of his goons approached us.

"Willing to come chat then?"

I breathed out heavily. "Let's go."

One of the short, stocky guys came up to me and knocked into my shoulder with the barrel of his gun. I'm assuming he thought it was intimadating but he really just looked stupid.

Tucker led the rest of us and made sure to keep me in view while he continued to play with Olivia's bracelet. A dumb ass smile stayed on his face the whole time.

"Go in." Jesús spoke from behind and nodded towards the door. The other guy with him pulled it open and turned a light on.

The inside of the store was rotting. It smelled as if something had died and you could clearly see rat droppings covering the tops of the counters.

"Probably should hire somewhere to take better care of your businesses." I shook my head as we stepped over the debris.

"Shut the fuck up." His stocky goon snapped.

"Through the first door." Jesús demanded as we approached a door at the south end of the business.

The door opened and we moved down a flight of stairs to an underground warehouse that had been built under the foundation.

There looked to be several storage containers spread out among it and probably a pretty hefty supply of weed and coke.

"Sit him down, tie his hands."

One of his men snatched a chair from a nearby table and pushed me to it. I sat back and held my hands out for him to tie me.

Jesús took a step towards me. I could tell he wasn't really enjoying my easy breezy attitude.

"You know what I want to do?"

"What's that?" I asked and blew cigar smoke at him.

He knocked it from my lips. "I want to rip your teeth out one by one."

He picked the cigar up from the ground and pressed the red hot embers against my skin. I gritted my teeth against the pain but continued to stare at him.

"Maybe we'll just take turns stabbing you. Just some slow, painful fun."

"And?"

"And...I'll decapitate you like you did my brother and deliver it to your fucking whore before I fuck her in front of it."

I laughed grimly. "You'll never have the fucking chance."

"Sure about that? I don't see anyone coming to your rescue, amigo.
"

"I don't need rescuing," I laughed. "Do I look like a damsel in distress to you?"

Jesús pulled his knife from his jeans. "Why don't we cut the chit chat and get started then?"

I grinned and then I just started laughing. I couldn't contain myself. This whole thing was just way too fucking funny.

"The fuck is wrong with you?" Jesús snapped and looked around at the others.

I kept laughing hysterically until the end of his pistol whipped against my cheek. I could taste metallic in my mouth as the blood pooled.

"Now shut the fuck up." He snapped and slid his blade against the fabric of my jacket.

I frowned. "This was my favorite one."

"You won't be needing it anymore."

"We'll see about that."

Before anyone had time to realize what I was doing, I used my foot to push against the edge of the beam next to me and flip myself backwards.

The chair broke as it hit the ground and I could hear the sound of shouting as the lights went out and several canisters clinked across the floor.

Heavy, grey smoke was filling the space fast and I used it as an advantage to cut myself free and make my move before they could figure out where I went in the dark.

I started moving quickly through the pitch black as the shouts continued and several rounds of gunfire went off. Several emergency lights started to illuminate parts of the building.

A hand touched my shoulder and I felt a gas mask cover my face.

"Boss, let's get moving."

"I want Jesús dead." I told him and took a deep breath. "I'm not leaving until I know he's dead."

Swarms of my men were rushing into the room and the gunfire continued to light up the darkness as the fight continued on.

"We have 10 minutes. Bombs go off in eleven minutes." Robin said.

"All I need is 7."

He tossed me one of the semi's and I started making my move. Robin kept on my tail as we rushed through the dark and took out several of Jesús' men.

Three of them started rushing from the left. I emptied both of the chambers in my pistols before unloading the semi on a fourth.

I emptied both of my chambers and reached out to grab my semi before unloading it on them.

One. Two. Three. Four.

All dead.

I smiled to myself as I heard the thump of their bodies and stepped over them.

"Move!" I barked out and motioned for several of my guys to rush past. "Clear this out now."

Robin and I started making our way towards the entrance where Jesús was when a bullet whizzed by the two of us and hit a crate from behind.

We both turned to find Tucker pointing a gun at us.

"Get out of the way, Tucker. You don't want to die over someone else's business."

"Fuck that!" He hissed. "You aren't going to ruin this for me. I'll kill you myself."

He raised the gun to us again and his finger edged against the trigger.

Before he could even think about releasing it, I had already fired two at him and buried both in his skull.

The close range impact caused blood to splatter on the wall behind him. His corpse hit the floor hard.

I reached out and yanked the bracelet from his dead wrist.

"We gotta go." Robin spoke up.

I looked around the room for Jesús. I wasn't leaving without killing him.

"Alessio! Less than a minute. Let's go." Robin snapped and several people rushed by us to leave.

"Do not let Jesús out of here, dammit!"

"Looking for me, bitch."

I looked over and found Jesús standing across from me. He had two .40 caliber in each hand.

"10 seconds!"

I grimaced and looked behind me at them,"Say hi to your brother for me."

Jesús locked his eyes on me and smiled.

The two of us raised our guns together and fired just as the building started to shake from the bombs.

Within seconds fire and smoke clouded my vision and I couldn't see him anymore. I felt someone dragging me backwards up the staircase.

"Off me!" I snapped as Robin tossed me out the door to the ground. "Fuck! Fuck!"

We all started putting some distance between us and the flames as several more bombs went off causing the underground structure to collapse on itself. The roar of the fire crackled and started to rip through the foundation of the shop.

"I wasn't going to let you die." Robin snapped as we started moving towards the cars. "The police are going to be here any minute. There's no way he got out, Alessio. We were at the exit."

I clenched my jaw and helped him toss the guns into the back.

Robin climbed into the driver's side and started the engine. I could hear the sound of sirens already in the distance.

Soon enough there would be a swarm of them on the scene.

We pulled out fast down the opposite street and I leaned against the side door. I noticed movement near the burning building.

A very familiar tattooed, bald head.

He smiled and waved his gun over his head at us.

Fuck.

Chapter 17

"I can't put her through this, Anna. Olivia deserves more than what I can give her right now. How am I supposed to even get out of this obligation with Monica?"

"Suck it up, Alessio! Figure it the fuck out."

I glare over at her but she continues on.

"You're going to be the don of this family, Alessio. Stop acting like you aren't! You take what you want and right now Olivia is upstairs. Don't think about Monica right now."

I know Anna is right. She usually always is.

I just can't stop thinking about the damage this is doing to Olivia. How am I going to figure this out?

"What would I do without you." I say playfully and she swats at me.

"You'd be lost," She chuckles. "I'm always here."

"I know."

"What are we doing about Jesús?"

I light my cigarette and toss her one. "I'll find him."

"What's Adolfo's opinion on this?"

I shrug, "I could care less."

"Really? Why does my opinion mean so little to you, Figlio?"

(Translation: son)

Anna and I turn to find him stepping out onto the patio. He's wearing his usual red satin morning rob and has a cigar dangling from his wrinkled lips.

"I have everything under control."

"You didn't inform me of your intentions last night, Alessio," Adolfo mutters and blows smoke out. "You know you need to run things by me."

"I had everything under control."

He puts a hand on my shoulder, "Yet, Jesús got away?"

I shrug him off. "I said I have this under control. If you want me to take on these responsibilities you need to let me handle things."

"I'm still in charge here, Alessio."

I shake my head. "Act like it then, Adolfo."

He looks over at me but I pay him no mind and turn around. I flick my cigarette butt to the ground and hear him speak up from behind.

"I know you are still fucking around with that little girl, son. Don't think for one second Monica won't kill her if she finds out."

I turn on my heel and rush after him. "Leave Olivia out of this. She's no business of yours."

"She is my business, Alessio."

"You're investing in her father's business, not Olivia. If you want to turn them into one of your drug rings, I can't stop you."

He smiles crookedly with the cigar still perched. "Should I run it dry and send your little girlfriend home to New York? You know it would take me less than 12 hours to ruin them."

"You know they could help increase a generous profit for you. You wouldn't ruin that chance." I remind him.

Adolfo's intentions were not pure at all. It killed me knowing Olivia didn't know the kind of business her father was partaking in.

Olivia's father works for a company called Vector Global. They try to assist their own clients with things like money management and helping grow their businesses.

Adolfo takes businesses like this one and uses it as a way to launder money quietly. They also see it as a chance to partner with other mafia organizations legally through Vector.

The business has had it's mafia ties for years and Olivia's father knows it.

Vector Global is dirty and his family has had no idea that they had been funding their salaries through organized crime activity under the surface and through shady clients.

When things got rough, they offered him a higher paying position in return for getting Adolfo to invest.

"Focus on Monica." Adolfo says.

"Monica is entertaining herself back in Venice. She'll be just fine without me until it's time."

"Her family wants to speed things up with the wedding."

My eyes narrow. "Her family or you?"

"Both." He shrugs and ashes the cigar. "We're ready to get this moving."

"How soon?" My jaw clenches. I had planned on this not being for at least another year.

"Two or three months."

"I need more time."

"I don't care what you need, Alessio. You'll marry her and then I want you to move back to Italy."

"That was not part of the agreement!" I snap and feel Anna touch my shoulder.

"I can do whatever I want. I'm still Don and if I want you to move back to Italy until I die, you'll do it."

"I never asked for this."

Adolfo laughs deeply. "None of us did, son."

Anna and I stand there in silence as he walks past us into the house. I can feel my entire body tingling with rae.

"You can't keep acting like this, Alessio." Anna speaks up.

"I don't care what he wants, Anna. I deserve to have a say in my own life. Mafia or not."

"You know it doesn't work that way for you."

"I'm aware."

"I'm going to be heading out to Italy in two weeks to handle some stuff with Alonzo and visit. Do you want to go?"

I shake my head. "I'm not leaving, Olivia."

She nods and steps off the patio. "I get it, Alessio, just make sure you don't let this drag on. Don't hurt Olivia."

I watch for a moment as she heads out towards her car and look back up towards my bedroom where Olivia still is.

I don't want her to hate me but I know my actions have upset her.

I head into the house and up the stairs. My bedroom door is still slightly propped from when I left.

"Olivia."

I look in through the crack of the door and see her flat on her back.

Her long dark hair is a complete mess around her face. I can hear her snoring a little under her arm tossed on her face.

Always sleeping.

I walk closer to her and sit on the edge of the bed. I reach out and brush my fingers against the exposed skin of her waist.

Her plump, pink lips are parted slightly and cheeks have a bit of a rose tint to them.

She has such an angelic look. I don't understand how someone so perfect and stunning would think otherwise.

She stirs and stretches her arms. "Alessio?"

"I'm here." I lean and kiss her head.

"Don't leave." She whines out and wraps her arms tightly against my neck.

I pull her close to me and press her stomach to my own. "I won't, baby. I'm sorry."

"I missed you so much."

I pull back a little and press her mouth to my own. I feel my own need and desire for her take over.

The want I have for her never ending or subsiding.

I feel myself slipping off the edge and I know if I don't get it under control it will be harder to slow down.

I want to match her pace. I need her to take charge.

"I love you, Olivia."

She smiles against my lips and pulls back. Her ocean Blue eyes lock with my dark ones.

I swear I lose myself in them every single time.

"I love you, Alessio."

I cup her face in my hands and kiss her again.

Her hands are suddenly moving from my neck and down my stomach. I feel her fingers play with the edge of my shirt.

Her touch leaves me scorching and I need more.

My grip tightens on her. "I want you so bad."

She responds with hooking her right leg over my waist and brushes her fingers up and down the lower part of my stomach.

"Do you want me?" I ask lowly.

She looks up from my shirt and blushes. "I do."

"You don't have to be afraid. I won't hurt you, Olivia."

She nods and nervously bites her lower lip. Just the sight of it drives me fucking insane.

"Okay." She breathes out. "I want to."

"Are you sure?"

She nods but she doesn't need to say anything. Just the look she gives me is enough.

Our mouths connect with one another feverishly and I pull her against my hard. My hands move from the back of her neck to her waist.

I move down to her neck and kiss the skin there. She rolls her head back and a little moan slips out.

I keep my eyes on her as I move down to kiss the tops of her collarbones.

Olivia locks her gaze onto me and moves her hands down to remove her top. She tosses it to the side and lays before me with her perfect, full breasts.

Her pale skin glowing and soft, full breasts bouncing with every moment. I move myself over her and nip at her pink nipples.

"You taste so fucking good."

I continue to travel down her stomach and feel her hands grab onto my hair.

She arches against me. "Please don't stop."

I move down to the edge of her shorts and she helps me slide them off of her. I finger the edge of her panties and admire her beauty.

"Please." She says again and looks down.

I hook my hands onto her underwear and toss them to the side.

She's dripping wet and the sight makes me hard instantly. I feel my erection pressing tight against my jeans painfully.

I kiss the skin there and slowly move down until the tip of my tongue is teasing her swollen clit. Her sweetness fills my mouth and I continue to create small circles on her slit.

Soft moans escape her and I muse at the sound of her ecstasy.

I take her in fully and her legs tighten around my head. I use one hand to hold her in place and the other to slip two fingers into her tight core.

"Fuck!" She gasps out.

I curl my finger inside of her slightly and pump it in and out as my tongue continues to swirl against her.

Within minutes her legs start to tremble and she screams out with pleasure as I drive her to the edge.

I feel her pulsate against my mouth as she reaches her climax. I try to hold her in place as she bucks against me as another wave takes over her immediately.

"Oh my god..." She pants.

I kiss each of her trembling thighs and look up at her. She lays there in stunned bliss and laughs a little.

"I'm not done with you." I warn and scoot her to the edge of the bed.

She watches as I toss my shirt to the floor and start to slip out of my jeans. I feel her hand take hold of mine and she positions herself in front of my waist.

I look down into her blue eyes and she watches me as she takes hold of the edge of my pants and pulls them down the rest of the way.

She looks down curiously at my boxers and pulls them down inch by inch until my full, rock hard cock is out and throbbing for her.

I hear a small gasp of shock come from her and she almost looks afraid.

"It's okay," I assure her. "I told you I won't hurt you."

She nods and takes hold of me in her tiny hands. I grip the edge of the metal frame and grit my teeth as she strokes me up and down.

Her pace starts to pick up as she works my shaft and I notice her bringing herself down to the tip. Her soft lips form a little circle as she takes the head in for a taste.

After a moment, she finds her rhythm and starts to explore.

She uses her right to continue to stroke me as she brings me in and out of her mouth. The warmth of her mouth and throat drives me to the edge as she continues to pump me into her faster and faster.

"Fuck, Olivia." I gasp and grab onto her hair.

I feel her lips curl into a smirl and she hooks onto my hips with her hands. I hold onto the back of her head and force myself deeper into her mouth.

She holds me in place as I reach my orgasm and release into her mouth. She looks up at me as the new taste fills her and swallows it quickly.

Oh my god. I really love this fucking woman.

"Turn." I tell her and motion for her to get onto her stomach. "Do not move."

I walk over to the nightstand near the bed and slip on a condom.

My hands grab onto her tiny waist and I pull her up into an arch. She skillfully lays her front half down flat against the bed and rocks her ass against my cock.

I lean forward and nip at the skin of her back playfully. She yelps a little and laughs as it's followed with a kiss.

I slide my hands back up and cup her full ass in my palm. I bring it up and down against her cheek hard.

She rocks into it and gasps. "Ouch!"

"Don't act like you didn't like that." I tease and another smack comes down against her bare ass.

She moans and moves her hips against me. I hook my free hand on her hip and position myself just at the edge of her core.

"Ready?"

She grips at the comforter. "Please...please fuck me, Alessio."

I move into her gently and watch her lips slide down the condom. I glance up as soon as I'm about halfway inside and notice her pained expression.

"Do you want me to stop?"

She shakes her head. "Please keep going."

I push myself the rest of the way a little slower and moan at how tight she is. She feels so fucking amazing.

"Are you sure you want me to continue?" I ask firmly.

"Yes..." She says softly and turns her head on the comforter. "It kind of hurts...but it feels really good too."

She experimentally rocks her hips against my cock and pushes me all the way in. I gasp loudly at the feeling and grab onto her hard.

I hang onto her as she continues to bounce her ass against me back and forth. Her tightness grabbing onto me with each movement.

"Fuck." I moan loudly. "You feel so fucking good."

"Faster, please." She begs.

I hold her in place and pump out of her again and again. Her hands grip at the blanket beneath us as I plunge deeper into her as fast as I know she can handle.

"Oh my god." She cries out.

It only encourages me to fuck her harder. I continue to push into her deep and hard as her moans turn into full blown screams. I feel her body stiffen up with my own as we both reached our climax together.

I feel my body start to go limp and explode with pleasure as she shakes against me and screams my name out.

I move out from her and fall on the bed. "Olivia..."

"Alessio." She says in between breaths.

I stare down at her and admire her perfection.

Every part of her. I could study her for a lifetime.

And she's mine. She is finally mine.

I don't want this to ever end. I want forever.

"Olivia..." I start and she looks up at me.

"What?"

"I want to marry you."

◇ ◇ ◇

O L I V I A

He's joking. Right?

This is a joke.

I stare down at the end of the bed for what feels like forever before he finally says something again.

"Please talk to me."

"You're kidding." I say bluntly.

He looks down at me offended. "I'm being serious."

"Alessio...don't you think this is all...a little fast?"

"That's why I said want," He explains and rests his head against mine. "I just want to know I can have my forever with you, Olivia. I'm in love with you...madly in love with you. I know things have moved quickly for us but I've never been so sure of something before."

"I'm only eighteen years old. I still have so much I need to do with my life."

He nods. "I know and that's why I don't expect an answer. I just want you to know what I want and when you are ready, I'll be here."

"Okay..."

He continues on, "And I know you want to move back to New York from school. I'd love to be part of that journey for you and...maybe buy you a cute little house so I can visit."

My breath catches, "I can't accept something so generous."

"I have plenty of time to convince you otherwise." He rolls his eyes.

He's lost his freaking mind! I know Alessio is impulsive but MAR-RIAGE.

"How are you feeling?"

I blush deeply. "Not bad...a little sore."

"It was perfect." He muses and kisses me.

"I'm sure you've had better."

"I haven't because it was never with you." He glares.

I shake my head at him and try to change the topic to something other than sex and marriage.

"Can we go see Giovanni and Beto?"

He seems to think about it for a moment before finally speaking again.

"I think they'd like that."

The two of us hurry through getting our clothes back on and he leads me down the stairs and through a hall I have never seen before.

It's completely bare from decor and looks pretty depressing.

"Why do you look so nervous?"He whispers in my ear.

"I'm not." I lie.

I don't know why I was a damn nervous mess but maybe it's just the mix of my mafia boyfriend proposing to me after we have sex for the first time and also being concerned for his family members who were shot.

Normal teenager stress obviously.

"They are just through that door." He says and motions to a door ahead of us with

clinic

written on it.

He holds the door open and we step into what looks to be some kind of waiting room. "Is this just for the Romano family?"

"Yes, usually for minor things, but we have a doctor on-call for emergencies like this. Dr. Tobias has been part of the Romano family for years."

"Tobias?"

He nods, "Very close family friend and medical doctor."

A door to the right of us opens and Anna steps out. Her dark hair is thrown up into a messy bun and she's actually wearing sweatpants.

I honestly wouldn't have recognized her at first if she didn't say something first.

"Hey," She smiles. "Good to see you up."

"You too," I reach out and hug her. "How is everything in there?"

"Stable."

"Can we go in?" Alessio grabs my hand.

"Sure. Nobody else is here right now." Anna waves back to the door. "I have something to handle so I'll see you guys later."

The both of us watch as she moves past us and heads out of the room.

"Is she okay?" I ask Alessio when she's gone.

"Yes. It's just a lot on her."

I nod and follow him through the second door and down another hallway. There's a door propped open and a weird mix of medical machines beeping and some kind of grunting noises.

"Suck it, bitch!"

"We'll see about that."

Alessio shakes his head as we enter."We have ladies present."

I step past him and find Beto and Giovanni both sitting straight up in their beds. Both boys have their eyes locked on a video game as they smash away at the buttons.

"Give me five seconds, Beto is about to die."

Beto snorts loudly. "It's not over til it's over, fat boy."

"It's muscle, fuck head."

I give Alessio's hand a little squeeze and move to sit in the chair at the end of their beds.

"BULLSHIT! I had your ass. You fucking cheated."

Beto throws him an annoyed look. "How? Please tell me how I cheated?"

Giovanni glares back at him for a long time before dropping the controller and looking at me with a big smile.

"Hello, Olivia. How are you?"

"I'm alright. How are you feeling?"

He shrugs and leans back to show me his bandaged wounds.

"I've been through worse."

"Well, it seems like you can handle it." I tell him and he winks in response.

"Round two when the lady leaves."

Beto just shakes his head and starts tapping on his phone. His dark hair looks disheveled and the loud machine I heard a few minutes ago is hooked up to him.

Compared to how he normally looks he was so pale today.

"What about you, Beto. How are you?"

He looks up with his dark, youthful eyes. "I'm doing wonderful actually. I told Tobias to let me off this damn machine, but he insists that I stay put until he says otherwise."

"Maybe for the best."

Alessio moves behind me and places his hand on my shoulder. I hear him speak up into his cellphone.

"Go ahead."

I look back at him and watch his face as he listens. He looks forward at Giovanni and seems irritated.

Alessio continues to converse in Italian for a few more minutes before his phone is back in his pocket.

"Is everything okay?" I ask.

He looks at Giovanni. "I'm leaving in ten minutes. How are you feeling?"

Giovanni puts his large arms up and his muscles ripple in his biceps. ""I've been waiting for this, baby."

Alessio rolls his eyes and looks down at me. "I have to take care of something in the city. I'm going to have Anna drop you off, I promise I'll see you soon."

I frown and want to push him for answers but I know he's not ready. "Okay."

His lips meet mine quickly. "I love you, Olivia. Stay safe."

Beto chirps from behind us. " Y'all are so cute but I have a question."

Alessio looks over.

"Can I come?"

"No."

Beto tosses his hand in frustration. The movement was quite dramatic even for someone like him.

"Why not? Tobias never has to know? I can help, please!"

Alessio scowls. "Beto, I don't have time. Please just follow the orders. We need you."

I can tell he wants to protest but instead he falls back into the hospital bed and picks the controller up from his chest.

Alessio puts his hand on the small of my back and guides us back towards the waiting room where Anna is already waiting.

"Come on." She says quickly and throws Alessio a glance as she hooks onto my arm.

She practically drags me through the house and out to the car waiting in the front. I climb into the passenger seat next to her and she pulls out from the driveway in a hurry.

"Is everything alright?"

"No, but Alessio will handle it. He always does." She says in an irritated tone.

"Can I confide something in you?"

I didn't know Anna very well but she had been a really good friend to me since I've met her. She seemed like she'd be one of those girls that always gave you the best advice.

"Shoot."

"Alessio said something to me this morning and I don't know...how I should take it."

"What do you mean?"

I blush a bit and look away. "Well, we took things to the next step for the first time this morning."

She laughs at my expression and shakes her head. "I'm assuming you two have done the deed and Alessio has declared his love?"

I can tell she's half teasing but something else with her statement almost sounds like she's not too thrilled with him.

"Yeah, but there is something else."

"Oh, really?" She looks at me.

I nod and nervously pick at the skin on my thumb.

"He said he wants to marry me."

Anna's brows raise and she looks back out at the road. "He did now?"

"Yeah..." I trail off a little from her harsh tone. "Is that a bad thing? I really didn't know what to say...or do?"

"I think that was for the best right now."

"I'm confused?" I say as she pulls sharply into my driveway.

She bows her head and sighs. "Alessio just needs to take care of his shit first before he goes off saying things like this."

"What do you suggest?"

"Just be careful, Olivia. I don't doubt Alessio's love for you but don't go jumping into things you both aren't ready for."

"Understood." I mutter and step from the car.

I glance back at her in hopes she'll give me something I can really hang onto but the car pulls away from our house without another glance.

I watch as she disappears over the hill and feel my heart squeeze. I turn to head inside and let my burning thoughts consume me for the night.

Chapter 18

"I found out last night Tucker resigned."

I look up at Kimberly as soon as she mentions his name.

After Anna had dropped me off back at my house, I hadn't heard very much from any of them.

I knew Alessio was at least alive because he sent me a text this morning saying he loved me but I had no idea what was going on.

It had been days and I had nothing.

I didn't mind it too much though because I really needed the time to breathe and think.

"Resigned?" I ask her and focus on the road ahead of us.

"Yeah," She shrugs and pops her gum. "Boss man said he left a letter on his desk. I guess he had to move back home immediately to Texas. Super vague."

I nod a little in response.

Did Tucker actually resign or was this something Alessio made up?

I knew he had gone after them but he didn't say anything about what had happened. I didn't push on it either because I'm sure the truth would just be too much for me to take in.

"What is going to happen now?" I continue.

"Guess we'll find out later."

She pulls the handles open to the school entrance and I stop in my tracks.

Austin's face is plastered all over the hall.

Hundreds of flyers and stunned students huddled around the posters. A couple of police officers walk out from the school office and Sierra follows behind them quickly.

"Sierra! What's wrong?" Kimberly hurries to her side.

She wipes at her red, puffy eyes and throws her arms around Kim's neck before breaking into a mess of sobs.

"Kimberly..."She says through broken words. "Austin is missing...they've been looking for him for days. His dad thought he may have ran off with his friends again like last time but...he hasn't come back."

Last time? I didn't know he had a history of disappearing.

Maybe this will keep Alessio and his family in the clear.

Kimberly reads over the flyer in her hands and tears start to spill. I stand there awkwardly as they pull each other in for a hug and reach out to bring me close to them.

I can't help but cry too.

I knew the truth and I couldn't tell them.

I couldn't take their pain away from this.

Austin is dead. Fucking dead.

Such a permanent sentence.

"I-I got to g-go."

"Olivia!" Kimberly calls out.

I don't stop though. My feet keep moving and I run straight to my new favorite hang out spot.

The girls bathroom to do all of my crying and stress puking.

I rush into the empty stall and curl myself into a ball. My body starts to shake as I break into a hysteric fit.

"I c-can't d-do t-this!" I cough out and bang my head against the stall.

Alessio and his family expected so much from someone like me.

I had to face these people every single day. I would have to see his father around the school asking questions and I would be the one to face my best friends.

How was I supposed to keep quiet? How can I just act so normal?

My phone starts to buzz in my pocket and I pull it out.

Alessio's name flashes across the screen.

Perfect.

"Hello?" I breathe out in a shaky voice.

"Olivia? What's going on?" He asks in a rough voice. It sounds like he just woke up.

"I can't do this, Alessio. They have pictures of him...everywhere."

"Olivia..."Alessio warns,"I know it's hard but you have to stay strong."

"I'm trying but this is not easy. I hate seeing my friends like this."

"You just need to be strong a little longer. This will pass, I promise."

I close my eyes tight. "How is this so easy for you?"

"It's not, baby. We've taken our precautions."

"Alright," I sigh and hear the restroom door open. "I have to go. Talk soon."

I hang up the phone and use my phone camera to make sure I don't look like too much of a mess before hurrying out of the room to English.

The entire school day is just the news of Austin scattering around the school.

According to the Westview gossip Austin had disappeared for almost a week when he was fifteen years old to hang out with some older friends of his in another town.

He went on an alcohol binge and apparently cocaine.

It was almost something new every single period.

People spreading rumors about him being with Sierra and wondering if she's hiding something.

People talking about how Austin used to say his dad was violent and an abusive drunk throughout elementary and middle school.

The worse of all…was the ones where my name got brought up when he talked to me at the party.

They would whisper and look back at me with curious stares. It made me sick to my stomach and I just wished I could get the hell out of there.

Sierra and Kimberly hadn't left one another's side so I was basically on my own and watching everything play out.

I tried to keep my head low and avoid any questions directed to me from other students since they knew we had all been friends.

I would just mutter out, "I really don't know. We stopped hanging out."

I was just grateful when the final bell rang and I could make my escape to the cafe.

Kim had called off for her shift after she found out about the news with Austin so I had the whole afternoon and evening to myself.

"Nice to see you, Olivia!"

I looked up to see our boss Edgar walking out from the kitchen. He's an older man in his 60's with thick silver hair and a crazy scar through his lower lip.

It had been awhile since he was around often since he left Tucker to manage but it was nice having him here. He always had a way of keeping the day fun and light.

"Hi, Edgar! How are you?"

"I'm doing well." He nods. "I assume Kimberly told you Tucker resigned."

"She did earlier today."

"Well, I wanted to know how you felt about a potential promotion?"

I stare at him in shock, not sure if I heard him right.

"A promotion? M-me?" I stammer out.

"Yes, ma'am." He grins showing his yellowing teeth. "Kimberly declined the offer and you've really grown here. She even recommended that I ask you about it."

I just continued to stare at him in disbelief. I've never been the manager of anything.

"What do you think?"

"U-uh, yeah! Why not. Thank you so much!"

He smiles warmly and tosses me a set of store keys.

"We'll be doing some training together this week. There isn't much you need to worry about but we are going to be hiring someone to help out in the kitchen so you don't have to learn that and two more baristas." He hands me a stapled guide.

"Thank you, Edgar! I won't let you down."

"I know you won't, Olivia."

◇ ◇ ◇

"Olivia Elizabeth Moore! I'm so freaking proud of you." Mom exclaims at the news.

As soon as I got home I erupted with the news from the cafe. She was so over the moon but of course it was short lived when she had to break to me that the school had sent out a call in regards to Austin.

I kept the conversation short like I had earlier in the day and tried my best to keep my heartbroken and confused expression plastered to my face.

She reached out and wrapped her arms around me tightly. I squeeze her back and smiled.

"Thank you, mom."

"Now," She starts up and walks over to the oven. "Your aunt called me this morning."

"Macy?"

"Yes, apparently she is having surgery this weekend and is going to need help."

"So...are you going to New York?"

She pulls out the casserole. "I am just for the weekend and until Thursday morning. I wanted to let you know in case you wanted to try to get some time off to visit your school."

"That's a good idea, I'd also love to catch up with Amy."

It had been months now since I had been to New York and with graduation literally around the corner I was more than excited to see my friends again, especially Amy.

Our little chats here and there wasn't cutting it out anymore. Plus, Aunt Macy is always a blast and full of surprises.

"I'm sure she'd love that," Mom grins at me. "I'll let her know tonight."

The next hour seems to move slowly as we wait for my father to arrive home from work. Over the past week he had been showing up almost two hours later than his normal time and just didn't seem like himself.

So when the door finally opened we stopped mid sentence and waited for him to walk into the kitchen.

"How was work?" Mom asks and stands behind his chair. "I made your favorite."

"Long," He groans and sits down. "Lot's of changes."

"Like what?" I ask.

"Just changes, Olivia," He says dismissively and pushes his food with his fork.

Mom looks up at me apologetically. "Do...do you want to talk about it later, Daniel?"

"No, Susan. I really don't. Please!" He shouts and slams his fist down.

She jumps at his reaction and backs away towards the sink to clean up. I watch silently as he fetches his whiskey from the top kitchen cabinet and heads back down the stairs towards the basement.

He had spent a lot of time down there trying to make it into some kind of man hangout/office space.

Usually it just seemed like he was drinking and watching football.

"I'm sorry mom."

She nods and pours herself a glass of wine. "He's just stressed out, baby."

"I didn't know it was getting this bad."

"The past week he has seemed pretty...closed off." Mom smiles sadly. "Try not to worry too much, Liv. He'll be okay."

"I understand."

"I'm going to finish up here and try to settle him down." She turns away and starts wiping down the counter.

Even through her smile I know she's so heartbroken. They've always been so close and best friends. I can't even imagine how this has been for her.

I hurry from the kitchen up to my room and pull a duffel bag out from the closet. I might as well pick out a few outfits for New York otherwise I'll do it last minute and probably end up with outfits that don't match at all.

Just as I reach back in the closet to grab my favorite black dress there's a weird sound against my window.

"What the f-"

clack

I walk over to the window and slide it open to find Alessio standing in the yard with a handful of rocks.

"Cell Phones exist and I'd appreciate you not breaking my window." I tease.

He laughs a bit and smiles up at me. He's so beautiful it just blows me away every time he's around.

The fact he even exists is just amazing to me.

"I missed you." He says with a whine.

"Well, I'm glad you decided to come see me then," I smirk at him. "You didn't have to go all Romeo and Juliet on me though."

"I'm a romantic."

"Very romantic," I laugh and shake my head. "Next thing you know you'll be scaling the house."

He goes silent for a minute and looks over towards the front porch."One second."

"Alessio!" I hiss at his retreating back as he's swallowed by the darkness. "What are you doing??"

No response.

Great, he's going to do something dumb and scare the shit out of my parents.

I look back to make sure nobody has ran up here to check out the commotion and back out towards the edge of the roof.

"Alessio!"

His face appears in front of me. "Quiet down."

I jump and grasp at my chest. He gently guides me backwards and steps through the window with ease.

I mold myself into his long and solid body and feel at home. Just being in his arms makes me feel so safe.

"I'm glad you do dumb things." I mutter happily.

"Anything for you."

"How have things been...back at home?" I ask and steer him towards the bed.

"Things are okay, baby. Just lot's of business."

I nod a little and think back to the conversation I had with Anna.

"I talked to Anna."

"About?"

"Well...us,"I frown a little. "She doesn't seem thrilled."

"What did you tell her?" He pushes back.

I look up at his face and search his expression. " I told her you said you wanted to marry me, Alessio. I didn't know this was a secret between us."

He sighs, "It isn't, Olivia, but I'd prefer to keep some intimate moments between us to ourselves. I know Anna has some good advice sometimes but let's keep this to us for now."

"I didn't mean to cause any trouble between you two."

"You didn't," He reaches out and cradles my face." She mentioned what you told her and I explained myself. I don't regret what I said and I still stand by it."

I tilt into his palm a little more and sigh happily. His thumb strokes my cheek as he speaks. "What's on your mind now?"

"Everything actually..."

"Care to share?"

"The Austin situation has been taking a huge toll on me."

"We'll handle it, Olivia, I know this is something you'll never understand or accept in my life,"He says softly and brushes his fingers against my lower lip. "I'm not asking you to forgive me for it, but I had to do it. If I didn't, I don't know what would happen."

"I won't say a word." I promise him. "It's hard but they won't get anything from me."

He smiles a little and kisses my cheek. "Now tell me something positive."

"I got a promotion."

"A promotion?" He muses and looks down at me. "I imagine Tucker's absence is part of that."

"He left a letter of resignation. Did you do that?"

"We needed it to look normal," He shrugs his shoulders. "He has family back in Texas. By the time they report him missing, his corpse will be completely disposed of."

I stiffen at the word he chooses.

Corpse.

"They'll never have closure then?"

"Let's focus on you right now," He shakes his head. "Tell me something else."

"I'm going to New York for a week," I smile up at him. "My aunt is having surgery so mom is going to help her out while I visit friends and see my art school."

I wait for some kind of excited response but he just stiffens and looks out towards the bedroom window.

"What?" I snap. His reaction pisses me off.

He stands up from the bed and turns towards me, running his fingers through his messy locks.

"Alessio? What the fuck?" I grab at his arm in frustration.

"Olivia, I don't want you going to New York right now."

I stare at him confused.

"What do you mean?"

"There's so much going on, Olivia. I just want to make sure you are safe." He says softly.

My head is reeling and before I even have time to think about my next response. I feel my attitude start to rear its head.

Maybe it's from the stress and everything else but I know it's coming.

"I don't need a babysitter, Alessio! I'm eighteen years old, I can handle myself for a week."

He glares down at me. "I told you I'd keep you safe. Right now a lot is going on and you could still be a target."

"Alessio!" I toss my hands above me. "I didn't ask for protection! I didn't ask for you to watch me every moment of the day! I sure as fuck didn't ask for you to boss me around."

He stares at me for a moment and before I have time to realize what is going on he pushes me down to the bed. Our mouths meet instantly and I feel his hands exploring all over my body.

My heart picks up as he kisses down my neck and my insides squirm with his heated kisses.

"Wait! Stop." I demand and push him back.

He pulls back a little and stares down at me with an unreadable expression.

"Please just let me talk," I beg and move out from underneath him.. "Obviously we need to talk about this."

He sits there for a minute and reaches over to hold my hand. "Please stay for me, Olivia."

"Alessio, I want to see the school and I need to see my friends."

"Can't I take you later?" He sighs and rubs at the stubble on his chin.

"Don't you trust me?" I argue.

"I do, Olivia. I just want to make sure you are safe. Why are you making it so damn difficult?"

"I'll be with my mom and friends!" I squeeze his hand a little. "It's only a week and I'd be more safe there, right?"

He stares down at me with pleading eyes and seems to be battling some kind of invisible argument in his head.

I know he means well and this is part of who he is but I know I can handle myself the same way I did before he came into my life.

"Fine," He says after a few minutes. "Mateo will be in the area though watching. I'll have a team on standby but you won't see them."

"Ales-" I start to protest but am cut off by another greedy kiss.

"Please..."He begs softly. "I promise he will be a shadow."

I roll my eyes at the thought of Mateo ever being a shadow. The Romano family sticks out like a sore thumb.

"Fine."

"You're the best." He smiles widely and kisses me again.

Chapter 19

"M y beautiful Olivia!"

I smile warmly at my Aunt Macy as we step into her apartment.

She still had boxes cluttering her living room that hadn't been packed. I'm pretty sure she had been here for at least five years.

Not to mention the fake plants and her seven cats really added that special touch.

Macy is my mom's older sister. There's about a five year difference between the two of them. She's a fit woman with silver streaks in her dark brown hair and a cigarette always in her mouth.

If she's not running a marathon she's smoking cigarettes. The irony in it all kills me.

"We've missed you, sis." Mom grins and they hug.

Macy wobbles a little as they break their embrace and tries to hop back to the couch.

"Tore my damn meniscus!" She groans loudly. "You'd think I'd learn by now."

"Maybe it is time to give the gym up?" Mom chuckles.

Macy pulls a cigarette out. " Hell no! I don't plan to slow down any time soon."

"You know you'll probably be down for a good 3 months." Mom bats at the smoke.

"I know, I know. Once you two leave, mom is going to come stay with me for a bit."

"Wow," Mom shakes her head in disappointment. "She couldn't have made it out to see us?"

Macy shrugs, "You know how she is."

"I know," Mom nods. "Maybe one day she'll take the stick out of her ass."

I roll my eyes at the two of them and pull my phone out to let Alessio know I made it here safely.

Be safe, beautiful.

I smile at his text but part of me wonders if Mateo is actually here already and looming in the shadows.

"What are your plans, Liv?" Macy chirps. .

I shrug," Probably going to see Amy and stop by the college."

She smiles and tosses me something heavy and silver.

Car keys.

"Take my car."

"Macy!" Mom snaps.

"She's 18 and she has had her license for three years, Susan."

Mom scoffs, "She hasn't driven since we left New York."

"Actually," I chirp up and eye my mom cautiously. "Dad let me take his car a few times when he worked from home."

She glares at her sister,"If she wrecks YOUR car, I am not paying shit."

"Get the wine, bitch. You need to calm down."

I laugh at them as I pull the door shut and head down her apartment stairs towards the little Camry.

I pull out my phone and quickly dial out to Amy.

"Wow! The bitch is alive."

I shake my head, "Missed you, whore. I'm in the city, let's hang."

"What are you doing in New York?"

"Aunt Macy is having surgery so mom is going to help her out for the week."

"So you're leaving again?"

I frown to myself. I hadn't been back in almost 5 months now and it really sucked how much I had missed my friends. My life had been so great out here.

"I got accepted to Cornell so I'll be back soon." I tell her.

"Such a smart, bitch," She laughs loudly into the phone, "Meet me at my place and we can go check it out."

I ended our call and drove directly to her house where she lives with her older sister and boyfriend, Matthias. She has been dating him for the past 2 years and it's honestly a shock to hear he wouldn't be clinging to her side on our little day trip today.

I had also decided after ten minutes of driving in New York traffic that I'd stick to cabs when I came back because it still is fucking nuts.

"Oh my god, I can't believe you are here!" Amy screams as I step out from the car.

Her blonde hair is pulled into a high ponytail and she has her favorite cheer sweatshirt on and black leggings.

We had so much in common but our interests were completely different. Amy was always boy crazy and loved cheerleading. She was a complete girly girl and was always trying to convince me to let her try makeup ideas on my face.

"I know! I'm so excited." I exclaim and hug her tightly.

"So," She wiggles her brows. "Any hot boys there?"

"Duh!" I snort and wave down a taxi.

"You don't want to drive?"

I glare at her. "God no."

We hop in the taxi together and head off to Cornell. The school is a complete dream and seeing everyone out and living their lives there made me want to go even more.

The Art department was exactly how I pictured it. Students crowded the halls and school classrooms with canvases and tarps laid out along the floors.

"You want to do this...forever?" Amy wondered.

"Absolutely," I nodded eagerly. "I love this, Amy, I always have."

"You are really good. I still have that canvas you did our sophomore year."

I smiled at her and noticed an unfamiliar girl walking up to us with dark purple hair and several piercings on her face.

"Hey! Are you guys new?" She grinned.

"Yeah, I am!" I tell her. "I won't be starting until the Summer though, I was just in the city and wanted to check it out."

"Are you in the Art program?" She asks and adjusts her lip ring.

"Yeah! I'm really excited."

"You're going to love it! I've been attending for a year now and the program is out of this world. I wish our instructor was here you would just adore him. He's a really great guy," She smiles and leans close. "He's also crazy freaking hot."

"Oh, go find him!" Amy teases.

"Anyways, my name is Jane." The girl says. "You'll see me around here a lot so don't be shy when you start. I'd be happy to help you out."

"Thank you! I really appreciate that."

She nods and walks back towards a group of people who were seated at the back. They were all so different from one another.

A mix of punk and art hipster.

I'm going to love this school.

Amy and I head back towards the front of the school together. "How are you feeling about it?" She asks.

My smile is huge," I love it so much, Amy."

"Come on, let's go get some coffee and you can tell me about Cali."

She takes my hand in hers and we rush across the busy street as soon as there's a break in traffic towards the little corner bakery.

"Bet you didn't miss the traffic." She laughs.

I look back at the cars lining the streets. "I kind of do."

"I'd be happy to trade places." She teases as we approach the counter.

We settle on two caramel latte and cookies before taking a spot at a little table in front of the store window.

"Tell me about your new home." She says as she takes a sip.

"It's a lot of fun. We don't live far from the beach and I'm walking distance to the school and my job there."

"That's good, babe. Any lover's in your life?" She winks.

My cheeks blush and she narrows her eyes at my expression.

"What's the name?"

"Uh," I say softly and nervously glance around for Mateo. "His name is Alessio."

"Ooo," She purrs. "Is he foreign?"

"Italian."

She shakes her head, "Lucky bitch! I bet he's a dream."

"You have no idea," I chuckle and roll my eyes. "He's over six feet and sculpted to perfection. All muscle and the most gorgeous black eyes and dark hair. I've never met a man like him before."

"Where did you find him?" She swoons.

"Shockingly, he attended my new school."

"Does he have any brothers?" She winks and I snort.

"He has a tank for a brother who would scare the shit out of you and the cousin is obsessed with polo's and Oakley's."

"The sunglasses?" She laughs loudly.

"I swear he owns at least 50 pairs."

We spend the rest of our time catching up on how she's been doing throughout her senior year and what her plans are.

I guess her and Matthias hadn't been doing good so she was considering breaking things off and attending school for a law degree.

It felt nice talking to someone outside from California. When I left early in the school year I felt like so much of me was left behind.

I have history here and Amy understands me more than anyone I know.

Today I was finally just able to relax. I didn't have to worry about people asking me thousands of questions about Austin or what the hell happened to Tucker.

No Romano mafia drama or anything else.

Just fun with a good friend.

Eventually 6pm had rolled around and Amy and I parted ways after a very long, tearful goodbye. I hurried back to the apartment to catch dinner with my mom.

"Are you ready?" She shouts from the living room.

I toss my hair back into a ponytail and settle on a thick black dress and some boots. I wasn't really used to the New York weather anymore.

I pass by Macy on the couch and look down at her. "Are you sure you don't want to come?"

She's still on the couch with her leg propped up and wine drunk.

"Go eat with your mom!" She waves me off. "I have plenty of chinese takeout, shitty tv, and my cigarettes."

I laugh and give her a quick kiss on the cheek before heading out with my mom. "Where to?" She asks.

We headed out onto the sidewalk heading into the city and I spotted my favorite Pizza place when I was a kid.

"Toni's?" I ask and she doesn't even respond.

We rush across the street together and right into the restaurant. The owner Antonio was standing at the front and had a big smile on as soon as he saw us.

"Olivia! Susan!" He cheers out.

Antonio is a long time friend of the families. He's a sweet, older man and has the best Pizza I've ever had.

"Antonio! How are you?" Mom says and pulls him in for a hug.

"Well! Doing very well. What are you doing here?"

"Macy is having surgery on her knee."

Antonio gasps,"What has she done now?"

"Tore her meniscus. She'll be needing some help for awhile." Mom rolls her eyes.

He shakes his head and yells something in Italian back towards a worker.

"Please sit", He smiles and guides us to a booth."Take your time!"

"What are you thinking?" I ask and flip the menu open.

" Not too sure..." She mumbles but her eyes are locked on her phone.

"Dad?" I question.

She nods and puts it away. They must be fighting again.

"He's just...not doing good."

"You can't make excuses for him all the time," I frown."You guys never fight like this."

"I know, Liv." She says quietly."He's under a lot of pressure."

"You're still his wife. He's supposed to be your best friend, vent to you when he's down. "

She eyes me,"I wonder who raised you to be such a smart woman?"

"Who knows."I smile at her.

"Mind if I interrupt?"

I freeze as I hear a familiar voice rip between us.

"Alessio?"

Why is he here?!

Alessio's dark locks are neatly styled back away from his face allowing the dim lights to cast shadows against the curve of his jaw line. He's dressed in his usual black on black attire and looks amazing as always.

My mom smiles at him and he reaches down to kiss her hand. "Good evening, Mrs. Moore! Pleasure to see you again."

"You as well, dear."

"W-what are you doing here?" I stammer.

Mom glares at me," Olivia! Be nice."

"I'm just...confused."

"I'm in town for business," He says casually. "I noticed you here and wanted to say hello."

"Really? Who are you here with for

business?

" I narrow my eyes.

He's a bad liar.

"Mateo," He points at a table behind him. "I'm sure you remember him."

Mateo is sitting alone at a table towards the back of the restaurant and awkwardly peaking around from his menu.

"Anyways," He continues, "I wanted to make sure I came over to say hello."

"I'm always glad to see you!" Mom smiles. "Your family is such a delight."

"You're too kind," He sa

y

s and grabs a champagne bottle from the waiter passing by.

"Grazie, signore."

He tells the boy and slips him a hundred dollar bill.

"My treat to you tonight, Mrs. Moore." He smiles as he pours her a glass.

She looks at me accusingly. "Aren't you Olivia's age?"

"Yes ma'am, but I know the Antonio family very well."

"Really?" She beams. "We've been huge fans of Antonio's pizza for over 10 years."

"He is the best," Alessio grins and his eyes lock on me. "So Olivia did you have a chance to see your college?"

. "I did, I love it."

"When will you be making the big move back to New York?" He asks and I hear the sarcasm lacing his words.

"As soon as I can." I say smugly.

"So, if you don't mind me asking," Mom interjects and motions for him to sit. "What are you to my daughter?"

I groan, "Mom! Please don't do the parent thing."

"Hush! I have the right to know."

"Well, I can assure you that I have nothing but the best intentions with Olivia. She means a lot to me and I would never do anything to hurt her," Alessio begins and keeps his black eyes on me. "She has really...changed me into a better person since I met her. I'm extremely grateful to have her in my life."

"Well, I love him!" Mom cheers and knocks my shoulder with her own.

The next half hour is complete torture with my mom deciding to share all of my my embarrassing phases I went through during school.

She decides Alessio needs to know about my obsession with wearing my Halloween cape for months when I was 7 and how I messed up in my elementary school Spelling Bee when I was 10 and messed up on the word chair.

Of course, he was a gentleman the entire time. She was laughing with him and they were chatting like old friends while I sat there in complete horror as she continued to spill all of my dirty secrets.

Here and there he'd throw me a little smile and my stomach would flutter.

This was the most normal I'd ever seen Alessio. He didn't seem like some dangerous killer.

He was just a normal boy.

"Well, it was a delight, Mrs. Moore." Alessio says politely and glances at his watch. "I do have some things to wrap up here tonight before I head back home."

"You aren't staying longer?" I frown.

" I wish I could, but I have other things to finish up in California."

"Do you mind if I talk to him privately before we leave?" I ask my mom.

She smiles and stands up from the table. "Not at all! I know I'm a pest, I'll just head back across the street and see you soon."

"Nice seeing you!" Alessio grins and kisses her hand again. "Tell Mr. Moore I say hello as well. He's welcome to connect with me when he needs."

"Of course, son," She beamed at him and gave me a tight squeeze. "Not too late, Liv."

I wait until she's left the restaurant completely and move back to my seat. Alessio follows quickly and wraps his arms tightly around my waist.

He kisses the side of my neck and turns my face towards him.

"I missed you."

"You didn't even give me a day." I tease.

"Is that an attitude?"

"If it is?" I challenge back.

His dark eyes narrow and a mischievous smile creeps across his face. "I have no problem fucking you in the bathroom."

I can feel the dull ache pick up between my legs and try to push them closer together.

"No! No!" I nearly shout and several people around us glance over.

"Not feeling adventurous?" He whispers and bites at my earlobe.

"Not here."

"I just wanted to see you at least," He mutters. "You make it hard to stay away."

"Do you actually have business here?"

"I do actually," He tells me and pulls me closer to him. "I'll see you when you are back in San Diego."

"Mateo stays?" I huff and glance back to where Mateo is. He's staring down at a piece of Pizza bigger than his face and scrolling through his phone.

"We discussed this, Olivia."

"I don't always need to be watched, Alessio. Can't I have privacy? Why can't we discuss this?"

"We have."

"

You

have."

He glares, "Let's talk more later."

I roll my eyes and he steers my face towards him until our lips meet. I melt in the moment and he pulls back to kiss my cheek.

"I'll see you soon, love. I'd walk you home but I am going to start receiving some pretty angry calls. Mateo will escort you."

"It's really fine! I can-" I start but stop when I notice his expression.

"Soon, beautiful." He smiles against my lips and kisses me again. "I love you, Olivia. I really do...and I hope one day you'll marry me."

My heart picks up quickly as I watch him exit the diner.

Only day one and I'm already ready to go home to him.

Chapter 20

Life has been good. Really good.

Once I came back from New York I immediately started my management training at the cafe.

We hired some new people and things have been thriving! The cafe was bringing in new customers and I was absolutely loving my new position.

Aside from work, the clock to graduation was literally around the corner.

My parents had been bugging me about a graduation party but I had been way too swamped to really think about anything else.

When I did have any free time I was always with Alessio.

I hadn't slept over since the day we had sex and I wasn't really sure why. He'd pick me up and we'd go eat and kiss before he'd take me right back home.

He seemed distant when we were together though. His phone was always in his hand and our conversations felt like they were just there to fill the awkward tension between the two of us.

Westview was still a complete mess. Austin's face was now plastered on every wall in the school and street I passed by.

Sierra didn't come near me at all anymore. Kimbery was trying her best to comfort her and make time for me when she could.

Seeing his face every day was driving me insane. I couldn't shake it away.

It was a never-ending nightmare and I was just ready to get the hell out of Westview High.

Kim and I were walking from our last class that afternoon. She hadn't really seemed like herself the past week and kept saying she didn't feel good.

We were taking our time to get there when she finally spilled what was on her mind.

"I think Joe is cheating on me."

"What do you mean? Joe is obsessed with you."

She shakes her head. "He never has time for me anymore. When I do see him, it is brief and he is always vanishing and not returning my calls."

I knew how that felt.

"Kim," I sigh and toss my arm over her shoulder."Joe likes you a lot. Honestly, I think it may even be more than that at this point."

She forces a smile. "You think so?"

"I know so."

She looks around and lowers her voice, "I'm still not feeling good...at all."

"What do you think is going on?"

She looks over at me nervously and presses her lips together. She has looked pretty pale lately and I remember she said she puked the other day before school.

Plus, her boobs are massive now.

"You're pregnant."

She panics and looks around at the other students. "Quiet! I don't know, Olivia."

"Kimberly!" I shout in a whisper. "You can't be pregnant."

"I don't know! I missed my period last week and I honestly haven't been tracking when I need to take my pill like before."

"What are you going to do...if you are?"

She shrugs, "Keep it? I don't know."

"Have you told Joe?"

She laughs, "Fuck no."

"He's the dad, Kimberly."

"I know...I just don't know if that is what he wants. He's an athlete and scouts are coming to the last game. What if he wants nothing to do with me or the baby because we could ruin his football career?"

I sigh, "You really need to tell him."

"Fine...just let me figure out if I am first."

I follow Kim through the crowded front doors of the school and we step out underneath the canopy there. I notice there's a cop car parked next to the curb.

I glance over at Kimberly but she just shrugs.

"Olivia Moore? Kimberly Simmons?"

We stop and turn to the right to see a familiar, older man walking towards us wearing a police uniform.

His short, blonde hair is pushed back with a pair of sunglasses. I could see a pen and notepad in hand.

"Officer Harrison." Kimberly speaks up next to me.

He smiles warmly at the two of us but his eyes linger on me longer than I'd like. I had only met him once or twice when we all actually hung out together before everything happened with Austin. His dad seemed okay at the time.

I knew Alessio said he was bad news though. Paying off street gangs and letting Austin get away with sexual assault and drug abuse.

Apparently, he was not a good man to his family as Austin was growing up. It seems like the Romano family isn't the only one keeping some secrets.

My stomach knots up as he looks us over. I almost feel like he can read everything clear as day on my face.

"How are you ladies today?" He asks warmly. "I was just checking in around here...trying to get some information."

"I'm so sorry about Austin, sir." Kimberly tells him.

"It has been really hard on his mother and I, but we aren't giving up."

Officer Harrison looks over at me again and something gives me the idea that he wants to accuse me of something already.

"Have either of you seen anything? Know anything?"

"No sir," I whisper. "I'm sorry."

"No worries, girls. I would like you two to come down to the station if you have anything that can help. Even from your last time seeing him."

"Of course, we will." Kimberly tells him and I fight the urge to smack her.

He smiles a bit again and stares me down one final time before turning back in the direction of his car.

"I feel so bad for him..." Kimberly mutters.

"Yeah."

◇ ◇ ◇

"Good job today, Michelle!"

Our newest hire glances up at me from behind the counter and smiles brightly. She's only sixteen but she has a lot of drive.

"Thanks for this, Olivia! My parents had been on my ass about a job."

"Well, we're so glad to have you." I tell her warmly. "We'll see you tomorrow at 4."

She nods eagerly which causes her blonde ponytail to bounce with the movement before tossing her apron off and leaving.

I catch Kimberly resting her head on a nearby table and shake my head.

"Are you going to do anything?"

"I'm sorry," She groans miserably. "I'm just not feeling good at all."

"Go home, Kim. We have like an hour left. It's slow."

She bows her head weakly." Are you sure?"

"Yes. Go home."

She gives me a sad smile before gathering her things up in her arms.

I can't believe there is really a chance she could be pregnant. It was hard trying to picture my party loving, crazy friend as a mom.

She seemed more like the cool aunt kind of like Macy.

I spend the next hour wiping down coffee stairs and bringing endless latte's to a group of middle aged hipsters taking up three tables in the back of the cafe.

One of them pulls out a guitar and they start singing some weird indie songs together.

At least they tip well.

I start re-stocking the cups against the back wall when my phone rings.

"Hello?"

"My darling, Olivia."

His voice melts me instantly. My insides are a gushy mess.

"You know I'm at work right?"

"Always working."

"Says you," I sigh and lean into the counter. "When am I ever going to spend more than an hour with you?"

"Aw, do you miss me?"

" Are you worth missing?" I tease.

"Want me to show you?"

My legs go weak. "Maybe..."

"This weekend? You are mine."

"Are you asking or telling?"

I roll

my eyes.

"You know I don't ask."

"Fine...Saturday AND Sunday."

He sighs, " I don't know if-"

I cut him off," Saturday and Sunday."

"Fine. Deal."

"Good," I smile to myself."Now I gotta go. Go do something illegal."

I could practically feel his glare piercing me through the phone.

"Talk to you later, love."

The line goes dead and I stare down at my phone like an idiot before a girly voice catches my attention.

"Ma'am?"

I look up and find a beautiful girl standing there in a tight, red dress and large sunglasses. Her light brown curls hang loosely against the low of her back and she looks as if she's some kind of high-end model. She smiles a little showing a set of perfectly white teeth.

"Hello! How can I help you?"

She removes her sunglasses and a pair of Green eyes pierce me.

It's the girl from the dance.

I think Alessio had said her name was Monica.

"Nice to see you again, dear."

Up close she's even more stunning. Everything about her screams wealth and beauty. Just being around her made me feel so inadequate.

"Oh! I'm sorry...I didn't even recognize you..." I trail off.

"No worries, darling. I was in the area," She smiles and looks around. "Love the place."

"T-Thank you."

"I saw you in the window and just wanted to say hello," She says and locks her green eyes on me. "Monica Rossi, by the way."

She stretches her hand out to shake my own. I can't help but notice how perfectly pampered she is.

"Olivia Moore." I nod.

"Ahh, yes. The girl who was dancing with Alessio." Her lips curl into a bit of a snarl.

"Y-yeah. That was me."

"You look so...well." She comments and looks me over with disinterest."I didn't expect you to be...a barista."

My brows scrunch, "Yeah...that's the life for me."

This fucking bitch.

"Good for you," She sneers and puts her sunglasses back on. "Have you seen Alessio lately?"

"U-uh...not for a couple of days."

She frowns at my response.

"Well...would you mind letting him know I'm looking for him," She tells me coolly. "We need to talk."

"Uh...sure." I reply uneasily.

She turns on her heel to leave but glances back over her shoulder.

"Oh...and let my fiancé know...his baby is growing perfectly." She smiles smugly. "

Ciao

, darling."

What the fuck.

◇ ◇ ◇

ALESSIO

"A little heads up would've been nice, Monica."

She rolls her green eyes at me and trails her manicured nails down my shirt.

I have been beyond busy since Olivia left and returned from New York. The police have been hot on the case of Austin Harrison, not to mention, I have other shit going on with the gangs Jesus decided to recruit to target the estate.

Austin's dad, Richard Harrison, has launched a full fledged investigation and I knew it was only a matter of time before he really tried to come after us for anything he could.

He never was a fan of the Romano family moving in.

Austin had completely been disposed of. It was disgusting and messy, but Giovanni was more than thrilled to put a bullet in that sick kid's head.

I wasn't scared by Harrison at all but more annoyed that he'd be sticking his nose around here.

Olivia leaving for New York had just really confirmed that Jesús still had an interest in getting to her.

He sent out a pair of his goons after Olivia and her mom when they left for New York but we were sure to take them out quickly.

He decided to retaliate by bombing a smaller warehouse of mine. I had a few guards watching over at the time who unfortunately did not make it out.

Things with Olivia when she came back to California were a complete mess. I knew I wasn't giving her the attention she deserved and she made that very clear.

I was dealing with so much it was hard to focus on her as much as I wanted to.

And to top it all off, Monica Rossi decided to show up.

"You aren't happy to see me?" Monica purrs out.

"Monica, I'm busy. Please."

"We have a wedding to plan, Alessio."

"I don't think that is the best thing right now." I tell her and cringe as she strokes my cheek with her long nails."We have too much going on here."

"What a perfect distraction then." She kisses my cheek. I can smell her disgusting perfume and cigarettes on her. "I'm sure Adolfo would be for it."

"Monica..." I rake my fingers through my hair. "Give me time."

She looks up and glares and opens her mouth to argue just as Adolfo steps into the main room with Anna following.

"Adolfo! Good to see you." Monica cheers and rushes to him.

I watch as they embrace and he eyes her up and down hungrily. I may not like the girl but watching a man in his 80's look at her like that is pretty gross.

"Monica, dear. Nice to see you! What are you doing here?" He asks and holds her close. "Alessio didn't mention you were coming."

She looks at me happily. "It was a bit of a surprise! Wasn't it, love?"

"It was."

Anna peers from Adolfo's side at me and looks just as pissed as I am.

"Special occasion?" Adolfo asks and pulls a cigar out."Are we moving the wedding?"

Monica looks at me with puppy dog eyes before rushing over to grab onto my arm.

"I was trying to talk to Alessio about it."

"I don't think it's a good idea right now, Adolfo," I tell him and feel her nails dig into my skin. "We have too much to handle right now."

Adolfo thinks for a moment. "Monica?"

"I would prefer sooner than later but if Alessio needs time..."Monica pouts like a child."I guess I can wait."

The muscles in my neck tense up as she trails her hand up the back of my jacket. I glance over at Anna and she stares back disappointed.

Disappointed in me.

"Give me two months." I grit my teeth.

Monica cheers joyfully and gives me a full kiss on the mouth before rushing over to Adolfo again.

"I'll call daddy! We'll arrange everything. I can't wait to be your daughter-in-law."

I frown as the two of them laugh together and head down towards the hall in the opposite direction to discuss themes.

Anna walks over. "You haven't said anything to Olivia."

"I know, Anna."

"She deserves to know, Alessio. You need to let her go."

"I need time."

She shakes her head, "You're out of time, Alessio. Two months! Seriously?"

"Anna...I love Olivia...I can't...I can't just let her go." I say defeated.

" Olivia, deserves the truth. If you love her, you'll tell her."

"I'll lose her."

"You care more about hurting her than losing her and letting her find happiness?" Anna accuses.

I stare after Adolfo and Monica with hate as they continue to talk huddled together like a pair of teenage girls.

The sight of them together like this makes me sick.

This should by my moment with Olivia.

I'd really never be able to have this with her. Adolfo has won.

Olivia deserves happiness with someone who can actually be with her. She needs loyalty and someone to love her always with no conditions.

I love her enough to let her be free.

"Okay...I'll let her go."

Chapter 21

"I can't do this, Olivia. I just can't!"

"Kimberly, get a grip. You can't just NOT find out and possibly pop a mini you in 8 or 9 months."

She shakes her head, "My parents will kill me! Graduation will suck and Joe might hate me!"

I watch her as she dramatically falls backwards on her bed and tosses her hand over her face.

"You both agreed to have sex, so it's his responsibility as well." I point out.

"Thanks mom." She groans and rolls into the pillow."Just end my misery if you love me."

I laugh and slap her butt. "Let's just go get a test and figure this out."

"If Joe backs out will you be the dad?" She looks up with sad eyes. "I can't do this alone."

I smile softly, "Kimberly, I would love to be your baby daddy."

"Okay, fine. I'll do it, BUT you need to spill the news between you and Italian boy."

"What do you mean?" I ask and try to act confused.

"Don't lie. I know you have something going on now."

"I thought we did but I don't know anymore." I shrug.

"I'm your best friend, you can tell me." Kim says and moves to curl up into my side. "I'm here for you, Liv."

I smile and settle into her. Ready to spill out as much as I know I can.

"We were dating."

"Were?" She questions.

"Well...let's just say this girl I met from a party his family had showed up at the cafe and dropped a major news bomb."

What Monica said in the cafe stayed engraved in my mind. I couldn't get what she said out of my head all night.

None of it made sense. Alessio had seemed so disgusted by her.

Why would he be in an intimate relationship with her? Is that why he went to Italy?

Thinking about it hurt so much.

"What do you mean?" Kim asks.

"She said she's engaged to him and pregnant." I blink back tears.

I look back towards Kim who is staring at me wide eyed. "What in the fuck? Engaged to Alessio Romano? I honestly didn't think he had an interest in anybody until you showed up."

"Yeah...tell me about it." I sigh loudly.

"Is she from here?Or somewhere else?"

"No, pretty sure her family is a friend of the Romano's from Italy."

"And...you believe her?" She eyes me.

"How would you feel if someone said the same about Joe?"

She looks away," You never know..."

"He's not cheating," I argue."I told you he is crazy about you."

"I just can't shake the feeling."

"So ask, silly."

She glares, "Why don't you just

ask

Alessio about his alleged baby mama and fiance."

"Alessio and I don't have the same relationship like you and Joe have," I frown to myself. "It's...different."

"Just make sure you confront him at some point," Kimberly says. "You guys have something special...don't let that just slip away."

" Fine...only if we go get you a pregnancy test though."

She groans out dramatically at the thought but doesn't protest even as I drag her from the house.

"What does any of this even mean? I just need to know if there is a gremlin in me."

I roll my eyes and snatch the box from her hands to read over the instructions.

"One line is negative and two lines is positive."

"So it doesn't say, "Congratulations! You're fucked!" That would be a lot easier." She groans out.

"Just take the damn test."

"I'm scared."

"Kimberly, you're eighteen years old. Take the damn test." I shove it back at her.

"You suck!" She shouts and goes back to the CVS bathroom.

I shake my head and look back at the shelves stocked with condoms and pregnancy tests.

Nice placement.

Aside from the cashier at the front and pharmacy technician at the back of the store we were the only two in here and I could tell the workers weren't too thrilled considering they are supposed to be closing soon.

After several minutes had gone by, I realized the cashier was watching me like I was ready to steal so I smiled back apologetically and knocked on the bathroom door.

"Kimberly?"

No response.

"Kimberly? Are you okay?" I ask through the door again.

There's a weird shuffle sound of feet before the door opens. She stands there with a blank expression.

"What?"

She bursts into tears and shoves it at me.

Two lines. Positive.

I pull her in for a hug, "It's okay, Kimberly! I'm here for you."

"I can't do this, Olivia. My parents are going to kill me!"

"They'll love you no matter what!" I assure her, "They care about you so much."

"What if this is a false positive?" She asks against my shoulder.

"Want to take another?"

She nods and wipes at her eyes. "Please?"

"Alright! I'll buy two more. Hang tight."

She hurries back into the bathroom and locks it behind her.

I turn and grab a few more of the tests from the shelves and head back to the front to have the employee ring them up.

"Olivia."

I jump as soon as I hear his voice behind me.

Alessio looks me up and down and leans casually against the shelf. His dark eyes look tired and his hair is a complete mess. I can tell that he hasn't shaved in days.

He's dressed in the usual faded jeans and leather jacket. Beautiful as always.

"W-what are you doing here?"

"I was in the area. How are you?"

"Fine."

His eyes land on the pregnancy tests. "You don't think you are-"

"Not for me." I cut him off.

"Kimberly?" He muses.

"It's private, Alessio."

"Have you been avoiding me, Olivia?" He asks softly. "I tried to call you last night when you got off from work."

"No, I've just been with Kim. You're always busy anyways."

He nods a little, "I know. I apologize for my absence."

"Sure," I roll my eyes and try to continue towards the front. "Some things never change with you, Alessio."

He catches my wrist and pulls me towards him. "Why are you being so difficult?"

"You have other things to worry about."

"What the fuck are you talking about, Olivia?"

"Monica."

He tenses up." Monica? What about her?"

"I saw her, Alessio."

"Where?"

"She came by my work."

"What did she say to you?" He asks and seems to be nervous.

"Don't play dumb."

He doesn't respond and looks away from me. The muscles in his neck twinge as he flexes his jaw in aggravation.

"That's what I thought,"I scoff and turn away again. "You're no different from any other asshole out there."

He moves quicker than me and within seconds I'm pinned between him and the pillar between the two isles. His mouth moves from my lips and down to my neck where he kisses the skin softly.

"Don't Olivia..."He begs.

"I can't do this."

"Please."

"You've caused enough pain, Alessio. " I push against him.

The words sting and hurt me too. I know I'm going to have to break his heart and to do so means I'll have to hurt myself in the process.

"Go be happy with Monica."

"Olivia, it isn't like that," He huffs angrily. "I don't want her."

"What's it like then? Please explain that."

"I want you."

"You are marrying her, Alessio!" I point a finger at his chest. "Why would you just marry someone you don't love?"

"Can we meet tomorrow and I'll explain?"

"I don't want anything from you."

"Olivi-"

I stop him. "No, Alessio! She's marrying you and is pregnant with your child. Go handle your business."

He freezes and looks at me as if I just slapped him in the face.

"W-what did you say..."

"PREGNANT! P-R-E-G-N-A-N-T," I spell it out slowly and tears roll down my cheeks. "She told me she's pregnant with your child."

His eyes seem to glaze over as something unsettling flashes across his face. I don't know what it is but I know I can't concern myself with it now.

I can't care anymore. I have to let him go.

"No..."He trails off and looks at me. "She..."

"Goodbye, Alessio."

I turn away from him and feel my heart squeeze in my chest.

He doesn't call after me or try to stop me this time.

I'm walking away from Alessio Romano.

And this time, I'm the one breaking his heart.

A

L E S S I O

I stare after her as she walks away and feel my heart shatter inside my chest.

She's taking a piece of me with her and I suddenly feel like I can't breathe.

I can't move. I just stay glued to that one spot.

I was supposed to be letting her go anyways. I should've been prepared for this.

This is for the best and easier if she breaks my heart, right?

That way I won't have to worry about her trying to get over me. I can let her move on and know she'll find someone better.

She can finally be happy.

The drive back to the estate is fueled with nothing but pure rage with fucking Monica. I hit 100 mph the entire drive and see flashes of red blur my vision.

By the time I arrived back there, I didn't want anything to do with anybody in this damn house.

I walk inside and toss my jacket down on the floor.

"What the fuck, Alessio?" Giovanni snaps as I walk by him angrily.

He flicks his cigarette out to the porch and follows me into the kitchen.

"Are you just going to ignore me?" He snaps and blows out smoke. "You just flew in here going at least 90."

"I need a drink."

He follows me silently as I pour out two shots of whiskey.

"Do you want to vent?" He asks.

Giovanni isn't one to really care about anyone or their emotions. For him to even ask was just weird.

"Just bullshit, bro." I shake my head and hand him a glass. "At this point, I'm tempted to just leave the country."

"You will once you are married," He points out and takes a drink. "Adolfo will want you in Italy for awhile."

"No. I want out. Like...just disappearing completely."

He glares, "You can't just leave."

"I know."

"So are you going to tell me why or are you going to keep me guessing?"

"I saw Olivia tonight," I take a drink, "Monica talked to her."

How? When?"

"She showed up at her work," I shake my head angrily. "she told Olivia about the engagement...and apparently she's pregnant."

"You're serious?" He gasps.

"I guess so."

"So I assume Olivia left your ass," He chuckles darkly. "Can't say I blame her."

I sigh and grab the bottle," I don't blame her either. I know Olivia is going to have a better life without me."

"What about Jesús? He's still out there."

"I won't let him get to her, I'll make sure he's dead before he ever gets the fucking chance."

Giovanni nods, "Understood. Are you confronting Monica? What if she really is pregnant?"

The thought of marrying Monica was horrifying enough. I really didn't want to have to raise a child with her too.

I know the few times I did have sex with her I was always sure to use protection. Knowing her she probably poked holes in them while I slept.

"Yeah, I'll have to."

"Just make sure you ask for proof. Monica can be pretty deceitful."

"I'll take care of her." I tell him and take a drink from the bottle.

The two of us glance up as the sound of bare feet echo across the marble floors and Monica's figure comes into view.

"Where have you been?" She barks out and pulls her robe close. "I've been waiting."

I glare at her and focus back on my whiskey. "Business, Monica."

"Always business, Alessio. You need to include me now on these matters."

I scoff," The fuck I do."

She narrows her eyes at me and without hesitation she smacks me hard against the face.

I feel my teeth hit against the top of the bottle and blood pools in my mouth.

Giovanni stares back at me in shock and waits for my reaction.

"Don't you talk to me like that!" She whispers angrily.

I rub at my jaw and grab her by the back of the neck. "Don't ever fucking hit me."

"I'll do whatever I need to do for you to act like a fucking don."

"I'm not the don yet," I sneer and squeeze it harder. "Adolfo still has command."

"Well according to your father, he's considering making you don after our wedding."

I let her go. "He told you this, why?"

"He likes me," She laughs coolly. "He's been like a little puppy."

"I'll handle my business with Adolfo. In the meantime, keep your hands to yourself."

I walk past her, whiskey in hand, before she grabs at my arm.

"I need to tell you something, Alessio."

Her voice is girly and soft now.

I turn back towards her and let my arms fall to my side as she wraps her arms around my waist.

"I'm pregnant."

I sigh at the words and rub the small of her back. Tears start pouring out from her.

"I heard."

"From who?" She says with big innocent eyes.

"You told Olivia." I slur out.

"Why are you still seeing her!" Monica shouts angrily. "I want you to stay away from her, Alessio."

"I had to handle some stuff and ran into her, that's all."

"She's trouble for this family!" She snaps with venom in her voice.

"It's done, Monica."

Saying the words hurt even with the alcohol acting as a temporary bandage.

It really was over.

Olivia Moore isn't mine.

Chapter 22

"You really can't hide this forever, Kimberly."

She looks up from her arms resting on the lunch table. "Sure, I can."

"A baby is going to come out of you." I point out.

"Keep your voice down!"

"It's been like two weeks since you found out and we are down to single digits until graduation! You need to tell them."

"I just want to focus on getting through this last bit of school." She groans dramatically.

I roll my eyes," Fine, but promise you'll tell Joe after graduation at the latest."

"Deal."

She goes back to being her usual moping and sad self as Sierra approaches us. I stare up at her blankly. I knew she had been around Kimberly a lot after school but she had made no effort to even come near me.

She looks a little better. Still tired and sad, but a lot more lively from the last few weeks.

"Hey."

Kimberly's head pops up. "Hey Sierra. How are you?"

"I've been better," She shrugs and sits down. "How are you all doing?"

"We're alright," I smile at her. "We were just talking about graduation coming up."

"Yeah, it's crazy how fast it's coming up...I've just been preoccupied." She mutters.

"I'm really sorry, Sierra." I tell her wholeheartedly.

I honestly do feel horrible. I wish I could take this pain from her.

I never really got to know Sierra since Kimberly kind of attached to me quickly but I wouldn't blame her if she hated me.

She had to watch her best friend start hanging out with the random chick from New York and then Austin flirt with me for days in front of her face.

I can't even imagine how that made her feel. I never stopped to think about it.

"It's okay," She smiles a bit."I did want to let you know that Austin's dad has been asking about you two."

My brows furrow, "Why?"

"He's been asking people to come down and just answer a few questions."

I look at Kimberly. "I-I uh..."

"We'll be there." Kimberly answers.

Fuck.

There's no way I can do this. I don't have Alessio anymore to keep me level-headed with this and now I have to try to lie my way through this.

No fucking way.

"It would mean a lot." Sierra says gently. "We just want to...have some closure...no matter how we find him."

"I understand..." I whisper and stare at the table. "Like Kimberly said, we'll be there."

"Thanks," She grins. "Are either of you attending any graduation parties?"

"Yea-"

Kimberly cuts me off, "Olivia's parents are letting her host one."

"Wait what?" I glare at her.

She smirks, "I talked to your mom when I was over the other day. She thinks it would be a great idea."

"Kimberly...that's a lot of work! Between the cafe, finals, and graduation....I don't know about a party right now."

She groans loudly, "Come on! It'll be fun. My parents are sticklers about parties and your mom seemed super excited."

I frown, "Fine. I'll hold a damn party, but you are decorating."

Her eyes lit up. "Oh, I got you. Don't you worry!" She turns towards Sierra. "I'll text you the details."

She smiles back at us and moves into a seat next to Kim.

They start up some conversation about colleges and I realize lunch is about to end.

"I'm going to head off to class." I tell them.

"Bye, Liv!" They say together and go back to looking at something on Kim's phone.

I head off in the opposite direction towards my next class and feel something tugging at the strap on my bag.

"Hey Olivia." Joe says from behind.

I turn around to face him and he smiles down at me shyly. It was odd to see him without his gang of sweaty friends and football gear. I swear this kid only thought about playing football in every waking moment.

"What's up?"

"Have you seen Kim?" He frowns. His voice sounds like something's been upsetting him.

"She was at the table back there with Sierra."

He nods, "Alright...she just hasn't talked to me much."

"She has a lot on her mind, I promise she is still obsessed with you."

Joe sighs and his dark green eyes light up a little.. "I'll take your word for it. Let her know I'm here when she needs me."

"You got it."

We give each other a little parting glance and I head back towards my class when I notice someone staring at me through the crowd of passing students.

Beto.

"What are you doing here?" I ask

as I walk up to him.

He's leaning against a locker and Westview's cheer captain is hanging onto him with her long nails while she flips her Blonde hair back and forth. Whatever she's saying must not interest him because he looks bored as hell.

"We were talking!" She snaps at me and Beto rolls his eyes.

"Great," I smile. "I'm talking to him now."

Nicole looks up at Beto with hurt eyes but he brushes her off.

"I'll call you, Nicole. Bye now."

She gasps at his response and walks away with a loud huff. Beto and I laugh at her retreating figure.

"Picking up chicks, obviously." He shrugs.

"The truth, Beto." I glare. "Did Alessio send you?"

"Yes and no."

"Tell him to leave me alone."

He looks down at me with his boyish features and big eyes. You really would never know he was ever affiliated with one of Italy's most dangerous mafia gangs.

He doesn't look like he could even hurt a fly.

"He misses you, Olivia. I'm really worried about him."

"What do you mean?" My voice shakes.

"He's been drinking... a lot. Most nights he doesn't even come home."

"Where has he been?"

"The clubs I suppose," He says and moves his fingers through his dark locks."Giovanni can't get through to him. Anna doesn't care to try anymore."

"What about Monica?" Just saying her name makes me sick.

"She's been up Adolfo's ass. She doesn't give a fuck about, Alessio. I promise you, Olivia, he wants you. Monica is not who Alessio wants to be with."

I glare, "They're having a baby, Beto. They are going to be MARRIED."

He nods, "I know that, but what you need to understand is in a family like ours...sometimes things are arranged."

"Arranged?" I clarify.

"Yes. Adolfo arranged Anna's engagement and he has done the same with Alessio. He's speeding things up because he knows it'll benefit him more than anyone else."

"Then why doesn't he get out of it?"

Beto scoffs, "He can't just get out of it, Olivia."

I sigh and lean against the locker next to him. "Doesn't change anything, Beto. Alessio has done enough to hurt me. He disappeared for months, fucked with my head, and he hid this from me."

"Olivia, you know everything Alessio has done or will do is for your benefit. He is trying to protect you from himself. We aren't good people."

"I don't need protection."

Beto cocks his head. "Seemed you really needed us when your ex boyfriend tried to get you killed."

"I had it handled."

He rolls his eyes, "Sure. You really are a true gangster."

I glare at him. "I didn't ask for your family's protection. It's my own fault if I get myself into stupid situations."

"Some of these things would've never happened if Alessio didn't fall in love with you."

My heart starts to hurt thinking about him.

I missed him so much. I was really trying to forget him but nothing was working.

I missed hearing his voice and holding him.

I just wanted to have him in my arms again.

"I gotta go..."

Beto grabs my arm. "Olivia, please just understand why we are still looking out for you. He wants to keep you safe."

I stare back at him and feel tears burn my eyes. Beto gives me a small nod and turns to head back to the exit.

"Thank you for coming down today, ladies."

Kim and I nod politely as Officer Harrison holds the doors for us to step into his interrogation room. Sierra had decided to join us for the little field trip to the police station.

The three of us take a seat across from him at the table in the middle of the room. I feel little beads of sweat form on my forehead under the heat of the lights.

I look over nervously at Kimberly as he pulls out a notebook and pen.

Kim shrugs and looks as cool as a cucumber. Of course, she has nothing to worry about.

Not like her ex boyfriend murdered the guy.

"Now...I know the three of you were very close with Austin," Officer Harrison starts. "Kimberly and Sierra specifically."

I glance over at Sierra who dabs at her eyes.

"Unfortunately, we have had a lot of dead ends in our investigation," He says and wipes at his brows. "I'd appreciate any help."

"I wish we had more information for you, sir. After prom, we didn't see him again." Kimberly tells him.

"Well, it seems Olivia here had seen him at the party."Harrison says and pulls a photo out from a folder. "Isn't that right?"

Kimberly and Sierra look over at me confused as he pushes it to me. It's a picture of me clearly very drunk standing next to Austin. Someone had taken a group photo together and posted it on facebook.

Of course, there would've been photos plastered everywhere from that night.

"Yeah?" I try to shrug indifferently."I had drank a little too much and almost fell. He was helping me."

"What else happened?" Harrison pushes.

Sierra looks at me accusingly, "Yeah...what else happened, Olivia?"

"Sierra there was nothing going on."

She glares, "Clearly, there was something going on. The two of you were always flirting before he asked me out. Austin even said you were so pissed when he rejected you."

I shake my head quickly. "Sierra, I swear to you there was nothing going on!"

Harrison puts his hand up to stop the arguing. "Ladies, I just need honesty here. My son is missing and we are terrified."

Sierra sits back in her chair and folds her arms. "I knew nothing about this, sir."

He looks back at me and waits. "Anything else, Olivia?"

"Sir, I was too drunk and he was helping me out. That is the end of the story."

He nods and jots something down across the notebook.

"Tell me the truth about your relationship with Austin. Are you sure there wasn't anything between you two?"

I can feel Kimberly and Sierra staring me down.

"What are you even talking about?"

"Like Sierra said, Austin even admitted to me that you were upset when he didn't want to pursue the relationship. Are you sure you didn't retaliate? Maybe have someone help you out?"

"No!"I shout and bang my fists down. "You are accusing me of something that never happened!"

"I need you to remain calm, Miss Moore." Harrison warns.

"Sir, your son KISSED me. He wanted much more than a kiss actually."

He glares back at me and looks back at the girls. "I'd like to speak to Miss Moore in private."

Kim looks over at me confused and stands up with Sierra.

"Sierra! I'm telling the truth." I tell her as she passes.

She looks over at me and frowns. "I'll never know the full truth, Olivia, but I wish you would've told me about this from the start."

I stare at them hopelessly as they exit the room and leave me alone with Harrison.

I groan and sit back in the chair.

"Miss Moore," He begins and pulls out more photos. "I need you to fill me in on something."

I sit up and examine each photo. All three of them include someone else this time.

Alessio.

One of them is him entering the house with Giovanni followed by a picture someone caught of Alessio entering the back bedroom and Giovanni standing in the kitchen drinking.

"Some students posted these online and they got back to us. Why would the Romano's be there?"

I look up at him. "Alessio used to attend Westview, sir. Maybe he wanted to party with his brother."

He nods, "I'm aware of that but I don't really understand this interaction." He points to the photo of him entering the room. "Another student snapped this."

The new picture is of Austin helping me to the bedroom and me slouching towards the floor.

"Like I said, I was drunk and he helped me. There was a bed back there and he helped lay me on it."

"I never saw my son leave in any of the other pictures following this, Miss Moore. We have already done a full search in the home and there's nothing. So where did he go? Did Alessio take him?"

"Sir, they just showed up to the party, I really d-"

"What are you to Alessio Romano, Olivia? Why was he concerned with going in there?"

I frown and look down at the picture of Alessio's face. "I'm nothing to him, sir."

"If you are keeping any information you could face jail time, Olivia," He warns me. "I need the full truth."

"I'm aware, sir."

"Did he take my son while you made out with your boyfriend?" Mr. Harrison snaps and points to the image of Giovanni.

"Sir, I don't know. Giovanni was just with his brother."

"I really don't know what to believe here. Austin tries to kiss you and you say he wanted more, right?" Harrison taunts. "So I have room to believe your little boyfriend here would've done something about that."

My chest tightens and I stare at him blankly.

"Kimberly already told Sierra all about the two of you flirting and Alessio Romano visiting you at work. It's very clear you had or have some kind of romantic relationship with him."

"Sir, I don't know what you want. I'm telling you the truth."

He grinds his teeth and puts his pen down. "Do you know who the Romano's really are, Olivia?"

"No, sir. I don't know them too well."

"You don't want to, Olivia," He shakes his head at me. "Stay away from them for your own good."

I try to nod a little and wait for him to finally give up and point towards the door.

"Get out of here but I'll be keeping tabs on you."

ALESSIO

"Alessio!

Svegliare il cazzo

! " (Translation: Wake the fuck up)

I stare at the dark ceiling above me and snatch the bottle of rum from rolling off my chest.

Olivia not being in my life has already really fucked me up.

I was never really into drugs and drinking, but every night I would spend as much time as I could in our clubs.

It usually consisted of snorting cocaine and drinking as much alcohol as I could before I blacked out.

I wanted nothing to do with anyone. Not my own family and certainly not Monica.

I wanted Olivia back more than anything.

I wanted to be the one to make her happy and give her everything I know she deserves.

I'm just lost without her now.

"

Ti butto giù la porta!

" Giovanni shouts out. (Translation: I'll kick your door down)

I roll my eyes and stand up from the bed. My head was already swimming with the liquor I had drank a little bit ago.

"What!" I snap and rip the door open.

He notices the bottle. "What the fuck is wrong with you?"

"Mind your fucking business."

"Alessio...this is ridiculous! You have business to handle."

I wave the bottle around sarcastically. "Always fucking business. I know this Giovanni, I'll handle my shit."

He shakes his head. "You are wasted."

"Bingo!" I take another drink.

"I'm worried for you. All you do is come home high and drunk."

"I'm young," I laugh. "Can't I live my life?"

"This is living?" He knocks the bottle with his hand.

"Don't most young people party?"

"This is killing yourself."

"Fingers crossed." I push by him.

I'm glad he didn't come after me this time. The last time I was this drunk he had come after me and slammed me into a wall.

We almost got into a fist fight that night but thankfully Beto talked me out of it. I knew I wouldn't survive a hit from him anyways.

He's right though.

This isn't living. This is just hell.

I'm living in my own personal hell.

I walk down the last set of steps and find Anna curled up with her husband to be on our couch watching TV together.

Alonzo decided to actually come out here for a change. I didn't mind the guy.

He was business smart and kept to himself. He's been a great connection of ours for many years and having him help manage so many shipments in Italy has been a blessing.

"Alessio, nice to see you." Anna acknowledges as I pass and I grunt in response.

She shakes her head. "I assume you are going to continue your day in misery?"

"Guess you could say that." I take another drink.

"You look like shit."

"You are shit."

"King of comedy!" She snorts.

I nod, "Finally you recognize it."

"You two are childish."

Monica's voice rings out and my stomach turns. This alcohol may be coming back up soon.

She plops down onto my lap in the recliner and kisses my neck. "I haven't seen much of you lately." She whines.

"I know."

"When are you actually going to spend time with me?"

I look down at her and she bats her Green eyes up at me.

"No clue, Monica."

"Ridiculous!" She throws her hands up. "My own fiance doesn't even want to spend time together."

"Don't take it personal, Monica. He's an asshole to everyone." Anna tells her.

Wrong. She needs to take it very personal.

I keep quiet though and try to refocus my attention on the bottle in my hand.

"I haven't felt so good," Monica continues her pity party. "This baby is killing me."

I look at her. "Have you had OB care?"

She frowns, "Not recently."

"We can take care of it here then. I'll take you right now."

"Why now?" She pouts and tries to cling to me.

"You need prenatals and need to check up on the baby. One of the nurses should be here, she'll do it for you."

Monica continues to push her lower lip out and holds onto me as if her life depends on it. I roll my eyes and grimace as she buries her face into my neck.

"Giovanni! Let's go." I shout and remove her arms from me.

"Where are you going?"

"Business, Monica." I shrug my shirt off and grab a clean one from a passing maid. "I'll be back later."

"But-"

She starts her protest again but stops when she sees my expression.

"Margo will take you to the clinic, "I inform her and motion for the sweet old lady to come over. "You'll be fine."

Monica looks back as if she wants to continue her pity fit but Margo takes her by the elbow and steers her back towards the clinic.

"Where to?" Giovanni asks as he comes into view.

"Business in the city." I tell him. "Where's Beto?"

"I think Westview High."

I raise a brow. "Why?"

"You know he loves cheerleaders."

"Yeah, I know. What else?"

"I know he swings by to make sure Olivia is okay too."

"Just...just make sure he doesn't say anything to her about it."

"I can't promise anything for that kid.

I knew it was wrong to still keep tabs on her so closely but I couldn't help it.

Jesús has still been around here and trying to gather up his little army of gangs the best he can.

He still had his eyes on her and I knew he'd try to get to her if he could.

The two of us exit the house together and head to the Porsche.

"So what are we doing?" Giovanni asks.

"Last night I had word that one of Jesús' goons was spotted in our club. I think he's planning an attack again."

"Which one?"

"Gold Lounge."

Giovanni groans, "Fuck. I really like that place. The dancers are so hot."

"He's not going to get the upper-hand this time. I almost killed him once, I'll make sure I succeed this time."

We step into the vehicle and I turn the engine on. As soon as we hit the side roads I'm already nearing 80 mph through the narrowing roads.

I just want to shoot someone in the face right now. I need to kill him.

"Slow down." Giovanni warns and grabs the wheel as we veer off.

"Why? Scared?" I tease and push down again.

90 mph.

"You've been drinking, Alessio. Let me drive."

"Just shut the fuck up."

He sighs and gives up but keeps his hand out towards the wheel. I keep my eyes locked on the road as the trees around us blur.

My vision starts to cross a bit and I blink excessively to clear it. My head is a complete fucking mess and I know the alcohol is starting to take a toll.

I try to keep the wheel steady as we continue to take the next curve and drift along it at high speeds.

I loved this shit. Driving was fun as hell when you owned a lot of land and no cops were around to try and stop you.

"Hello?" Giovanni says loudly into his phone.

He glances over, "It's Anna."

"Speaker."

He hits the button. "How long will you be?"

"Why?" I ask and look at the speedometer.

105 mph.

"Something is going on with Monica."

I frown, "What do you mean?"

Also, why does she think I care?

"I went to make sure everything was going okay and she was arguing with the nurse."

I roll my eyes. "And? Doesn't sound like news to me."

"I don't...I don't know if something happened, but they couldn't find the baby on the ultrasound."

Giovanni and I stare at one another.

"What-"

"Alessio! Look out!"Giovanni's shouts as I lose control of the car.

I hit the brake hard but it's too late. The trees come up fast as we skid off the road.

Before I have time to realize what's going on my head hits something hard and everything goes black.

Chapter 23

"I'm fat."

I roll my eyes at Kimberly who is now analyzing her " baby bump" from every possible angle.

"Still look thin to me." I tell her.

"Well you get to stay skinny!" She groans and falls onto my bed dramatically. "I'm going to be a whale."

"You'll be okay."

"So..."She starts and moves onto her side. "What's the plan for your party?"

"Do I really have to do this whole graduation party thing?"

I wasn't in any kind of party mood. When I wasn't with Kimberly, I was trying to study and prepare what I could manage for the upcoming art show.

I haven't really painted in what felt like months now. I had no inspiration anymore.

"Please!" She begs. "I just need an escape."

"As long as you don't invite the whole school."

She glares, "I'm not that dumb."

"You are full of surprises."

She laughs and pulls her phone out."I know, I know."

There's a knock on my bedroom door. My mom walks in carrying a load of clean laundry. Her dark wavy hair down and framing her face and bright blue eyes.

"Hey girls!" She cheers and sets the basket down. "I have news."

I sit up on my forearms. "What news?"

She claps her hands together. "Aunt Macy and some of your friends are coming in from New York for the party!"

I break out into a smile. "Are you serious? Amy?"

She nods, "Amy, Katherine, Cleo, and Macy. I tried to contact Michelle but no word yet."

I can't believe it. My childhood friends are coming to California!

Kimberly pouts, "I thought I was your friend."

I laugh and smack her shoulder."You are my friend! You can have more than one."

"I suppose."

"How many people should I expect...to be at this party?" I ask my mom.

"Up to you, dear. Just don't go too crazy." She says to me but her eyes stay locked on Kim.

"Hey! I'm not doing anything." She protests.

Mom laughs and just shakes her head as she makes her exit.

"So have you decided on a place in New York?" Kim asks.

"No." I frown.

I had been trying to do my own research while I had some free time. Aunt Macy and Amy had been kind enough to even go view a couple and send me pictures.

They were all so expensive and I was a nervous wreck on how I was going to have enough saved by the time I had to move.

Macy offered her place for a few months but I wasn't really thrilled with the idea of living with a ton of cats and her excessive smoking habits.

"I did find a cute little loft but I don't know." I tell Kim. "Kind of pricey. I started packing a few things but now I don't know."

Her eyes flick over to the only two boxes packed in the corner of the room. I had started on a few things but with so much time left and barely any money who knew what would happen now.

I just couldn't really focus on anything and finding a job out in New York would be a bit of a challenge with me stuck here.

"You have Summer break to figure it out." Kim points out. "Why not stay at the college?"

"Eh, I'll have to see what they have to offer again."

"Talk to Edgar." She says and stretches her legs into the air. "I think he has a cousin or something that owns a coffee place in New York."

"Really?"

"Yeah, but you gotta double check with him."

I smile and wrap my arms around her. "You're the best!"

She laughs, "I know."

◇ ◇ ◇

"Hey, Edgar! How are ya?" I smile as I walk into the shop.

"Doing well, dear!" He greets me and comes out from behind the counter.

"Have you been here late?" I ask and notice how tired he looks.

He nods, "Only some nights. I'll be alright, dear."

"I had a question for you," I perk up. "Kim mentioned you have a relative that owns a coffee place back in New York?"

"I do, why?"

"I'll be starting college after Summer break, I'll have to move back to New York. Can you possibly help me out? With a good word or something?" I put my hands together.

Edgar waves me off and laughs. "Of course, dear. I'll talk to Frank about it and let you know."

I squeal and give him a huge hug."You are the best!"

Edgar's deep chuckle fills the air but my phone starts to buzz wildly in my pocket. I reach down and read off an unfamiliar number.

"Hello?" I say into the receiver.

"Miss Moore?" The voice responds.

"Who is this?"

"This is Officer Harrison."

My stomach flips over.

"O-oh. H-hello."

"Can you come down to the station?" He says sternly. .

I look at Edgar who is just watching me with a confused expression. "I'm working."

"Understood. Please make time to stop by." Harrison continues.

"U-uh. Okay. Have a nice day." I say and the line goes dead.

"Everything okay?" Edgar asks.

I nod, "Absolutely."

ALESSIO

I'm dead.

Okay...I'm probably not dead but my body hurts a lot. There's no way I could be alive after that.

Maybe I can finally be out of misery for good now.

"Oh my god! Alessio! Baby are you okay?"

Fuck. I am alive.

Or I got sent to hell since Monica is the devil.

"Monica, please step back." A deep voice commands.

Dr. Tobias?

"Is he going to be okay?" Another voice.

Anna's voice.

"Yes, he's fine. I've administered a large amount of painkillers. He's lucky nothing aside from his car was damaged."

Fuck! I loved that car.

I should've wrecked the Cadillac.

The last thing I really remember was being pretty drunk and driving into the city with Giovanni. He got some kind of call about Monica and the baby.

I lost control of the car and we went off the road. I had spun the wheel to the side just in time to miss a tree and the car flipped over.

I deserve to be dead.

"I can't believe he fucking did that." A new voice.

Giovanni's okay. Thank god.

"

Idiota!

" Anna shouts.

"Where's Adolfo?" Giovanni asks.

I'm really not even shocked he wouldn't be here. I feel like if it was any of our funerals he would do anything to not go.

"Business." Monica mutters.

"Punch him in the nuts, I bet he wakes up." Beto's voice rang out.

My eyes started to flutter and I felt my hands instinctively curl into fists causing him to bust up laughing.

"F-fucking hit me...I dare you." I cough out.

"Oh, Alessio!" Monica cries and sits on the edge of the bed. "I didn't know if you'd wake up again!"

I look past her to find Beto, Giovanni, and Anna all together. Giovanni looks like he made it out with a few scratches if that. Beto is obviously amused and Anna is annoyed which is never new with her.

"You are real fucking dumb." Giovanni laughs and walks over. "You almost fucking killed us."

"It was fun though right." I smirk. "Kind of like real life GTA."

"Except we can't re generate, Alessio."

"That's the fun part."

Anna rolls her eyes, "He's emo as hell right now. It's all the alcohol and drugs."

"Shut up!" I try to sit up.

I look down at my body and see all of the deep bruising across my stomach and chest. They had me hooked up to some kind of drip and it felt like there was a knot on my forehead forming.

"What's the damage?" I ask Tobias.

"I really don't know how you made it out alive," He shakes his head. "The car is totaled but you banged your head on the window and Giovanni was lucky enough to make it out with a minor cut."

"Not easy to do." I groan from the pain in my ribs.

"Just take it easy for now, Alessio." " Tobias states.

"Gotcha, doc." I shake my head and look at Monica. "Can you all leave? I need to talk to her."

All of them get up to leave the room quickly. I catch Anna giving me some kind of look of distress before the door shuts behind them.

"I'm so glad you are-" Monica begins but I stop her.

"Explain." I demand.

She stares at me blankly. "W-what do you m-mean?"

"Anna said she found you fighting with the nurse about the baby." I tell her. "They didn't find one."

Monica nods and looks away. It almost looks like she's forcing herself to cry.

"I lost the baby."

"Monica..."I run my fingers through my hair. "Don't lie to me."

She looks at me in disbelief. "Don't accuse me of being a liar, Alessio!"

"We both know you weren't pregnant."

"I was too!" She cries out and falls onto me. "I've just been so stressed over the wedding and everything else, I did this."

I shake my head and start to feel bad.

Maybe...maybe I'm being irrational.

What if Monica really was pregnant and had a miscarriage?

This was supposed to be our child. My child.

"I'm sorry." I whisper and try to wrap my arms around her. "I'm sorry, Monica."

She sighs heavily and moves to rest her head against me. "No, I'm sorry, Alessio."

I move over on the bed and let her curl up to me. I lean my head back and stare up at the ceiling.

I didn't know what to do at this point.

OLIVIA

I was getting really into my study guide when a very familiar ass plops right on top of my desk.

"What the fu-" I start but catch Mr. Conroy giving me the eye.

I smile at him sheepishly and glare up at Kim.

"What Kimberly?"

"Party...tonight...you and I...let's go." She says excitedly.

"You can't party." I remind her.

"I can dance, but I can't drink." She shrugs.

"What if you get hurt."

"I'll be okay, you'll be there and Joe will be there."

I groan, "Do I even have a choice?"

"Nope!" She pops the "p".

"Who is even throwing this party?"

"I think Joe said it was a football buddy. Probably will be the biggest party of the year and we are about to graduate so let's have some fun."

"Fine!" I throw my hands up in defeat. "I'll go and watch you have fun."

She glares,"You know you'll have fun."

"As long as I'm drunk, who cares." I snort and she laughs.

"Miss Simmons!" Mr. Conroy shouts from the front of the room. "Are you even in this class?"

His aged eyes look exhausted behind his thick rimmed glasses. I stifle a laugh as he glares at her and puts his hands on his hips.

She smiles flirtatiously at him and twirls her hair around her finger. "No, sir. I'm not but I just love watching a real man teach."

He grimaces, "Inappropriate, Miss Simmons. Get to your class."

Kimberly sighs and gives me a little wink before heading out of class.

I was ready to just get this whole day over with.

"Olivia! Kimberly! What's up?"

I smile over at one of Joe's friends. I didn't really know the guy but he seemed pretty nice.

The music was already blaring and the entire house reeked of marijuana. Someone tossed us both a beer and I took Kim's from her hands.

"Hey Kyle!" Kim smiles.

He's a pretty good looking guy. Nice build and pretty tall. He looks like the kind of guy you'd see living in California in the movies.

Beautiful golden hair and bright blue eyes. He has a killer smile and abs that would cause anyone to swoon.

"How are you ladies?"

"Good," I nod. "How's the party so far?"

He grins and waves his hand around. "My biggest one yet, baby."

I blush a little at his choice of words and notice Joe walking over to us.

"You came!" Joe kisses Kimberly and pulls her close. "I'm so glad you are here."

"Of course!" She chuckles and wraps her thin arms around his neck. "I am always down for a good party."

"Drink?" He offers and she looks at me.

"She has a bit of a headache so I think water would be best for her tonight." I interject. Kim throws me a grateful smile.

Joe nods and wraps his arm tightly around her waist before steering her in the opposite direction.

Kyle looks over at me and reaches out to pop the cap off of the beer in my hands.

"Are you excited to graduate?" I ask him.

"Hell yeah! I got a scholarship so I'll be able to continue football in college."

"Congratulations! You deserve it."

Kyle flashes a bright smile and I catch his eyes roaming up and down my body. Kimberly had talked me into wearing one of her showy crop tops and a pair of ripped jeans.

It was not at all my normal style but she said she needed me to wear it since she was apparently too "fat" now.

"How about something a little stronger?" He offers.

"Sure! Why not."

He flashes a coy smile at me and places his hand on the lower of my back. The two of us head through the kitchen packed full of some football players trying to do some kind of karaoke together to an Eminem song.

He reaches up and gives some of them high fives as we pass by and heads over towards the counter.

He hands me a red cup and I laugh. "Mr. Popular around here?"

He shrugs, "Football really helped me during my high school career. I used to be new to Westview as well."

"Really?"

He nods and takes a drink, "Yep. Junior year was my first year here. I used to play football back home in Florida before I moved."

"Nice to know I'm not the only one."

"Not at all," He teases and tilts my cup up towards my mouth. I grimace at the bitter taste.

"Not a vodka fan?" He chuckles and grabs a can of soda from the counter.

"Not straight." I gag and quickly take a drink.

"Well, I got plenty of chasers for you." He smiles softly and hops up onto the bar-stool. "So what is your plan after high school, Olivia Moore?"

"Art school!" I nod and take another drink. "I'll actually be heading back to New York when semester starts."

"Aw, that's too bad." He frowns playfully. "I would've liked you to see me play at least once."

"Really? Why's that?" I ask and feel my cheeks redden.

"Well..." He leans in closer to me. "I have to admit you are one of the cutest girls I've seen at Westview. I think we would've gotten along really well if we had more time."

"Wow...u-uh, thank you."

"Everyone just assumes the football boys only want the cheerleaders," He shrugs his shoulders. "I prefer the ones who have depth to them and are creative."

He reaches over and picks something off of my shoulder. I feel goose-bumps cover my arms from his touch and look over at the crowd of people now dancing in the livingroom and trying to do the macarena.

Part of me feels wrong for even talking to Kyle. I was still so hung up on Alessio.

We weren't together though.

I deserve to move on and enjoy my youth.

"You okay?" Kyle asks.

I smile a bit and shake off my thoughts. "I'm perfect!"

"Want another drink?"

I nod, "Yes. Please."

After my third cup of vodka with Kyle, I was already feeling like a total drunk mess. The nerves were totally gone and we were having the best conversation ever.

He was really easy to talk to and actually funny as hell.

Everyone always said the guys on the football team are just so cocky and stuck up, but he seemed like he was down to earth.

Plus, he made me feel good. He'd go out of his way to touch my hair or cheek and it made me feel nice.

I felt wanted.

"What are you thinking?" He yells over the music.

"I'm just glad I came!" I slur out. "Thank you for being so kind."

"Of course," He smiles and leans into me again. His mouth is only a few inches from mine now. "I really am glad you came, Olivia. I like talking to you."

"Me too..." I trail off and stare into his eyes.

He wastes no more time before his mouth is on mine in seconds. My arms move up around his neck and I feel his hands hook onto my hips as we break into a full make-out session against the island in his kitchen.

I feel my head going light for a moment as he pulls back and smiles down at me. "Want to go upstairs? It's quiet and we can be alone."

My heart is pounding in my chest and I can't deny the desire building up in the pit of my stomach. I had only been with Alessio but the thought of giving it a go with Kyle was really tempting right now.

I nodded a little and he steered the two of us through the crowd of students so we could make it up the stairs.

I tried to keep my attention on my own feet so I wouldn't end up falling on my face and embarrassing myself in front of him.

The party was in full swing now and I couldn't see Kimberly anywhere. Kyle looks back and gives me a reassuring smile before tossing open a door at the top of the hallway.

"Welcome!" He cheers out.

Football trophies and music posters line the walls. His bed is neatly made but there's a bit of a B.O. smell that seemed to be coming from a pile of clothes on the floor.

He notices my wandering eyes and smiles sheepishly."I haven't done my laundry yet, so I apologize if it smells like sweat and grass."

I snort, "It's fine."

"So..."He starts and looks down at me. "What do you want to do?"

My heart was pounding so loud now I was sure he could hear it. I decided to let instinct take over and pushed my mouth against his again.

Our feet moved us in the direction of his bed and I heard him moan against my lips as I reached down to take his shirt off.

He tossed it over his head and helped me pull my own shirt and shorts off. The two of us laughed loudly as I stumbled over my own feet and we fell onto his bed together.

He looked down at me in my silky underwear and bra and ran his fingers up the curve of my stomach.

"You're beautiful."

I reached up to kiss him again and felt his hands explore all over my body. He felt so warm and toned.

It felt really good. I really liked the way we molded together.

It seemed natural.

I just...I had thought my second time would be with Alessio.

I thought maybe it would just be him forever.

That was dumb though. I'm only 18-years old...I have forever to have sex and it can be with whoever I want.

"Are you alright?" Kyle asks when he notices I stopped kissing him.

"Of course."

I kiss him again and he pushes himself deeper against my body and moves his mouth from my neck down in between my breasts.

I arch myself against his lips and he trails his fingers down to the edge of my panties.

"Please." I beg.

He smiles up at me and hooks his finger around my underwear. My entire body is on fire and I'm just so ready for him to fuc-

The door opens.

My eyes pop open and I scream as a flash of light shines in the room before the door shuts again. I try to cover my chest with his duvet and Kyle shields his eyes from the glare of the strobe lights from downstairs.

"Who the fuck? Occupied, bro. This is my room so get out!" Kyle snaps.

Whoever is in the door is shielded by the shadows and steps completely inside the room. My eyes blur for a few seconds before I finally focus on his face.

"Alessio!" I gasp out.

He looks beyond fucking pissed. His eyes are locked on Kyle and he looks as if he's ready to pull his gun out right now.

Even through his anger I can't get over how breath-taking he is. It was almost like seeing him for the first time again.

I studied the curve of his jaw and full lips. How the shadows covered his black eyes and the small amount of light in the room casted along the sharpness of his cheekbones.

His dark hair lay in a messy fashion and he was dressed in the usual black on black attire he favored.

He finally looks at me. "Get up, Olivia."

Kyle stands up and pulls his jeans back up. "She's with me, bro."

Alessio looks at him threateningly. "She's leaving with me,

bro .

"

I can't help it anymore. The interaction between the two of them sends me into a complete fit of laughter and within seconds I'm crying from the laughs rolling from me.

They both look over at me with a mix of annoyance and confusion.

"What!" Kyle snaps.

"Nothing about this is humorous, Olivia. We're leaving, get up." Alessio demands and pulls me up by my arm.

I tense up as soon as he touches me and yank myself back away from him. He glares down at me and the fury is very clear on his face.

It doesn't matter how drunk I am. I know what he did to me.

"Don't touch me!" I snap. "I hate you."

He continues to shoot daggers at me with his eyes but it doesn't completely shield the hurt that is there too.

"Let's go, Olivia."

Kyle points between the two of us. "Are you guys...like dating?"

"Something like that." Alessio mutters.

Kyle looks at me and shakes his head. "You should go, Olivia."

I stare after him apologetically as he tosses his shirt on and starts to hurry out of his room. "Both of you need to leave before I throw your asses out.

Alessio moves his hand to expose the gun at his waistband. "Don't try your luck with me tonight."

Kyle eyes the weapon for a moment before throwing me a look of concern as the door closes behind him.

"I'm not going anywhere with you." I tell Alessio and move away from him to put my clothes back on. "I want nothing to do with you."

He tries to grab my hand. "I need to talk to you, Olivia."

"Why?" I throw my hands up. "This is over, Alessio! We aren't together anymore."

He looks down at me. "I love you, Olivia."

I stare up at him hopelessly and don't know what to say. Hearing those words gave me so much joy but I just hated it now.

I wanted to hide and disappear from everything.

"I'm leaving." I tell him and try to move around him.

He grabs my arm and blocks me from the door. "Alessio, move!" I snap and try to push to the side.

He says nothing. He just holds me in place and lets his arms close around me tightly.

"I love you, Olivia."

I look off to the side of us and try to keep my eyes from him. I knew I'd be crying within seconds if he continued.

He tilts my face up towards him. "Olivia."

Our eyes meet and I feel my lower lip tremble as the tears start up. He wraps his arms tightly around me and hoists me up so my legs are secured to his waist.

Our mouths meet and I feel my clothes coming off again and hitting the floor in a heated whirlwind as we move back towards the bed.

His mouth moves down to my breasts as he hungrily takes each one in his mouth and kisses me there over and over again.

I moan out as his mouth moves down and he uses a freehand to take his shirt and pants off.

My eyes wonder up and down the curves of his stomach and abs. I run my fingers along the ridges there and move down slowly.

He grabs my hand and holds it there. I hear him sigh for a moment and he closes his eyes.

I need him. I can't take it anymore.

"Come here." I demand.

His hands start moving all over me again and I feel my breath coming out quickly as he kisses back down my stomach until my panties are sliding down my legs.

I feel his tongue move against my swollen clit and cry out in ecstasy as he takes me in his mouth. His arms circle around my thighs so he can rock my hips against his tongue as he fucks me with it.

Two fingers come inside of me and I feel him curl them as he moves them back and forth.

"F-fuck!" I moan out and grind against him feverishly.

"Cum for me." He whispers and his fingers curl more. "Cum for me, baby."

"Oh, god!" I cry out as I feel my climax taking over.

Every part of me bursts into light as I feel my body cum hard against his mouth and hand. I shake hard from the orgasm and my chest heaves quickly with my breathing.

"More." I beg and bring him back to me.

Alessio moves his hand down to his groin and exposes himself to me.

He is huge and very erect.

How did that ever fit inside me?

"Fuck me." I tell him and he smiles back in response.

He pulls me down to the edge of the bed and pushes inside of me with no warning. A moan mixed with pain and need comes from my lips.

"Are you okay?" He pants out as he rocks into me again.

I nod, "Yes. Please don't stop."

He looks down at my naked body as if he has never seen it before. So much desire and need in his eyes as he holds me in place and fucks me as hard as he can.

I can't stop the excessive screams coming from me as he continues to pump into me faster and deeper. I can't take it any longer.

I know I'll be coming again within seconds.

"Shh." He whispers. "Your friend may not like us fucking in his bed."

I shake my head at him and he pushes himself deep inside of me. He holds me there and gazes down at me.

"You were going to fuck him, Olivia." He says in a rough voice. "He was going to fuck what is mine."

I stared at him desperately. My head is swimming.

He pulls out a little. "He couldn't ever fuck you like I can."

I nod up at him and bring his hand to cover my mouth as he continues to elongate his strokes so they come back in as deep as they possibly can.

"Do you want to fuck Kyle still, Olivia?" He taunts me.

"N-no. Please."

"I'm going to fuck you every chance I get." He warns and starts to pick up speed. His other hand comes down onto my neck and I feel my eyes roll. "I'm going to show you what you were giving up."

I couldn't speak anymore. I could barely fucking think.

"Tell me you want me to fuck you hard." He demands.

"Fuck me hard, Alessio." I beg loudly and grab his wrist. "Please..."

He stares down at me as his speed picks up and his hand squeezes the side of my neck. I can feel my second climax getting closer and try to stifle my screams as he fucks harder than I'll be able to recover from the next morning.

I hear his breaths coming out hard and I realize how badly I want him to cum for me.

I want him to feel good too.

I lock my legs tightly around his hips and hold him there. I use the momentum to push myself back into him as he pumps into me and it drives him absolutely mad.

He releases my neck and grabs onto my hips. I feel his nails dig into my skin and wince a little from the pain there.

"Fuck." He groans out and pulls me closer to him. "Dammit, Olivia."

The building desire to cum washes over me again and I try to hold back my screams as he reaches his own climax at the same moment.

The both of us hold onto one another as it takes over. He holds onto me with one hand and flips both of us onto our backs.

He reaches up to wipe the sweat from his forehead before wrapping his arms back around me.

I sigh and look up at him happily.

"I love you, Alessio."

Chapter 24

"**F**uck! Alessio!"

"Shhh. You're going to wake the whole house up."

I roll over onto my back and feel my breathing coming out fast. I was on cloud nine and I never wanted it to end.

Alessio looks over at me and smiles. "Did you enjoy yourself?"

"I always enjoy sex with you." I laugh and push my hair away from my face.

"Or you're good at faking it," He teases and kisses my cheek. "Are you excited for graduation?"

I groan loudly at the thought of walking in front of thousands of people. I had been so ready for this day and now I just felt terrified and unprepared.

"What if I fall?" I whisper.

He laughs and runs his fingers down my cheek. "I'll be there to encourage you the whole time."

"You aren't going to walk?"

"No," He tucks his arms under his head. "I have my diploma plus, I'd rather watch you."

"There won't be any other visitors?" I ask him hesitantly. The thought of another Monica showing up was enough to make my stomach hurt.

After Alessio had found me at the party, I went back to the house with him and we spent a good two or three hours talking about everything that had happened.

Anna had called Alessio when she caught Monica fighting with the nurse. She had tried to play it off as a miscarriage but the nurse was positive there was never a baby and Monica was not pregnant.

Anna threatened Monica that night but tried to fight back by saying she'd get Adolfo involved for trying to ruin the agreement.

Alessio told me about the car accident with Giovanni and that had really messed me up. Knowing he could've died that day and we never would've had our true closure hurt a lot.

There was so much I wanted to experience with him. It just really put into perspective how human he is.

He confided that Monica continued to try and play off the miscarriage until he was able to gather all of the facts. She realized quickly she couldn't continue her charades and disappeared in the middle of the night.

Alessio said his father was more than pissed about the marriage being called off since it voided the contract but I was just glad to have him all to me.

No crazy girls or made-up babies.

Just Alessio and myself. Finally.

He intertwined our fingers together. "None, love. Just you and I now. Now talk to me about New York?"

"Macy found a pretty affordable place there...I'd be all moved in no later than the first week of July."

Alessio sighs,"Why won't you let me buy you a place? Or at least help with your rent?"

I stand up from the bed and grab my shirt. "I don't want anyone thinking I am accomplishing all of this due to my rich boyfriend."

He sits up and grabs onto my waist. "I have nothing to do with this. This is all due to your talent and intelligence."

"Let's just take this slow with the whole buying me a home and such," I tell him awkwardly.

"Fine," He huffs in defeat. "Have you been studying for your finals?"

I glare at him. "You are talking to me. The girl who has literally been obsessed with her grades since birth."

He smiles and pulls me onto his lap. "My smart girl."

I shrug and wrap my arms around his neck. "I guess so. It's just a nice distraction especially with stuff going on with Sierra and Kim."

"Like what?"

"Well...Kim is pregnant."

He laughs, "Can't say I'm surprised."

"Don't be mean," I snap and bat at his chest. "What if it was me in her situation?"

"That's different because it would be

our

child." He muses.

I roll my eyes, "You say that now."

He scans my expression. "Are you trying to tell me something?"

"No!" I gasp in horror. "No pregnancy here."

He nods, "Good...but if it ever-"

"Alessio!" I interject. "No pregnancy voodoo on me."

"Fine! Fine! No pregnancy voodoo." He laughs and holds his hands up in surrender. "Now what's going on with Sierra? Still trouble with Harrison?"

"Well...he has been blowing up my phone, wanting to make sure I know to talk to him if I find anything out. Sierra has just been dismissive when she's around me. I'm assuming she still thinks something was going on behind her back."

Alessio reaches over and cradles my face. "Don't worry about Harrison, we'll make sure he stays off your tracks."

"Please don't kill him, Alessio," I narrow my eyes. "I can't handle more on my plate."

He locks his pinky with my own. "I pinky promise, love."

"We'll see." I tease him.

He pulls my face towards him and distracts me with a heated kiss. I immediately lose myself in the moment as we fall back onto the bed.

"Are you ready?"

Kim looks over with her eyes full of excitement. Her entire graduation gown and cap is completely covered in gold glitter from her makeup.

I grab onto her as we enter the auditorium. "I can't believe the day is finally here!"

We take our seats with our graduating class towards the front of the room near the stage. Behind us seas of families and friends start pouring in to fill the lower and upper levels.

How the hell am I going to find anyone in this?

"I am even more excited for your party though!" Kim leans over. "I'm so ready to not think about school right now."

"I know! Are you going to stay anything to Joe yet?"

She frowns. "After the party."

"Promise?"

She locks her pinky with me. "I promise!"

The principal suddenly walks out and approaches the podium. His voice shakes a bit as he addresses the crowd.

"Good evening Westview High students, family, and friends!"

The crowd grows quiet as he continues on with the speech. "I want to thank you all for coming out tonight in support..."

I peer around the sea of people sitting behind us and try to find anyone that I recognize. There has to be at least a few thousand shoved into this building.

"Hey, Olivia."

I turn to the right and notice Sierra moving to sit by us. Her short hair is in little curls and clipped at the sides with silver barrettes.

"Hey, Sierra! You look gorgeous." I compliment her. I'm honestly a little shocked she's even speaking to me.

"Thank you," She grins and looks away awkwardly. "I want to apologize for my behavior before over Austin. It was out of line."

"It's okay. I completely understand."

She shakes her head, "No, it wasn't! I should've been a better friend to you and I was just feeling jealous. I'm so sorry, Olivia."

I take her hand in mine. "Thank you, Sierra. I really appreciate it."

She smiles over at me and pulls me in for a hug. Kim decides to interrupt the moment and pops her big head in between the two of us.

"Are we besties again?"

"Yes!" Sierra cheers and holds us close. "I love you guys!"

We all three laugh together for a moment and realize they have started to announce names to receive their diplomas.

"Victoria Davidson...Angela Davis..."

"Shh! It's going to be our time soon." Kim whispers.

The line of students pours down the center aisle as the list continues on. I finally hear my name called and stand up to take my place.

My heart pounds quickly in my chest as I walk up the stairs and reach the administration members.

"Ms. Moore, congratulations and good luck!"

I smile kindly at him as he hands it to me and walks down the opposite stairs towards the back of the auditorium with the others. I notice a group of people waving wildly at me and someone hollering.

Giovanni, Beto, Alessio, and Anna are all sitting together and cheering. All of them are matching in black and look so out of place next to the other people around them.

"Woo! Fuck yeah, Olivia!" Giovanni booms and several people shush him.

I shake my head at him and look over towards Alessio. He looks so beautiful.

His black hair neatly styled for the occasion with his all-black suit. He's clapping for me and looks so proud.

"I love you!" He mouths as I pass by and I feel my cheeks heat up.

The line of graduates makes it out the back doors and onto the front lawn to greet their friends and family. I pull my cap off my head and look around for my family.

"Olivia! We're so proud."

I turn at the sound of mom's voice and am nearly knocked over by her. She's already cried all of her makeup off and is nearly in hysterics.

"Mom! It's okay."

"My baby girl is done with high school!" She cries and pulls back to look at my face. "I can't believe it."

Dad eyes me from her side. He doesn't look very thrilled for whatever reason but he does manage a smile still.

"Congratulations, sweetheart."

"Thanks, dad." I pull him in for a hug. "I'm glad you were able to make it."

"Wouldn't miss it for the world," He mutters into my hair. "You did good kiddo."

"Mind if I steal her for a moment?"

I look over to find Alessio standing behind us. He smiles down at me but I catch my father glaring at him.

The tension between them grows and I look between the two of them confused.

"I don't -"

"Dad!" I interject and stare back at him. "It's fine, I'll see you and mom in a bit."

He doesn't take his eyes off of Alessio. "Fine."

I watch silently as he steers my mother away and the two of them head back in the opposite direction to meet up with Kimberly and her parents.

I look over at Alessio and am completely puzzled by their interaction.

"Know anything about that?"

He wraps his arms around my waist. "I don't actually. We've never had any issues, but I don't handle much with him directly as far as the business goes."

"His behavior has been really weird and erratic lately."

"Hmm," Alessio mutters and purses his lips. "I'll see if I can figure out if anything has been going on between him and Adolfo."

"You're the best." I smile and pull up to bring his mouth down to mine.

Someone grabs me by the arm and pulls us apart.

"There she is! Big graduate over here."

I roll my eyes as Giovanni skips around the two of us and showers me in a mess of confetti.

"Really?" Alessio picks the tiny pieces off of his suit.

"It's confetti, cry baby. You won't die from it." Giovanni snickers and looks over at me. "How do you feel, Olivia?"

"The same...just with a diploma in my hands."

"Get excited! Get drunk, do something." Giovanni cheers and Alessio glares at him. "I'm just saying bro, she deserves to do something fun."

"She will do something fun with me." Alessio looks down at me and grins.

"Gross! Don't need to hear about your sex life." Giovanni fake gags and Beto moves around him.

"Congratulations, Olivia!" He says warmly and puts something in my hands. "Just a little something you can add to your bracelet."

Inside the tiny black bag is a gorgeous charm that is shaped like a graduation cap with the graduating year. I hold it in my fingers and watch as the sun reflects off of the gold.

"Thank you so much, Beto! This is beautiful." I pull him in for a hug.

"Of course! You deserve it."

Anna pops up next to him,"Don't forget me!"

She hands me a little box and bounces up and down on her toes like a little girl.

"You didn't have to-"

She glares at me and shakes her head. "Open it."

Inside is one of the most beautiful necklaces I've ever seen. It's a layered Topaz necklace with matching earrings.

"I know you don't really like fancy, but maybe you can wear it on one of your dates with Alessio."

"Oh, Anna!" I gush and hug her tightly. "It is so beautiful!"

Alessio pulls me back to my side and turns me towards him.

"She also bought it because I want to take you out to dinner tonight." He leans his forehead with mine. "The only condition is that it has to be out of the state."

"How is that supposed to work?" My brows furrow.

Alessio glances at his brother. "I have a private jet, Olivia."

"Since when?" I gasp.

I don't know why I found this surprising considering the amount of money they have but I had never heard of them having an airplane.

"Since forever," He teases and kisses my head. "It's easier and more discreet to fly privately."

"Fine! Fine! I'll go with you on your crazy dinner date."

"Where to?"

"Well..." I trail off and don't know what to even say.

"Would you like to visit New York for the evening? I'll take you out to eat, call up any friends you want?" He offers.

"Are you sure?"

"Of course," He promises. "Let's get going."

"I'll just have to let my mom know I'll be spending the rest of the day with you."

"No need, I already talked to her."

I glare, "Are you two best friends now?"

"Something like that." He teases me and we wave goodbye to his family before he escorts me back to his car.

He had decided on a beautiful all-black Bugatti.

It was one of the coolest cars I've ever seen but also terrifying as fuck considering Alessio doesn't know how to obey traffic laws.

"A Romano can never settle for something...humble?" I laugh as the butterfly doors expand out.

. Several people around us gasped at the sight of it and quickly started taking pictures as we climbed inside.

"Humble is boring."

The entire drive is completely horrifying and I think I had my eyes shut the entire time. Alessio was having the time of his life with the windows down and some metal songs on full blast.

I didn't even know he listened to music! Him doing anything normal ever was still so weird.

When we finally arrived at our destination I was grateful when the engine turned off and I could actually let go of the "oh shit" bar.

"How do you not get pulled over?"

He shrugs, "Threaten the police or bribe them."

"Rich people." I roll my eyes at him and look down at my outfit. "Should I change?"

I had opted for a really cute black dress my mom bought me for the occasion. It was simple but had hints of silver throughout the fabric and paired nicely with my wedges.

"You look beautiful," He says as he helps me from the car. "Olivia, I'd like you to meet our piolet for the evening. This is Mr. Ambrose."

A tall man with a tanned complexion approached us. He was dressed in the typical pilot outfit you usually see and looked to only be a few years older than me.

"Pleasure to meet you!" He bows his head. "I'll be flying for you both tonight. If you have any questions, don't hesitate to ask."

"Thank you, Mr. Ambrose." I smile and look back towards Alessio.

"Shall we?" He asks and takes my hand in his.

The two of us walk hand in hand up towards a massive jet with "Romano" sprawled across the side in Gold italic.

"This...this is yours?"

Alessio laughs, "Belongs to the Romano family."

"Wow!" I say and look it over. "Unbelievable."

"Just wait." He teases and pulls me up the stairs.

Inside the jet is set with black leather chairs and a beautiful red wine-colored sofa. There's a fully stocked bar off to the right and a tray set out with an array of cheese and fruits next to a bottle of champagne.

"Wow!" I admire and pick up the bottle. "This is beautiful. How often do you use it?"

"When we need to travel under the radar."

"Good for illegal business?" I eye him and pop a strawberry in my mouth.

"Let me worry about the details, gorgeous." He muses and pulls me close by my waist. "Now sit tight."

Alessio gently pushes me back towards the sofa behind us and his knee pushes my legs apart.

I feel his mouth come down against the sides of my neck and his free hand traces up the length of my spine.

"Want another present?" He kisses my neck. "I'd be happy to help you join the mile high club."

"M-maybe on the way back," I tell him breathlessly. "I've never been in a jet and I'm a little scared."

He kisses me fully on the mouth and moves to sit beside me. "Just relax and enjoy, love."

Mr.Ambrose steps into the cabin and bows as he greets the two of us. "We'll be heading off now, sir."

"Wonderful," Alessio states and sits in the spot next to me. "We're ready to go."

I watch him as his hands move to harness me into my seat. He notices my terrified expression. "Do you need anything to ease the nerves?"

"No," I shake my head. "It'll probably make things worse."

He nods and kisses my cheek. "Let me know if you change your mind."

The jet roars to life and we idle for a few minutes before it starts to take off down the runway. Alessio muses silently at my terrified expression and squeezes my hand in reassurance.

I try to keep my eyes shut tight as the engine continues to roar loudly and starts to ascend into the air. I feel my stomach flip and grab Alessio's arm.

"It's okay, Olivia," He whispers in my ear. "Look outside."

He pulls back the curtain from the little window and points out to the city below us.

Everything looks so small and detailed from this height but the view is incredible. He certainly has set a high expectation for our dates.

Our trip to New York only takes us a couple of hours on his jet and soon enough we are landing in a private airport and exiting the plane together.

I decided to invite Amy out to dinner but I wasn't really sure how hungry I was now that I stuffed myself on two glasses of champagne and cheese.

The door opens and the stairs slowly extend out from the plane reaching the runway. I try to take the first step down but apparently, I didn't do a very good job.

"Woah there lightweight!" Alessio laughs and grabs my elbow.

"I'm not!" I glare at him and he releases me as we reach the landing.

"Let's get to dinner."

"Are we taking a cab?"

"No," He smiles and motions to something behind me. "We're driving that."

I follow his gaze and find a stunning black Lamborghini parked there. Under the soft lights along the road, it almost looks like the paint has hints of purple in it.

"How many cars do you have?"

"Not mine."

"What do you mean? Giovanni's?" I look up at him.

"Yours." He says simply.

"Shut up!" I gasp. "You're so mean. That's a cruel joke."

His hands reach out to cradle my face. "I'm not joking. I purchased it yesterday when I said I had business to attend to."

"You came all the way to New York...to purchase this car?"

"Wasn't a hassle at all. I want you to have something special."

"Alessio..." I start and look over at the death machine again. "I've never driven a car like this."

"You'll be great," He promises. "It's an automatic and we can keep it safe here until you officially move."

"Are you sure? This is...so much."

"Olivia," He pulls my face up to kiss me. His lips are warm and I feel myself melting into a puddle. "I love you and I wanted to do something for you."

"Okay...okay."

He wraps his arm around me tightly and leads us over to the car. Thankfully, he decides to drive tonight and holds up the passenger door for me.

The interior is all black leather and the new car smell hits me as soon as I buckle into the seat. I run my fingers across the smooth material and smile.

The car rumbles to life and Alessio looks over at me.

"What do you think?"

"I'm terrified of it," I admit honestly.

He rolls his eyes, "I'll teach you my tricks."

And just like that he is back to his normal self and speeding through the busy streets of New York. While the best that he can since the streets are always full here.

Compared to him having the time of his life back in California watching him drive like this here was somehow a lot more terrifying because he decided to just merge in and out of traffic repeatedly.

We don't talk much the entire drive to the restaurant but I don't mind since it gives me time to marvel at the city. I always missed seeing how it looked late at night. Everything felt so alive at this time.

"Amy is going to be meeting us here shortly. " Alessio says and pulls down a side road.

The car stops in front of a restaurant called Carmines. A red canopy leads the way towards the entrance displaying the name brightly on the side.

There's a long line of people standing outside along the sidewalk waiting to get in. Everyone looks to be dressed in suits and fancy dresses.

"This is insane," I tell Alessio as I take in the crowd. "I've never been here."

"It's amazing Italian food," He muses and leans over close to my face. "I know Italian is...your favorite."

My cheeks heat up again and he kisses my cheek. He comes over to my side and helps me out of the car.

He guides us past the long line of people waiting to get in and walks right up to a young kid standing at the front next to some guys working as security.

"

Piacere di vederti, Marco.

" Alessio nods kindly. (Translation: Nice to see you, Marco.)

"Ah! Mr. Romano. How are you, my boy?" Marco cheers and reaches out eagerly to shake Alessio's hand. "It's been forever,

Sì.

"

"It has," Alessio smirks and looks down at me. "This is my girlfriend, Olivia. I have a reservation tonight for the two of us plus one."

"Of course! We have the private dining section reserved for you." Marco tells him and ushers us inside quickly. I can hear people behind us groan impatiently as we are led inside.

"An entire private section?" I hiss at Alessio under my breath.

He smirks but doesn't respond as Marco pulls back a door opening up to a gorgeous private dining room with a bar, pianist, and several tables set with candles and roses.

"I'll have someone be with the two of you shortly, Mr. Romano," Marco says as we take our seats. "Please enjoy!"

I look around at the expensive decorations and candle-lit chandeliers hanging gracefully from above.

"This is...amazing."

"I'm glad you like it." Alessio reaches across the table to hold my hands. "Your other present just arrived."

I followed his gaze and spotted Amy being escorted into the room by Marco. Her blonde hair has been curled and she's wearing a maroon dress and black pumps. She blows Marco a kiss and looks around the room in awe before she sees me.

"Ahhhh! Olivia! BITCH! This is amazing."

I laugh as she runs up and hugs me tightly. The two of us squeal together like we are twelve before her eyes land on Alessio at the table.

"Ohhh! So this is the charmer," She muses at me and reaches out her hand. "Nice to meet you."

"Pleasure is mine," He takes her hand and kisses it politely. "Always glad to meet a friend of Olivia's."

"So," Amy starts excitedly and grabs a bottle of red wine. "What are we having?"

"Amy, we aren't twenty-one!" I scold her.

She looks over at Alessio who waves her on. "It's alright, Olivia. Marco is the son of the owner. They don't mind if it's under the Romano name."

"How do you know him anyway?" I ask curiously.

"Long time family friend," He grins a little and pours three glasses. "Marco's a good guy and his family has helped us out a lot."

"Really? Like what?"

He eyes me for a moment. "Another time, love."

Amy is too busy chugging down wine and picking at the bread on the table to even take notice of what we are talking about. I purse my lips together but decide not to push the conversation as our waiter comes up to the table.

"Ready to order?" The young boy asks and looks at Alessio nervously.

"Yes!" Amy groans hungrily. "I'll take the stuffed mushrooms, Ravioli, and Eggplant Parmigiana."

"Woman with an appetite," Alessio chuckles and pulls a cigar out. "Penne Alla Vodka and clams, please. Your famous cheesecake for dessert." The waiter nods and tries to write down quickly as he speaks. "Olivia...have you decided?"

"Uhh...the shrimp scampi and garlic bread sound wonderful...with a little side salad."

He nods and jots it down before setting another bottle of wine down on the table for us.

"This is SOOOO fucking fancy!" Amy shouts way too loudly. "I've never been to Carmines! Have you, Liv?"

"No, I haven't. It is nice though."

She pours another glass. "You've been keeping this classy guy with good taste hidden in the dark?"

I roll my eyes and look at Alessio's smug face. "No...we've just been stuck in San Diego."

"Well, I'm so excited you are here tonight and invited me! Are you excited about your party Saturday? I can't wait to fly out."

"Well," Alessio starts up, "I'd be happy to have your friends and family use my jet for the special occasion."

Amy looks at me and bread falls from her mouth. "He has a FLIPPING jet!? Who is this man, Liv."

"U-uh...he's just lucky." I laugh awkwardly. "Are you sure your family would be okay with that, Alessio?"

"Of course, I'd be more than happy to have Ambrose fly them."

"Yes! Oh my god! A private jet! Freaking amazing." Amy throws her hands up.

"Slow down," I hiss at her as she grabs the new bottle. "Little class, Amy."

"Don't go acting all different on me now because of your new boy toy" She sighs and takes a sip.

I frown. "I'm not different."

The young waiter arrives holding three platters along his arms as another girl dressed in white and black follows behind folding out a tray to hold the food.

They place the piping hot plates of food in front of us and bring out another bottle of wine considering how fast Amy is going through the two we already have.

"It's so good!" Amy says with a mouthful of food. "Wow! Literally...just wow."

"Very good."

Alessio picks at his food across from me but has his eyes stay locked on something on his screen. I try to kick his leg under the table and he glances up at me. Something about his expression tells me he's not thrilled.

"Are you okay?" I say quietly.

He looks over at Amy eating and scoots back a bit from the table. "Excuse me, ladies. I'll be right back."

Amy and I watch as he puts his phone to his ear and heads back towards a hallway where the bathrooms are.

"What's that about?" Amy asks.

"Not sure...he has a lot of family business to tend to."

"So, Olivia," She wipes at her mouth. "Tell me the truth about this Alessio Romano. He's definitely not your average California guy."

" You're right, he's not. His family is just well off...he moved from Sicily years ago."

"I'm totally jealous, girl! He's so freaking hot."

"Amy! You have a boyfriend," I remind her and twirl my fork around the pasta. "He'd be so sad if he heard that."

"I'm allowed to look! Plus, you know things are shitty right now anyways."

"I guess so..." I shake my head.

"Would you mind if I steal Olivia for a moment, Amy?" Alessio suddenly asks from behind us.

I turn in my seat towards him and look at his face. His jaw is set and he looks incredibly tense.

Something must be really wrong.

"Of course! I have food and alcohol!" She winks and waves us off. "Take your time."

He takes me by the hand and guides me back towards the hallway he entered before. His legs are moving too fast and I feel myself start to trip over my own feet.

"Slow down!" I shout.

He releases me and turns around with his hands in his pockets. His shoulders are hunched and he looks like he's about to hit the wall at any moment.

"What is going on? You're acting so weird." I grab his hand. "Please say something."

"We need to leave...soon." He says darkly and stares at the wall behind us as he talks. "I'm so sorry for ruining the night."

I study his face for answers. "What happened? Is everyone okay?"

He shakes his head. "There's been an attack on the Romano Estate."

Chapter 25

"Would you like to explain what happened, Mr. Romano?"

I glance up at the light annoyingly swinging overhead. Officer Harrison is sitting across from me with his notebook in hand doing the same shit he always does.

"Sir, I already told you I was out of state with Olivia and her friend celebrating graduation."

His lips form a tight line. "So you just go out of state the same night there is a massive explosion that occurs on your family's estate."

"I don't know what else to tell you," I sigh and pull out a cigar. "May I?"

He leans over with his lighter to ignite the end. I puff on it for a moment and let the smoke cloud up in between us.

"Do you know of anyone targeting your family right now?"

"No, sir."

He puts his pen down. "This doesn't just happen, Alessio. There were multiple families camping in the woods that evening when it happened."

"And did any of them report seeing someone flee the scene?" I ask and blow a smoke ring.

"No, but there is clearly something going on here."

"Ask my father then," I ash the cigar on the table. "Adolfo may be your man with all the answers."

"Look, you little shit!" He snaps and knocks the cigar from my hand. "I know your family is up to something, Romano. You all think you are so smart but I've heard about you out there on the streets. You are no good and I'll get the upper hand soon enough to lock your asses away for good."

I pick up the cigar from the table and take another puff. "I'll be waiting then, sir."

He glares at me and swipes the smoke away from his face before standing up from his chair. "If you have information, call me."

I stand up and grab my jacket. "Of course."

"Yeah," He looks at me strangely. "Any information on my boy, Romano?"

"No, sir. Nothing new. I'm sure he will show up soon enough."

"We'll be in touch, Alessio. Make sure Olivia knows the same." He folds his arms. "I'm not like these other cops here. I know when something is going on."

"Of course, you aren't sir. Have a wonderful rest of your day." I say respectfully and step out from the room as the door slams.

"Ooo," Anna muses from her seat. "Tough crowd, huh?"

"I guess so," I passed her a cigarette. "Nothing we haven't been through before."

"I can't say I blame him," She starts as we head out towards the car. "It's not like every day you hear about a local billionaire's mansion under attack."

"Any word yet?"

"Well, we're lucky nobody died but clearly Jesus is getting closer. He's probably still using someone else so he doesn't have to get his hands dirty."

"Thought so," I ran my fingers through my hair. "We'll get him. I swear."

She leans against the car. "What if he's not even in California?"

"I'm sure of it. He wouldn't want to miss the show."

I'll take your word for it. What's the plan for today?"

"Giovanni and I have some stuff to handle, but I need you to go with Beto."

"Why Giovanni?" She groans.

"He's over 250 pounds of pure muscle and good with a glock." I shrug.

"Whatever! I'll see you at Olivia's party." She says to me in hops in her.

I watch as she pulls away from the lot and lean against my car, phone to my ear.

"Giovanni...Be ready. We attack in thirty minutes."

OLIVIA

"Oh my goodness! Olivia! This looks amazing."

"You think so?" I smile at her. "We found a lot of this at the dollar store."

"It looks really good, plus I'm going to gain another 10 pounds with all this candy." She pops another smartie in her mouth. "Now hand me some decorations so I can help."

I point to the box of stuff behind her.

"So...how have you been feeling? With...everything?" I ask her.

She picks up some streamers. "Alright, I guess. The morning sickness comes and goes, but I've already gained some weight and I'm not even in my second trimester."

"Have you decided when to tell your parents?"

She shakes her head, "I've been going to the doctor before work but I'll tell them soon."

"What about Joe? He needs to know too."

"I know...you said after the party. I'm keeping my word, I'm just nervous." She sighs and sits on the floor.

I sit next to her and hold her close. "You can do this, Kimberly. Joe loves you."

"You're right, I know he does."

"Love you!" I lean my head against her shoulder as the front door opens.
I hear a bunch of familiar New York accents hit me like a truck as we're
ambushed by everyone running up the stairs with gifts.

"Olivia!"

"Hey! Oh my god!" I shout and am nearly knocked over by all of them.

I look around at them as they all hold me close and cry happy tears. Aunt
Macy and Amy came and they even brought Cleo and Katherine along.

"I've missed you so much!" Cleo cries out and wraps her arms around my
neck. "I can't believe it's been so long already."

It feels like it's been years since I've seen her face. Unlike Amy, Cleo was
a friend I had since birth because her mom was best friends with my mom
since high school. She kind of stands out from the group with her baby
pink hair and lip rings.

She's always been a really good friend though and recently came back
home from studying abroad in France.

"I'm so glad you're here!" I tell her and turn to greet Katherine.

"I missed you so much, girl! We have to catch up!" She says and flips her
long red hair back. "I really can't believe this is your new place! It is huge."

"Right!" I laugh at her expression.

"So," Amy interjects and pushes between the two of them. "Is this rich
Alessio coming tonight? We REALLY loved his plane, by the way."

I nod," He is and he'll be bringing his siblings and cousin."

"Male cousin and brother?" Amy winks.

"Yes." I groan out.

"I can't handle so much sexy in one room!"

"Amy, you have a boyfriend." Cleo glares at her.

"I'm just looking!"

"Aunt Macy! How are you feeling?" I turn my attention towards her and
realize she's still on her crutch. "Are you healing okay?"

She kisses my cheek. "I'm doing okay, I missed you so much!"

"Mind if I interrupt?"

Everyone turns as the Romano's enter the home. Anna looks beautiful as always with her hair in curls and White dress suit.

The boys were all in matching Black slacks and long sleeve shirts. I don't think I've ever seen Giovanni in anything but a tank top or shirtless.

Alessio caught my eyes immediately. He looked so amazing tonight. He was freshly shaven and his hair slicked back with gel.

I couldn't get over how perfect he was. Everything about him was so addicting and surreal.

"Ladies, I'd like you to meet the Romano's. This is Anna, Giovanni, Beto...and Alessio." I say as I introduce them.

The girls stare at them in complete shock. I feel like forever passes before someone finally speaks up.

"Drinks?" Amy smiles and her eyes stay on Beto.

Anna moves around the boys. "Please and thank you."

Alessio walks up to me and his hands find my hips. "How are you?"

I push up to meet his lips. "Better now that you made it."

"Ew!" Beto fake gags from behind. "Get a room."

Alessio laughs against my mouth and continues to kiss me hard. I feel electricity run through my body and want more.

I needed him now.

"Thank you everyone for coming!" I turn at the sound of mom's voice. "We are thrilled to be celebrating our only daughter and closest friends starting the next chapters in their lives tonight."

Dad steps out from the hall to stand next to her. I notice he spots the Romano's and something strange flashes across his face.

I glance up at Alessio but he stays watching my mom speak.

"Please enjoy the night!" She smiles and raises her glass. "Tonight I'll turn the other cheek, Olivia, but don't get too wild on us."

I roll my eyes and hold up my champagne along with everyone else. Kimberly holds up her Dr. Pepper from the sofa with a miserable expression.

"Cheers!"

Mom walks around as everyone disperses to chat and eat. "I'm so proud of you."

"Thank you," I hug her close. "I don't want to leave you guys in a few months."

"I know, baby," She smiles sadly. "You are going to do so amazing though!"

"Thanks, mom." I hold her hands.

"We're going to turn in early, but you all have fun." She hugs me again and tears start to flow. "I just can't believe you graduated high school."

"Honey, let the girl have her fun." Dad chuckles from her side. "Congratulations, kiddo." He wraps his arms around me tightly.

"Thanks dad, I love you."

He pulls back and kisses my cheek quickly before straightening back up and watching Alessio. I feel the room almost vibrate with the tension between them.

I turn back towards Alessio as my parents walk upstairs. "Are you ever going to explain why he looks at you like that?"

"It's nothing."

"Don't lie to me!" I scoff and cross my arms. "You saw his face."

"He isn't a huge fan of the family."

"Seems like it's mostly you." I point out.

"Olivia," He sighs and cups my face. "Enjoy the night, love."

"Fine."

"Joe! You came!"

I look over as Kim springs up from the cough and runs right into Joe's arms. He holds her close and kisses her.

"Of course! I wouldn't miss this for the world." He laughs and reaches over to do a bro bump with Alessio. "Nice to see you man."

"Likewise."

Kim looks over at me and I offer her a reassuring smile. She looks back up at Joe nervously.

"Can I talk to you real quick alone?"

"Is everything okay?" He frowns.

"Yes, let's just go chat."

She looks back at Alessio and I with her eyes wide before they exit through the front door together and step onto the porch.

"What's that about?" Alessio teases in my ear.

"Kimberly is breaking the news now."

"The pregnancy?"

"Quiet!"

"Oh, stop." He snickers and leans his head against mine. "Come with me."

"Where to?"

Everyone around us is dancing to the pop music my mom put on and drinking. Amy is very noticeably flirting it up with Beto and it looks like Katherine is trying to get somewhere with Giovanni but he is too busy flexing his muscles to care.

"They won't miss up," He says in my ear. "We'll be fast, love."

He guides me through the kitchen and out onto the balcony. I shiver as the breeze blows over the both of us and he wraps his suit jacket around my shoulders.

We embrace one another silently and stare up at the moon.

"Beautiful tonight." He whispers.

"It is."

"You're more beautiful though."

"Liar."

"I mean it," He turns me towards him and tilts my face up. "I love you, Olivia."

"I love you too-"

"Wait," He stops me with a kiss. "I love you and...I know I scared you when I said I want to marry you, but-"

"Alessio, please not tonight."

"What do you mean?"

He holds up a box. "This...this is not an engagement ring, but it is a promise...that you will be my wife one day."

"A promise ring?"

"It's beautiful, Alessio. Thank you." I look up at him in admiration."T his is...amazing."

He dips me backward playfully and kisses down my neck. I laugh wildly and slap at him as he puts me back on my feet.

"It's perfect." I smile at him.

He leans down and kisses my head. "I'll be right back."

"Olivia?"

Someone cloaked in black steps towards me quickly with a white cloth. I don't even have time to scream before their hand closes over my face and everything goes dark.

Chapter 26

"Ahh! She's awake."

I blink through the dark and try to focus my vision. I can't make out who is in front of me but it looks like I'm in some kind of warehouse.

"Where am I?" I ask weakly.

"Don't worry about all the details right now, love."

Someone steps towards me wearing a ski mask with a phone in his hands.

"W-who are you? What's going on?" I panic.

"I'm offended you don't remember me." He smiles and flashes his gold teeth. "I've missed you."

"Jesús."

He grabs a chair and pulls it up. "I've been waiting for this, Olivia. I thought I could get my hands on you when you ran away to New York, but Alessio has made it pretty difficult."

"I have nothing to do with this!" I shout desperately.

He nods, "I know that. You are my...leverage."

"Leverage for what?"

"Obviously to get Alessio here," He says and pulls a knife from his pocket. "When he gets word that I have you he'll be here quickly."

"You won't win this."

He points the end of the knife at me. "What do you know? You are just some random girl who got mixed up with a mafia family."

"I know enough," I argue back. "Alessio's family is dangerous."

"Yet you stay with him," He laughs. "He kills people for fun and you stay with him. They decapitate humans and pour acid on their bodies. Do you like the idea of that?"

My stomach turns at his words. "You aren't better."

"Oh, I know I'm no better," He says simply. "I at least admit that I'm a bad man with very, very bad intentions."

"What do you want from me?"

"I want your boyfriend to give himself up to save you," He folds his arms behind his head. "Plus, I'm not the only one who needs you for something."

"What?"

A light illuminates something behind him and I spot two people tied up to chairs with duct tape on their mouths.

I try to squint through the poor lighting and realize who they are.

"Oh my god."

My parents.

"Please! Let them go!" I beg him. "They have nothing to do with this."

"This isn't for me," Jesús says and looks over his shoulder. "It's for him"

A man steps up next to him in a long trench coat and hat. Something about him looks oddly familiar as I take him in.

"I know you," I say oddly. "I've seen you before."

"That you have," He tips his fedora. "Nice to see you, Olivia."

"What do you want? Why are you here?"

"I'm a long time friend of the Roman's," He begins and pulls his gloves off. "I'm sure Alessio has mentioned my name. You can call me Dr. To-bias."

I stare at him in shock as he removes his hat. He looks over at me and I realize immediately why I recognize him so well.

Something about his voice struck a memory in me again and I realized why.

He's the man from that night. He's the man who attacked me in the alleway.

He was at the prom.

It's him.

"It was you." I say bluntly. "I saw you in the alleyway all those years ago...you were at my prom,"

"I was instructed to handle you," He says simply. "It was nothing personal."

"I was only twelve years old!" I shout and fight against the rope. "What the fuck is wrong with you! You attacked me!"

"The reason I also needed you here tonight is because of him," Tobias says and looks at my dad. "Your father is not who you think he is."

I look over at the both of them in confusion. My mom's face is covered in tears as she stares back at me. My dad doesn't take his eyes off of Tobias as he moves closer to them.

"Dad? What the fuck does he mean?"

He stares back at me and shakes his head. His eyes are full of shame.

"Do you know anything about your family history?" Tobias asks. "Has your dad ever told you anything about his past?"

"I don't...I don't understand."

"Interesting. Why don't we have daddy tell you himself."

Jesús reaches over and rips the duck tape from my fathers lips. He groans out in pain as the skin on his lips tear.

"Dad? What's happening?" I beg him. Mom looks over at him and cries harder from the blood pooling on his mouth.

"I'm so sorry you two are in this," He says sadly. "This is my past catching up to me."

"What do you mean?" I look over at my mother but she seems just as confused.

"I wanted to keep this from the both of you," He explains and looks at mom. "I really am so sorry, Susan."

"Dad...I don't understand."

"Years before I met your mother I was living in Moscow with my father. My birth name was Ivan Kuzentsov and I was born and raised in Moscow until I turned sixteen. My father was the boss of a very big organization...a lot like the Romano's." He begins and looks over at me.

I stare back at him in shock. I don't know how to process what he's even saying.

Jesús walks over again and pulls the tape from my mom's lips. She cries out in pain and spits the blood at him.

"Daniel, I don't understand," She shakes her head. "What are you trying to say?"

"My father, Edgar, was the leader of the Moscow mafia. It was all I ever knew of him and I spent years under the organization," His head hangs in shame. "When you met me, I had found my escape but he kept finding ways to suck me back into his life when he needed my help."

"Sucked back in?"

"When Olivia was three and I told you I had to go on that week long business trip, I wasn't really in North Carolina."

"Where the fuck were you, Daniel!" Mom shouts angrily.

"I flew to Moscow to meet up with him. I never wanted you to know anything of my life there or who my father was." He looks over at her sadly. "We flew to Sicily together with his team because he wanted to facilitate an attack on Adolfo Romano's estate. He wasn't there when Edgar entered the home."

"Oh my god," I say in shock. "Your dad killed Alessio's mother."

"He did and I'm so sorry," Dad looks at Tobias. "I didn't want her hurt and I sure as fuck didn't want to be there. The only way I could have my life with you Susan was to be there when he needed me. I had to help get them in so they could catch them off guard. They weren't expecting Edgar to retaliate the way he did."

"Adolfo was always loyal to Edgar," Tobias snaps at him. "The day your father killed her was the day he sealed his fate."

"I'm just telling you what I know...what he wanted us to know," He continues. "All we ever knew was the treaty was broken."

"What happened to Edgar then?" I ask him.

The guards killed him," Tobias responds. "He knew he wouldn't make it out alive. The moscow mafia has never been able to compare to the Romano's."

I look back at Tobias. "Why was I even targeted then? I knew nothing about my father's past."

"Revenge."

"Olivia has nothing to do with this!" Dad shouts and Tobias turns to hit him with the back of his gun.

He grunts in pain and spits blood at the floor.

"Shut the fuck up, Ivan!"

"Why did we move here, Daniel?" Mom asks him. "I want the truth."

He looks over at her weakly. "A truce, Susan. Adolfo wanted a large cut of Vector's profits because they have been run by the Moscow mafia for fifty years now. They use it as a front to move illegal products safely."

"So you don't do the work you even say you do?" She shook her head in disbelief. "I don't know what to believe anymore."

"I'm sorry, Susan."

"Why would you involve my daughter and I in this, Daniel!" She shouts at him again. "What have you done!"

"I don't know what else to say, Susan. I'm so fucking sorry.

She looks at me and all emotion drains from her. "I hate you."

Dad looks over at her but doesn't say another word as the reality of her words sink in.

"Why are you even partnered up with him then?" I ask Tobias and look at Jesús.

Tobias clears his throat. "There's something else nobody aside from Adolfo knows. I'm his younger brother and the only full blood brother."

"W-what? I thought Michele and Mateo-"

"They only share a father." Tobias reminds me. "Adolfo and I came from the same father and mother."

"So...what does that even mean? What does that have to do with you two working together?"

He laughs darkly, "Jesús and I both want something similar. He wants revenge and I...well...I want Alessio out of my way."

"He's your family!"

"Adolfo doesn't want him to lead this family," He begins. "When we were younger, I was left with our mother and Adolfo was torn away to become next in life for don. He never wanted Alessio to be the next don."

"Why even waste his time then? Why wouldn't he just admit who you really are?"

"He's weak," Tobias shrugs. "It's always the son who becomes next to take over. It has been that way for hundreds of years but Alessio has failed again and again. His fate is what he deserves for his disloyalty."

He continues, "He also broke Omerta, didn't he?"

I feel myself grow cold and look away from him. "You can kill me but just leave Alessio out of this. Get your revenge on me and become don."

Tobias backs up for a moment laughing before he turns around and slaps me painfully across the face. My head whips to the side and I taste blood in my mouth.

"You're such a dumb little girl," He scolds me. "Let's see how you like it when I hit mommy."

"Don't! Don't fucking touch her!" I scream at him.

"Please!" Dad cries out. "Please...just kill me! Please don't touch my wife."

Tobias lowers to his level and nudges his gun under his chin. "That would be too easy for you, Ivan."

"Don't let them suffer for my family's mistakes."

"Wouldn't it only be fair though? Eye for an eye?" Tobias smiles.

He turns and points the gun directly at my gun. I scream in horror as he rests it against her head and try to break through the rope.

"I'm begging you."

Tobias stares back at him amused as he digs the gun further into her head. Tears stream down her face and I just sit there helpless.

There's nothing I can do. I can't save her.

"Goodbye, dear," Tobias taunts and drags the gun down her cheek. "I'm sorry it had to end this way."

She stares back at me with her big blue eyes and I feel my stomach squeeze. Tobias looks over at my dad as a loud gunshot rings out around us.

I squeeze my eyes shut tight and try to not look at whatever lies before me.

"What the fuck!"

I open my eyes and realize there's a thick smoke building between us followed by the sound of something metal scattering across the floor. The gun Tobias had is on the floor and I can see him holding his leg in pain.

"Mom! Dad!" I scream as the smoke thickens.

"We're here!" Dad shouts back and coughs. "She's okay, Olivia!"

I look around desperately as flashes of light shine through the room as several more rounds of gunfire ring out.

"I got you."

I jump and look up as a pair of hands touch my hands to un tie them. The person moves around the chair wearing a gas mask.

"Who...who?" I cough as they press a mask to my face.

"It's Anna. Just hang on."

I nod weakly as she slips a knife under the rope and helps me stand up from the chair.

I breathe deep through the mask and feel my chest burning. I try to look around for my parents but can't see what is even a foot in front of me.

"Where are my parents?" I ask her.

"Meeting us at the van," She grabs my hand. "We have to get out of here before they go off."

"Time before what?"

"The bombs."

"B-bombs?" I say in horror.

"Yes, Olivia. Alessio has to blow the building up."

She pulls the two of us through a door and I hear several more automatic rounds of gunfire behind us followed by someone screaming.

"Where did Tobias go?"

"We'll handle it," She says and rips the mask off. Her face covered in dirt. "I'm so sorry, Olivia. We had no idea he was involved."

"Did you all...hear everything?"

"Not everything," She shakes her head. "Why?"

"Uh-" I start but there's a sound of something exploding. The building next to us shakes violently and she grabs me by the elbow.

"We need to go now!"

"Will Alessio be okay?" I panic as we rush towards the black van.

The door slides open and an unfamiliar man with an automatic rifle helps us inside.

"Olivia!" I hear my mom cry and spot her tucked behind him next to my dad.

"I'm so glad you are okay!" I cry and wrap her in my arms.

My dad looks over from the corner of the van. His face is covered in black and blue bruises. "I'm so sorry, Olivia."

I scoot in between the two of them and rest my head on his shoulder. "I forgive you."

"I should've protected you two better." He shakes his head. "I should've stopped you from being around the Romano's."

"Dad." I start and he looks down at me. "I know who he is and I love him."

My mom looks at me in horror. "Olivia, you can't be part of his life, hunny."

"I've already been in his life, mom. He makes me happy and he protects me." I tell them both. "I'm in love with him."

They both look at each other and sigh.

"We'll talk more later," Mom says quietly. I nod my head and lean over onto her shoulder.

The drive to the Romano house is quick and Anna motions for me to get out of the car with her.

"What about my parents?" I ask her.

"They'll be safer at the house for now. We have six different guards watching." She tells me.

I look back at mom and dad. "Are you guys going to be okay?"

"Yes, hunny. We love you."

"I love you too." I tell them and give them both a hug. "I'll see you guys soon."

The door closes and I watch as it speeds down the road and disappears into the dark."

Anna and I look back up towards the mansion and it's eerily quiet and dark.

"Did everyone go?" I ask her.

"No," She shakes her head in confusion and looks at the guard next to her. "Something feels off..."

He looks at her and waits for her instruction.

"I want a full security check on everyone now."

She pulls some bags out of the van and nods towards the house. "Stay close to me."

We head up the stairs together and walk through the double glassdoors. The entire house is dark and there doesn't seem to be anyone around.

I've never seen it so dark and empty before.

"Don't move!" Anna hisses and immediately disappears down a dark hallway.

"Wait!" I call after her. "I can't see."

I start waving my hands around wildly and try to feel for anything that seems familiar. I probably look dumb as hell trying to find my way through the massive pitch black room.

"Anna!" I hiss out again.

I tip toe slowly across the marble floor and listen to the sound of my own footsteps. I feel the edge of the couch.

"Living Room." I announce to myself and walk around to the front.

I find the arm of it and try to make my way to the seat.

My hand touches something that feels like slack pants.

It's a leg.

I gasp and jump backwards. "Hello?"

The figure on the couch shifts a little and I can make out the silhouette just barely through the darkness.

"Not exactly." The deep voice replies.

I try to turn to run from whoever it is just as I smack right into a new person. Something comes down over my head and I feel myself tossed over someone's shoulder.

Just my fucking luck.

Chapter 27

Alessio

"She's gone. We need to go now."

Giovanni pulls away from kissing on Olivia's red head friend and looks at me in confusion.

"Olivia? She was just with you?"

"I know!" I run my hand through my hair anxiously. "I stepped out because Robin reported a suspicious vehicle in the area."

"Alright..."Giovanni pushed the girl off him. "I'll call you, cutie. Business calls."

"Alessio!" Anna runs down the steps from the upper level. "Her parents are gone. The door was left open."

"It's fucking him!" I snap and punch the wall. "God dammit! Why didn't I say out there."

Anna tries to put a comforting hand on me. "Alessio we will get them back."

"Let's go,"I shake her hand off. "I want everyone outside in 5 minutes."

All of them start to follow behind me and I look back to see Beto trying to tell Olivia's flirty friend that he had to go. That girl was a damn leech.

"Hey!" I turn back and see Olivia's aunt wobble out. "Everything ok?"

"It is," I nod and look back at the house. "Can you maybe take everyone out into town or something?"

She stares back at me confused. "I don't understand?"

"There's a situation going on and I think you all need to get out of here for a little. Take my card and if you need to get a hotel, that's fine. Let everyone know Olivia will be joining them soon and it was a surprise for her graduation." I explain to her.

She eyes me suspiciously but takes the card. "Okay...I don't understand but I know Olivia loves you, so I'll trust you."

Our eyes meet once more in understanding and I turn back towards the van where Robin is waiting.

"We located him," Robin announces. "They are in a factory off of 84th street. It was marked off as condemned years ago."

"And Olivia?"

"We have a group doing surveillance around the perimeter now, sir."

"Alright," I turn towards Anna. "Take my car and go alone. I want you in and out with Anna. Martin will meet you there as well to get her parents. Do not linger."

She nods but her dark eyes are wary. "Are you sure about this?"

"It's Olivia," I say angrily. "I have to get her out of there."

"Why would they take her parents though?"

"Who knows what his motive is right now," I tell her. "I just want them safe. Go now."

She turns to head in the opposite direction from us as Robin starts up the car. I grab a bag of weapons sitting behind the chair and Giovanni snatches two automatics from it.

I look back towards where Anna is and catch her watching us anxiously.

I knew she was nervous for tonight because Alonzo would be involved. She knows he'd never do anything stupid but he's going to be part of this family too.

"Here." Giovanni tosses me the AR-15. "Full force, bro."

I roll my eyes at him but take it in my hands before strapping it over my chest and pulling out my two pearl handled pistols.

"These are my only other two loves." I announce proudly.

Giovanni shakes his head at me and tosses Beto some ammo but I notice he hesitates.

"Are you sure about this?"

Beto glares. "I can handle myself."

"We could use you-" I start but he cuts me off angrily.

"Let me prove I'm still valuable to this damn family," He says in frustration. "You almost killed yourself in a car accident and didn't have to lay in that damn bed for weeks. I don't need you guys always watching out for me because I'm not muscled up like the two of you."

"Beto I never said you wer-"

"I need this, Alessio," He continues on. "I really need to redeem myself, please just let me have this.

I look over at Giovanni and he just nods. "Okay, Beto. We understand."

"Any trouble on the inside though and I want you both to look out for yourselves first," I tell them. "Let me handle Jesús."

They both nod and I hear Robin say something from the front. The car pulls around to a very large and dark building. The lot is completely empty and it looks like it hasn't been touched in at least twenty years.

"There's Diego and Alonzo." Robin announces as the engine shuts off.

The doors pull open and we all step out together. I peer around the roof but don't see anyone up there acting as snipers.

"Status?" I ask as Diego approaches us.

His bad eye is covered with a black patch and I notice he has a new cut on his lip from the fist fight he got into with Giovanni the other night when they were drunk.

"He did have two snipers on the roof. We took them out immediately."

I shake my head, "Sloppy...very sloppy Jesús."

"Any sign of Olivia or her parents?" I ask Alonzo.

"They are inside," He says and folds his arms. "I spotted at least 15 inside with them spread out through the room and armed. He has Olivia and her parents held hostage but there's one more thing...Tobias is here."

"Why?"

"We aren't sure but it could have something to do with Olivia's father."

Giovanni looks at me confused. "Her dad? Why?"

I sigh, " Adolfo hinted at Olivia's father being Russian a few months ago. I overheard him talking with someone on the phone and questioned him but the topic was changed. We never talked about it again."

"Do you think he meant Russian mafia?" Beto asks.

"Only one way to find out," Alonzo says and tucks his gun. "Let's get this going."

"Alright," I start and wave for them to move in. "I want the van waiting for Anna to bring out Olivia and her parents. Canisters first and then we send the first wave. I want Giovanni and Beto moving with Diego. Alonzo keeps close to me with Robin. If you see Jesús give me the chance to kill him, but he doesn't leave here alive."

"What about Tobias?" Beto lights up a cigarette.

"Let me...let me figure that one out." I say and run my hands through my hair.

I never pictured Tobias being involved in anything with Jesús. It just didn't make any sense at all.

If he is playing for the wrong team I'll have no choice but to kill him.

"Alright!"

We all turn as Anna comes up and straps her guns to the holsters around her thighs.

"You're so sexy when you're strapped." Alonzo compliments and kisses her quickly.

"We have people to kill!" Giovanni scoffs and Anna glares over at him.

Diego rolls his eyes at them and looks over. "What's the word, sir?"

"Ask Zander what his status is."

Diego pushes the little button on his earpiece and requests Zander's current position with the team scoping out the building.

He nods in response to whatever Zander says and looks back up, "Olivia's father has been brutalized by Tobias. They are threatening to kill the mother. They are ready to enter."

"Fuck! Move now."

We approach the building quickly and I hear several canisters hit the floor. There's the sound of someone firing a gun and everyone enters immediately.

I pull my gas mask on and pull out my guns. I can already hear gunfire ringing out heavily as we approach the building together.

"Go! Go!" I order and rush inside the thick gas filled warehouse. Giovanni and Beto stay close behind as we move quickly.

I can hear a female voice yelling at someone and I can only hope Anna has made it to Olivia safely.

If anything happens to her tonight, I really don't know what I will do.

"Left!" Giovanni yells and turns to fire at someone.

We all watch as a big man falls to the ground, lifeless.

"One! Two! Three!" Beto laughs manically as he fires into several men coming at him.

I shake my head at his childish antics as he starts posing with the gun. He really did miss this.

"There!" Giovanni grabs my shoulder.

Emerging from the smoke in front of us I make out a tattooed skull and black gas mask. Jesús steps forward with an automatic strapped to his chest.

He has just a pair of blood stained jeans on and it looks like he's already been shot in the shoulder by someone.

"Alessio! You fuck. Glad to see you made it." Jesús taunts and fires at a box near us.

"You took what's mine, Jesús. I will kill you tonight, I promise."

He shrugs, "What can I say? The ladies just love me."

"I'm not here to play games." I warn him. Giovanni and Beto start covering my side as several more men run towards us.

Jesús doesn't take his eyes off of me as his men drop like flies.

"I'm going to decapitate you, Alessio. I am going to send your head to your precious bitch just as you did with my brother." Jesús howls with laughter and tries to sneakily move to the side for a weak spot.

"You'll never get close to her again."

"Obviously, you aren't a good protector. I've had my hands on her twice now."

I fire towards his foot and he flinches.

"Watch your fucking mouth."

"I've been waiting for this moment, Alessio."

Giovanni bellows from the side, "End this! Kill him now."

I wave him and Beto off. "Go! Now. I will handle this. Find Tobias."

"I don-" Beto starts but stops when he sees my expression.

"NOW!"

They both continue to stare at us for a moment before moving in the opposite direction towards several more men running towards them.

I turn my attention back to Jesús. "It's been a pleasure.

He cocks his gun, "Goodbye friend."

I watch as he lifts the barrel of the gun and aims at my head. I smile beneath my gas mask and feel my fingers twitch.

Not for my gun though. I have something else in mind for him.

He releases the trigger and I move to the side just in the nick of time to toss my both pairs of gold handled daggers I had in my holster.

Jesús notices them at the last moment as they plunge into his left side and lower thigh.

I wanted to watch him suffer. I wanted to see him in pain.

This was the side of me I never want Olivia to know. The side of me that shows no mercy to my enemies.

"Really should wear protective gear." I laugh and walk up to him.

"Fuck!" He coughs and tries to pull at it. "You fucking coward!"

"Me? A coward?" I laugh darkly. "You were never a fucking threat to me. You were never a match for me, Jesús. You thought you could kill my girl, take her parents, and fuck up my property. You were nothing more than a boy with a gun...just like Alejandro.

He looks up and I can make out his face twisting into a horrific glare. I smile down at him as I raise my gun to his temple.

"See you in hell."

The bullet shatters his mask covering his face and embeds into his face. The shot rings out loudly around us and I watch as his body slumps to the floor.

"No coming back now," I kick his side with my boot. "Enjoy your reunion with your brother."

Giovanni hurries back to my side and notices a very dead Jesús covered in blood on the ground in front of us. "We need to go, Alessio."

"Where's Tobias?" I ask

Beto steps up next to us. "He's gone. We can't find him anywhere."

"Let's go."

The three of us hurry out of the building together and back in the direction towards the vans parked at the end of the lot.

"Losses?"

"Few of Jesús' men made it out through the back when the canisters went off. We lost five guards from what I could tell, but Xavier is doing a count."

My head bows, "Fuck..."

"It's done, man. Jesús is dead...we don't have to deal with this anymore."

I toss the mask down. "We'll always have something challenging us. We need to extend training times, I want everyone at peak performance."

"Move out!" Robin calls.

Everyone hurries into the vans quickly just as the sound of sirens in the distance come to check out all of the hell that just broke out in that warehouse. I was grateful to see Anna's car was long gone.

"Status on Tobias?" I ask Robin.

He looks back at me in the rearview mirror and mutters into his ear piece.

"No word, sir."

"Get me word immediately on why he was there and what his motive was with Daniel Moore. Run a background on Mr. Moore as well, I need to know more of his history."

"Done."

"What are you thinking?" Giovanni asks as he starts putting equipment away.

I shrug my shoulders, "I'm not sure really. I think something had happened previously when Adolfo met up with him because there has definitely been some tension. I think he has some kind of Russian tie."

"He works for that business Vector right?"

"Yeah, they are shady as hell."

"I'd assume Olivia's father is aware then." Giovanni pointed out.

"Time will tell."

The rest of the drive back to the manor is silent as we pull up quickly towards the gates. The entire estate looks dark aside from the few headlights shining brightly as we pull up the driveway.

I pull the phone out and try to dial her.

No answer.

I try Anna.

"What the fuck..."

Beto looks over, "What's up?"

"I'm not sure if they took the phone Olivia had on her but Anna isn't even answering."

Robin tries it as well and watches my face.

"Nothing."

"Fuck!" I hit the door. "Find them both immediately and find fucking Tobias!"

Mikael in the driver seat hits the pedal hard and speeds up towards the front of the home and stops right in front of the set of stairs there.

"Let me know when you find him!" I call back and head inside immediately.

There's nothing. It's completely dark almost as if the power had been cut.

And it's so silent.

Giovanni comes in behind me and waits. We move quietly through the front hall and peer around in the darkness.

The only time we had no guards like this was during lock-downs or when Adolfo called them out for something extremely important.

"Here," Giovanni tosses me an ear piece and I turn it on. "They are waiting for you to give them the green light."

I nod at him and speak, "Find Olivia Moore right away. Status on her parents?"

Alonzo speaks, "Dropped off at home with several guards on watch.

"Olivia and Anna have to be here. Find fucking Adolfo!"

I release the button on the ear piece and look at Giovanni. He's extremely on edge and looks ready to attack someone.

"Left wing." I order and he moves quickly.

I decide to walk in the opposite direction and head down a hallway towards the only place I would think they'd try to hide Olivia in if Tobias was up to something.

The entire bottom level of the cellar was completely underground and spread out a few miles due to the size of the estate. We had used it primarily for storage of weapons and even had a training facility down there.

The hallway was dark but I could make out a small amount of light pooling beneath the door there. The chain looked to be broken.

I pulled the door back slowly and tried to keep as quiet as possible. There were several sounds coming from the room below and it sounded like someone was arguing.

I take the steps slowly as the staircase winds down towards the platform. I pulled my gun from my jeans and kept it close to my chest.

"This is fucking insane! What is happening?"

Mateo is down here.

"I told you! Listen brother, this really is the best thing for us." Michele is speaking now.

"This? THIS! For 75% of the investment. You did this for money!?" Mateo shouts.

Someone else laughs and it sounds like Adolfo.

"Shut up! This is not the time to argue. We need to handle matters here, men." Adolfo rumbles. "Tobias?"

My hand stands up on my neck and I feel my finger inch towards the trigger.

"If I do it...you promise the deal is done?" Tobias asks him.

"A deal is a deal," Adolfo responds. "Don't forget Daniel and Susan Moore. I want them both dead this time."

"Understood."

"You're all fucking insane! What is wrong with you all!" A voice screams out and it seems like it's Anna's.

"Business, Anna. This is all the best for the family. I wanted you to be there right alongside us, but you all failed. You let an outsider into our world and you all knew what Alessio had done." Adolfo explains. "It's best for Tobias to take over."

As in...don?

What the fuck.

"Alessio will fucking kill you before you get the chance!" Anna yells back.

"Shut up!" Tobias screams and there's a loud crashing sound. I hear Anna yell out in Italian. "Michele get this shit done."

"Michele!" Anna pleads. "You know this is bullshit, right?"

"I need this, Anna!" Michele argues. "I'd actually be second in command and the increase is worth it. I know you don't understand but the family needs this. Plus...Tobias is his blood brother, it only makes sense."

Brother?! Blood brother?

"How did we not know? How could you hide this?"

Tobias sighs, "It took years for us to even know. Our father wanted Adolfo to take over so he took him one night from mom and left me. I spent years living a normal life and studying medicine. When Adolfo finally showed up and offered me a job, I accepted it. I wanted to know him...we wanted to have the relationship we had ripped from us as children.

"So why not Mateo or Michele? They've been here. If you didn't want Alessio, why wouldn't you pick who has been working under you for over twenty years now and is still family?" Anna argues.

"Tobias has done more for this family than you can imagine," Adolfo begins. "He's been working for me in secrecy outside the clinic for over ten years now. I make the decisions, daughter. I wanted Alessio to step up but his disloyalty to keeping our family secret and safe is broken."

"You're fucking sick!" Anna yells at him.

"Well, my dear, it's really been a pleasure." He says simply. "Michele please don't waste more time."

"I'm sorry!" He says brokenly.

"No-" Anna cries out.

The sound of a gun firing rips through the room.

Chapter 28

"Wake up!"

I cough violently as something wet splashes against my face. I try to blink the liquid away and a stone room comes into view.

Something moves quickly in front of me as my vision steadies.

"Again."

More liquid hits me in the face and I feel some of it get into my mouth. Warm and dirty tasting water.

"She's up," A voice mutters and I hear footsteps come near. "Should I do it again?"

"No, that's enough."

I try to focus on the figure in front of me and squint against the harsh lights to see an elderly man walking towards me.

He tips his fedora in my direction and leans closer towards me. A cigar hangs on the edge of his lips and he smells strongly of whiskey.

"Sweet, young Olivia."

"W-who are you?" I stammer out.

He steps back and smiles. He has to be at least in his late 70's or 80's. He's basically all wrinkles and his hair is nearly all silver except for a few black strands mixed in.

His smile widens to show his yellowing teeth. "I'm so happy I'm finally meeting you."

"Who are you?"

"My boy never introduced me," He says and clicks his tongue. "Adolfo Romano. Pleasure to meet you, darling."

It never really hit me that I'd never met Alessio's dad. I assumed with him being the don it wasn't going to happen anyways. I'd heard about him a few times through the house but he was almost like a phantom to me or just a name.

Putting a face to him felt so surreal.

He puffs oh his cigar, "A little star struck?"

He moves towards me again and blows a cloud of smoke towards my face. I cringe away from his closeness and cough.

A figure near him moves closer to us and I see the edge of a gun through the shadows.

"What do you want?" I cry out and try to rock against my restraints.

You'd think I'd be some kind of escape artist by this point.

"Well, you see..."He starts and looks back at someone. "It's more what I need from you, dear. Your family is unfortunately the cause of my late wife's death and my dear boy, Alessio, well he just can't seem to learn what is best for him and this family."

"I have nothing to do with that!"

He nods and his dark eyes run over me. "I'm aware of that but revenge is necessary at this point, darling. I should've taken care of this when we had the chance."

"I don't understand..."

"We've met before, dear." He smiles again. "I'm sure my brother filled you in."

I think back again to that night in New York when Tobias attacked me.

There had been a second man in the shadows with a heavy Italian accent.

It was him. Adolfo had really hunted me down at the same of twelve to avenge his wife. I was an easy target and I usually was always walking alone at night from the shop or school.

Who knows how long they'd been watching.

Mom always stayed home but my dad had been working from our home office for almost a year at this point. I could've been dead at any moment.

I had been living for years with a target right on my family.

He continues, "Forgive me, dear. It's just how this life works and it seems your father decided to wrap you and your mother up in this. So selfish of a man to try and hide his past from his loved ones knowing how deceitful his own father was."

"Your guards killed my grandfather that day. Isn't that your revenge right there? He didn't get away with it." I plead with him. "I'm so sorry for what they did, but my family doesn't have anything to do with this."

"You can't even imagine how painful it was, "He explains and looks down at the ground. "I should've been there for my wife knowing how bad things had gotten with the Kuzentsov mafia. I never expected Edgar to grow some balls and initiate a full-blown attack on my estate. That was my own mistake, but he only lost his life. Your father still was there to assist in her murder and then run back to his perfect family."

"He didn't..."I start and shake my head. "My father didn't just let it go...I'm sure it ate at him every day."

"He had no consequences...until now." He glares at me. "The Kuzentsov family knew the murder of the Sicilian mafia's wife would give them the upperhand. It would unleash a full war for years to come...he wanted the control of the ports, weapons, money. He needed the advantage."

"An advantage?"

"This is a business, Olivia," He explains. "Edgar and I started having some differences and he figured he'd take the opportunity to push himself further and gain the control he clearly desperately wanted in Sicily over my territory."

"So...this happened because you had a fight with him?" I roll my eyes.

He glares at me and before I realize what's happening I feel something whip across my face. Adolfo pulls his hand away and smiles widely.

"Knock the little attitude off," He spits out. "It had nothing to do with a fight, girl. It had everything to do with who was going to be the top in this business."

He leans closer and a snarl creeps across his face. "How do you feel knowing your precious father killed your boyfriend's mother? Doesn't that eat at your core?"

I feel tears fill my eyes. "I'll never hate him, Adolfo. I know Alessio wouldn't hold this against him either."

"Are you so sure?" He taunts and his cigar gets closer to my cheek. "What if Alessio hates you too? You are the daughter of a murderer."

I close my eyes tight. "Shut up! If you're going to kill me, just do it. Stop the mind games!"

"Oh, I will," He muses and peaks behind him. "I'm just not ready yet."

Tobias steps from the shadows and pulls Anna along with him. Her mouth is taped and she has blood smeared across her face and hair.

From what I could tell Tobias also had a few scratches on him. Anna definitely put up a good fight.

I look back at Adolfo. "Anna has nothing to do with this!"

"I know," He nods and grabs a chair from behind him. "Tie her."

Tobias grabs Anna by the back of her hair and drags her to the chair next to me. I watch as she struggles with him and tries to fling her head back towards his nose.

He groans out in pain and pulls her harder by the back of the head as he shoves her into the chair.

He moves to quickly tie her to the back but loses his balance when Anna kicks out her tennis shoe and nails him right in the chest.

"Bitch!" He groans out and slaps her hard across the face.

Anna glares back at him through the pain as he finishes securing her feet to the legs.

Adolfo smiles warmly at her. "Your mother would be proud of you my dear."

She continues to stare at him as he moves closer to her and leans in close.

"I'll miss you all," He says sadly and touches her hair. "I'm sorry it has to be this way, but it's just business, darling."

"What is your plan here then?" I snap and draw his attention. "Kill me and your children? For what reason?"

"Not that it's your business, but my children have betrayed me." He says simply and walks back towards Tobias. "They let you into our lives. A traitor."

"They didn't know about my family!"

"I'm an old man, Olivia," He explains and pulls his gun out to admire it. "I need something fresh and Alessio just isn't going to work out. My brother here was always pulling through for me over the years, he has shown true dedication and leadership."

Tobias nods a little and smiles over at him proudly.

"Tobias has risked more for me than any of my children have. He has put himself on the line time and time again."

"So you'll kill your children? All because of my family and because I know who you are?"

He sighs," They sealed their own fate, child. They should've killed you from the beginning. You've been such a risk to this family and have ruined quite a few plans I had in mind." He chuckles darkly.

"Alessio should've been punished for his betrayal, but instead he drug his siblings and cousin into his bullshit."

"Why not just tell them about Tobias then and send them away? I'll cut all ties if it means saving their lives."

He smiles and kneels down before me. "I like my plan better."

I felt a chill creep along my spine. Hearing him talk about the murder of his children so easily really proved that he had no remorse for the death of them.

He would relish in it.

"Let's get to it," Adolfo nods and motions for Tobias to step forward. "Anna first."

I look over at Anna in terror and our eyes meet. She gives me a little nod and looks back up towards Tobias as he closes in on her.

This was it. There was no way out of this.

"I'm so sorry, Anna." I whisper brokenly and look away.

"Wait!" A new voice calls out.

We all look up to see Mateo step out from the darkness and head towards us quickly. Just as he reaches Adolfo, I realize someone else has stepped out from behind Tobias with a gun drawn.

Michele glares back at his brother and both of them raise their guns at one another.

"This is fucking insane! What is happening?" Mateo snaps.

Michele continues to stare back at him. "I told you! Listen brother, this really is the best thing for us."

"This? THIS! For 75% of the investment. You did this for money!?" He says frantically and looks over at Anna and I.

"Shut up!" Adolfo stops them and laughs. "This is not the time to argue. We need to handle matters here, men." He turns towards his brother.

"Tobias?"

He looks back at Anna. "If I do it...you promise the deal is done?"

"A deal is a deal," Adolfo nods his head. "Don't forget Daniel and Susan Moore. I want them both dead this time."

"Understood."

He takes a step towards Anna and rips the tape from her mouth. She coughs a mixture of spit and blood on the floor.

"You're all fucking insane! What is wrong with you all!?"

"Business, Anna. This is all the best for the family. I wanted you to be there right alongside us, but you all failed. You let an outsider into our world and you all knew what Alessio had done." Adolfo explains. "It's best for Tobias to take over."

"Alessio will fucking kill you before you get the chance!" She argues.

"Shut up!" Tobias snaps and kicks her chair. She topples over and hits the ground hard. "Michele!" He turns back towards him.

"Get this shit done."

He steps forward a little hesitant as if he didn't expect Tobias to pass the task off to him. He looks over at us and something shifts in his expression.

I couldn't figure out if it was remorse for what he was about to do or not. He didn't look like the man I had met before.

His eyes were dark and he seemed so far away.

"Michele! You know this is bullshit, right?" Anna shakes her head and laughs.

"I need this, Anna!" Michele says with almost no emotion. "I'd actually be second in command and the increase is worth it. I know you don't understand but the family needs this. Plus...Tobias is his only true blood brother. It only makes sense."

"How did we not know? How could you hide this?"

Tobias speaks up. "It took years for us to even know. Our father wanted Adolfo to take over so he took him one night from mom and left me. I spent years living a normal life and studying medicine. When Adolfo finally showed up and offered me a job, I accepted it. I wanted to know him...we wanted to have the relationship we had ripped from us as children.

"So why not Mateo or Michele? They've been here. If you didn't want Alessio, why wouldn't you pick who has been working under you for over twenty years now and is still family?" Anna argues.

"Tobias has done more for this family than you can imagine," Adolfo begins. "He's been working for me in secrecy outside the clinic for over ten years now. I make the decisions, daughter. I wanted Alessio to step up but his disloyalty to keeping our family secret and safe is broken."

"You're fucking sick!" Anna yells at him.

"Well, my dear, it's really been a pleasure." He says simply. "Michele please don't waste more time."

Michele takes a step closer to her and raises the gun.

"I'm sorry."

"No!" She cries out.

I try to look away from the scene as the tears continue to pour down my face. There's a loud bang that erupts through the room and I brace myself for the next one meant for me.

I can hear a mixture of yelling and gunfire again as the room grows louder with the chaos. I start to panic and barely can hear myself scream over the ringing in my ears.

Something grabs me and shakes me hard.

"Olivia!"

I hesitantly open my eyes and find Alessio in front of me. His dark eyes roam over my body for any wounds.

I look past him and realize Tobias, Michele, and Tobias are gone. Mateo is leaning against a pillar and looks to be injured in his left shoulder.

I look to the chair at my right and realize Anna is gone.

"Where is she?!" I panic.

"They took her," He says as he cuts the ropes at my wrists. "I shot Michele in the hand and they fired back. Adolfo tried to use Anna as a shield he knew I wouldn't hurt her."

"Mateo?" I ask him softly.

He looks over his shoulder. "He jumped in front of the bullet when Michele fired back."

Mateo looks up at him and smiles weakly.

"You didn't have to risk yourself like that," Alessio says to him. "We need to get you to the clinic."

"I couldn't let them kill either of you," Mateo says and cringes from the pain. "I'm so sorry this is happening, Alessio."

Alessio nods in his direction and helps me to my feet. His arms wrap around my waist tightly and I melt into his familiar embrace.

"We need to find Anna," I say into his chest. "They are going to kill her."

He tilts my chin up towards him. "I won't let her die, Olivia."

"Do you know...everything?" I ask him sadly.

I feel my heart swell in my chest at the thought of Alessio hating me for what my father helped my grandpa do.

I wouldn't blame him though. I apparently had a dark family history too.

He smiles down at me and kisses my cheek. "We'll talk later, love."

I nod and grab onto his hand. The two of us turn to find Mateo trying to tie a poorly ripped piece of fabric around his upper arm.

"Clinic," Alessio points at him and lets go of my hand. "Take Olivia with you."

"No!" I beg and pull him backwards. "Let me go with you! I can help."

"Olivia," He cradles my face. "I can't put you at risk, love. I'll be okay, I promise. I have to get moving, this underground level is massive and they could be anywhere by now."

"I'll take her with me," Mateo promises him. "Let me know when you find Michele."

"I'm sorry if I have to kill him."

"He's a traitor...they all are." Mateo responds. His voice is full of hurt.

"I'll do everything I can to win him back," Alessio promises and grabs onto Mateo's good side. "You can count on me."

Alessio pulls away and pulls me back to him again. His mouth finds my own immediately and I feel my own tears spilling down my face as we kiss each other hard.

I didn't like this kiss though. It felt wrong.

Our embrace was full of pain and uncertainty. I didn't know his fate.

This could be the time Alessio didn't return to me.

This felt like a goodbye.

"Please be safe." I whisper against his lips.

He pulls away and rests his forehead against my own.

"I love you, Olivia."

Chapter 29

"This way."

Mateo nods towards the staircase ahead of us. He's already not looking too great and is looking pretty pale and sweaty.

As concerned as I am for his current state I just couldn't seem to pull my eyes from where Alessio disappeared.

Was this really our last time seeing one another? Would I wake up and find out he wouldn't be coming back to me?

Alessio is smart but his father is the don of the family. He would have more than just Tobias and Michele there to back him up.

Alessio could be walking right into a room full of people ready to kill him on sight.

Besides...did he really have enough hate towards Adolfo to kill him? Could he go through with actually killing his father?

Deep down...I knew a lot of this was my own fault.

If my dad would've never said yes to the job change, I wouldn't of ended up here. And even if I did, I should've listened to the rumors about the Romano family.

I should've kept my distance. Maybe I would've settled down with some other California boy or found someone in New York when I went back.

Or, I would've been just fine on my own. Alessio's life would've moved on without me interfering with any of it.

Adolfo would have no reason to have a grudge against him for telling me about the family.

I should've moved on the moment I laid eyes on him. I let my own curiosity put me here and now several people I care about could be murdered tonight.

"Miss Moore?"

I look back at Mateo. His face glittering with beads of sweat.

"Please, Mateo. You're always so formal." I smile gently. "Just call me Olivia"

"Force of habit," He chuckles and I help guide him onto the first step. "I'm sorry you are involved in this."

"Don't apologize. I love Alessio and I decided to be part of this."

He shakes his head. "Alessio would've never wanted this for you."

I frown at him and look ahead as we move slowly up the stairs. "Do you think he'll be okay?"

"He's smart, dear." He assures me. "Alessio always finds a way to get out of any situation."

I nod a little but try to keep focused as we approach the door leading to the upper level. Mateo's weight was growing increasingly more heavy as he held onto me.

"Which way to the clinic?" I ask as we step into the hall.

"That way, "He points a shaking hand in the opposite direction. "Right down the hall and through that last door."

I shift his weight onto me and we continue to move through the darkness. The main level was still eerily quiet and dark.

It was almost as if everyone had evacuated.

"Too bad Tobias turned out to be a traitor," Mateo groans. "I could've used his medical expertise."

"Do you guys have someone else?"

"Yes, don't worry about me. I just want to get you somewhere safe."

The two of us try to move as quickly as we can through the great room. There appears to be some kind of movement just outside the double glass front doors but inside is so still I can hear our hearts beating.

"Quickly," He whispers and looks around the dark. "You never know who is hiding."

I pick up our pace a little and set my eyes on the doors ahead of us. The only thing really driving me was knowing how much Alessio needed me to help him with this right now.

The unknown though was what was driving me insane.

"Mateo!"

The two of us turn towards the voice coming from our left and the sight makes me sick.

Michele walks up to us slowly with his clothes soaked in red blood. I notice some gauze tied around his wounded hand.

"Fuck you!" Mateo growls and draws his gun out.

"Brother," Michele holds his hands up. "It isn't what you think. I had to trick them into thinking I was in on everything. I found out what they were doing weeks ago when Adolfo found me in his office."

"What did you find?" I ask him.

"Everything..."Mateo shakes his head. "He had family photos with To-bias in it. There was a signed contract detailing Tobias to take over the family." His eyes land on me. "I even saw some stuff about your family."

I try to push down the pain of my family's past and look away. It was just too much to think about right now.

"So why are you here now? How?"

"I'm supposed to be killing you," Mateo admits and my body grows cold. "I also had to fix my hand up."

I glare at him. "So why aren't you trying to kill me then?"

"I'd never hurt Alessio like that," He says and looks at Mateo. "Or my brother."

"How am I supposed to fucking trust you?" Mateo coughs up from the pain.

"Please, Mateo." Michele steps close. "Let me help you."

"I got him," I pulled Mateo back towards me. "Maybe you can find something else to do."

"Olivia, I really mean no harm to you," Michele says to me. "I know you can't trust me, but I really just want to help."

"So the investment was a lie? The second in command?" Mateo asks.

He nods," Adolfo was using it to keep me quiet but I'm sure it would've been retracted. At the rate he was going, I'd imagine he would've wanted to kill off everyone aside from Tobias."

"So much for brotherhood."

We approach the clinic door and a plump woman steps out from it immediately. Her eyes widen as she takes in Mateo.

"Oh, god!" She says and grabs onto him. "I'll take it from here."

"Can I come?" I ask and feel Michele standing behind me.

"We're on lockdown, hun. You really need to get to a safe room." The aged woman replies. "The don put out an alert to all staff and guards. You need to get going."

I watch as they both disappear through the door and look back towards Michele.

"Well, if you really need to kill me this would be the best time."

"Olivia," He groans and runs his hand through his shaggy locks. "I'm really not going to kill you. I don't agree with anything Adolfo is doing. This is betrayal on the entire family. Our father would've been disappointed in him, but I think he feels this is some twisted way to pay his respects to him by taking his brother in to follow his footsteps."

"I just-" I start but stop as footsteps come near us.

We both look over at a man clad in black with a massive gun heading in our direction. His hair is cut short and he has a patch over his left eye.

"Found her!" He says into an earpiece. "Alessio has asked me to take you to your room. My name is Robin."

I glare up at the big man. He reminds me a lot of Giovanni.

"I don't want to hide anymore. Let me help."

"We are not to discuss this," He looks over at Michele. "Can we still trust you?"

"I already told you," Michele sighs and pulls out a cigarette. "I'm only here to help Alessio. Adolfo has no idea of my intentions."

"Where is Alessio?" I ask Robin.

"He's handling this," Robin grabs onto my elbow. "We need to get going."

"I'll take her." Michele offers.

Robin nods a bit but freezes as someone yells something at him in Italian on his earpiece.

He replies back and I hear Alessio's name thrown in.

"Why did you say his name?"

"It's fine."

"Don't fucking lie to me!" I bang my hand against his chest.

He narrows his eyes. "Go to his room."

"Not until you tell me."

Robin's expression changes and he looks at Michele.

Something is wrong.

"He found Adolfo and there was a gun fight," Robin begins. "Some of the guards decided to stay on the don's side and…"

"And what?"

"I-I can't, ma'am."

"And WHAT?" I demand and hear my voice shake.

Robin looks down at me and his voice lowers.

"Alessio has been shot but -"

I don't want to hear anymore. My body turns ice cold and I turn away from them.

I hear what sounds like a gun being fired in the distance and take off running.

Robin and Michele call after me and I hear them yelling for me. I don't look back and head right into the action.

I'm done being the room who needs to be saved.

ALESSIO

"Give it up! You know you aren't going to kill her!"

I'm a fucking idiot for not shooting him first.

Mateo is injured and Olivia is a complete wreck. Now Anna is being held hostage and I have no idea if she's okay.

As enraged as I am, the thought of killing my own father felt extremely daunting.

One of us had to die tonight.

And I plan to make that person him.

"Come on, old man!" I call into the dark corridor. "Why would you hide from your own son?"

My voice bounces back to me and I peer down into the darkness. The hall seems to grow more narrow as it continues on and a musty smell starts to build really showing the age of the home.

"On the way."

"Copy." I respond to Giovanni in my ear piece. "Make sure someone is on the way to Olivia."

"On it."

The little speaker crackles in my ear as it's turned off. Something moves ahead of me through the dark.

I pull my gun up and keep it in front of my body. My pace slows to a crawl as I inch through the pitch black halls.

"Stop playing games."

The shuffling grows louder and starts moving towards me. I fire in the direction of it and hear a shriek.

A massive fucking rat appears from the shadows and runs right over my shoes.

"Dammit!" I shout and rake my fingers through my hair.

"Alessio."

I turn towards the voice and raise my gun again.

"Calm down!" Beto snaps and pushes the gun down. "Giovanni is on the way with the others. I tried to alert everyone but...apparently something is going on."

"What else could possibly be fucking happenign right now?"

Beto glares at me, "Shut up, dude. Listen...some of the guards are on Adolfo's side."

"Like who?"

"Well let's just say our go-to team is safe and not turning against us."

"What are our numbers looking like?" I ask him.

"Well," He starts and pulls out his ear piece. "Adolfo has already ordered them to meet him on the opposite end. They are in a shipment room and waiting for us."

"Should've known they'd pick weaponry to hide in." I shake my head.

Beto rolls his eyes at me and pulls out two glocks to load them.

"We need to get moving. Where's Giovanni? I also need a status on Olivia."

"I'm here, bitch!" Giovanni's voice booms as he steps into the small pool of light. He has two pistols in each hand and his favorite AK-47 strapped to his back.

He looks like a kid in a candy shop.

"You good?" I laugh at him.

"I'm so fucking ready," He muses and flex his arms. "Nobody tries to kill my sister."

"She can handle herself," I remind him. "We just need to get there before Adolfo gets impatient."

His expression softens. "We'll get her back, bro."

The three of us look at one another and take a moment. There's no guarantee we'd be together again.

We had no idea what was waiting for us.

I could lose any of them tonight. Adolfo was dead set on killing his own and I may not be able to save them.

We start moving down the dark halls again and in the direction of the location Adolfo was said to be in.

The dark grows as we move deeper into the cellar and I feel something creeping over me like a shadow.

It was just a sickening feeling. Something felt so wrong and I couldn't shake it off.

I just had to get there.

I have to kill my father.

◇ ◇ ◇

"There. Are you ready?"

I glance back at Giovanni as we peak around the edge of the wall.

Adolfo is casually sitting at a table in the middle of the room playing cards with Tobias. Several guards are stationed among the crates and loading up guns.

In the far right corner I make out Anna. Her hair is tossed about and her face looks to be swollen.

"Where are they?" I ask Beto. He holds a finger up. "I need to know where Olivia is right now."

Giovanni pipes up." Where's Michele?"

"I've put out an alert for him, "Beto assures the two of us. "Alonzo and Diego are on the way now, they are bringing 12 with them."

"Anyone else?" I ask and scan the room.

Adolfo had at least twenty men in here with them.

"They are all we have."

"We got this,"Giovanni grins through the shadows. "We don't need the numbers. We have plenty of skilled men."

"Skill we got from him." I remind him and nod towards Adolfo. "Don't forget who has the upperhand here."

"Not very don-like of you." Giovanni teases.

"Obviously, he never wanted me to be don," I sigh and look back at the room. "I would've been fine with just a normal life...one with Olivia."

He nods a little and breaks out into an ongoing show of extremely vulgar jokes to lighten up the mood as we wait for the others. I look back over at Adolfo and watch.

His cigar hangs loosely on his lips as it ashes against the table. His fedora on top of his head.

He looks so calm. He wasn't nervous or concerned at all.

He was completely fine with what he planned to do.

I can't believe I ever trusted him. The man who brought me into the world was the same one to fuck me over in the end.

The same one who was planning my funeral.

"We're here."

The three of us turn around at the deep voice speaking from behind and find Alonzo leaning down next to Diego. They have a bag with them and start handing out the guns and ammo.

I watch as several more take place behind them and begin loading up on weapons.

Everyone was silent and the tension was high. I knew they were all nervous and scared.

They all had family back home in Italy. They had so much at risk too.

Now they were expected to kill the Sicilian don.

"Plan?" Diego asks us.

"Let the three of us go first," I tell them. "I don't want to go in too quickly."

"I'm coming," Alonzo says and locks his eyes on Anna. Her head is bowed now and I can see a trail of blood oozing from her beaten in lips. "If they don't die by your hand, I'll kill them immediately."

I put my hand on his shoulder, "I know you're upset but we have to be smart in this Alonzo. We'll get her out safely."

His jaw flexes and I see his finger loosen up on his trigger. "Fine."

I look back at Giovanni and Beto.

"No mercy." I say to the both of them. "Do not hold back. These are not friends or family any longer."

I look back at the rest of my men. "We need to get Anna out safely. She's my first priority here."

"I'll do it," Alonzo says sternly. "I need to get my girl out of there."

"Alright."

Shouting picks up from the room and we all look back around the corner. A guard has started taunting Anna and apparently she bit him.

He slaps her across the face hard and her head turns to the side. A stream of blood pours from her mouth and she spits it at the ground.

"Hurry!" Alonzo growls out.

I nod and we all stand up from our spots. The three of us move in quietly to the room with Alonzo waiting in the shadows.

The guards in the room spring up immediately at the sounds of our shoes and draw their guns.

I hold up my hands as we move towards them and look back for Giovanni and Beto to follow my lead.

Of course, Giovanni opts for his middle finger.

"This is what you wanted, right?" I ask Adolfo. He looks up from the cards in his hands. "We're all here."

"My boys!" He cheers excitedly and stands up. "So glad you could make it."

"Cut the shit, Adildo!" Giovanni mocks his name.

"Classy," He sighs and steps away from the table. "You've always been the sarcastic one."

"Let Anna go," I say to him. "Tobias can have the mafia, I just want Anna safe."

"You know it doesn't work like that, son," He shakes his head at me. "We live and die for the mafia. Unfortunately, you broke something that can not be forgiven. You took your family down with you and now you all have to pay."

I laugh at him. "You've just been so ready to kill your own children."

"It's not a want," He shrugs his shoulders. "This is business and I need to set an example. You shouldn't have let that Russian slut into this."

My body tenses and my vision crosses with red. "Olivia has nothing to do with this."

"Her grandfather murdered your fucking mother!" He shouts and slams his fist down. "He killed her and her father was there the whole fucking time! Do you not care about your own mother?"

"It's time to move past this, Adolfo."

"I'll let it go when I've killed all of the Kuzentsov family," He smiles at me. "That includes your girlfriend."

Anger rages through me and before I can even think my guns are drawn. The guards around us all raise their weapons.

Adolfo smiles at the scene unfolding before him and pulls his gun from his waist.

"Don't be stupid," Tobias speaks up from the table. "He's your father, Alessio."

"Who plans on murdering his children and my girlfriend," I turn my gun towards him. "Fuck the both of you."

"You failed, Alessio! You're weak." He laughs and pushes his peppery hair back from his eyes. "Your dear father is near the end of his time and you were supposed to step up. He's lucky to have had someone like me working in the background for him all of these years. You could've had it all! You just had to pick a Kuzentsov bitch."

"We knew nothing of the Kuzentsov being associated with Olivia's family. She didn't even know."

"Weak, Alessio! So weak!" He roars with laughter. "You should've let her go! You told her of your family and put your family at risk for some silly crush you have. Now we have to try to off the little bitch all these years later since the first time didn't work out."

"Excuse me?"

Tobias looks over at Adolfo and back at me with a taunting grin as he steps closer.

"That's right..."He starts and slides his pistol from his pants. "When your dear was just a measly twelve years old, we found them in New York. She was easy to target, but it didn't work out. We'd been after him for years, we just didn't know Ivan had changed his name."

"What the fuck is he saying?" I snap and look at Adolfo.

"We found her walking home one Winter,"Tobias continues on. "I had her pinned and should've slit her neck right then but that old bitch had to interrupt the fun.

"You..."I trail off and stare at him blankly. "You tried to murder Olivia?"

"I did and I plan on finishing the job tonight."

Within seconds I felt myself come undone. His words had unleashed something in me and without signaling the others I snapped.

I moved quicker than he could and fired directly at his chest. Tobias flew backwards from the impact and hit the table behind him hard.

The room around us erupted into a show of gunfire.

Bullets start flying around us and our men who had been in the shadows step out before us.

Adolfo's eyes linger on his dead brother for a moment before he finds me again. He roars with anger and whips his gun up to fire.

I try to move out of the line of fire but nearly miss as the bullet hits my thigh.

Burning pain rushes up my leg and I grab onto it as blood starts to soak my pant leg.

"Fuck! Alessio!"

Beto grabs onto me and drags me backwards until we are shielded from the gunfire.

I ignore him and finish wrapping some fabric above the wound. I wasn't ready to stop now.

"Get out of here!" Beto shouts loudly. "Get to the clinic."

"No!" I snap and look back towards Adolfo. He has a new cigar lit and is casually watching the chaos. The guards around him do everything they can to shield him. "I need to fucking kill him now."

I push back up onto my feet and move Beto out of my way.

"Give it up, son!" Adolfo shouts and turns to shoot a guard rushing him in the head.

Mikael's body falls to the ground. He had been with us for the past twenty years.

"I have no problem killing everyone in this room!" He sings joyously. "I may be an old man but you don't have my experience or the numbers to win this!"

"You're wrong!" I shake my head. "I'll see you in hell."

I raise my gun again and our eyes meet. The ends of our barrels pointed directly at one another as time seems to slow down to a crawl.

This is it. This is the moment that changes it all for us.

I release the trigger.

The lonely bullet seems to soar through the air slowly as it heads towards his skull.

I step to the side and pray I miss his next shot meant for me.

Except...

Oh no... what the fuck!

Why is she here! Why is Olivia here!

I see her immediately. I feel the room change as I take her in.

Everything about her changes something in me the moment I lay eyes on her.

Her stunning beauty and grace. Her innocence.

I lock onto her eyes. Blue and terrified.

She's scared but something in her expression tells me she is determined to do whatever she came here for.

Her long dark locks rush behind her as she runs right into the middle of the room.

I've had dreams of this. Nightmares.

Every single dream would be her dead in my arms. Her skin pale and lips blue.

Drained of life.

She'd have a single wound. Bloody and fresh.

Yet I'd always wake up and she'd be there. She would always be okay.

I'd feel her warmth and soft skin. Relish in her each time.

I couldn't save her in my dreams but when I woke up she was always in my arms.

I was okay. She was okay.

This time...this time I'm not dreaming.

She did the one thing I had feared. The one thing I never wanted her to do.

Olivia ran directly in front of the bullet.

The bullet meant for me.

Her eyes were locked on my body as it impaled into her. She stumbled a few feet and her eyes widened with confusion and pain.

I watched as her body started to hit the floor and ran after her.

I screamed her name over and over again as she lay in my arms. Her head rolling to the side and eyes barely focusing.

She looks up at me through the anguish and tries to smile. Her soft fingertips brush against the edge of my cheek drenched in tears.

Her lips part as she whispers weakly, "I saved you."

Epilogue

I'm dead.

I know I'm dead.

There's no way I could've survived. This was it for me.

This had to have been the end of the road. After everything, this should've been what sealed my fate.

I don't know why I did it.

All I remember was seeing him. I saw his face and I saw what was meant to kill him.

Something in me broke and I felt like I needed to save him.

I had to risk myself for him after everything he's done for me.

I felt like it was my time to be the hero. To be superwoman.

Except it involved a bullet embedding itself into me.

And damn…it hurt so fucking bad. The pain was brief before everything went black but I remember it burned.

I don't know how the Romano's are so fearless when it comes to guns.

It was so painful but seeing Alessio's face had made it worth it.

Taking the bullet though didn't ease the hurt he would heal. I remember hearing him scream my name over and over. Everyone around him was shouting and he looked terrified.

I took Adolfo's bullet but he was still in pain.

Seeing that look on his face would stay with me forever. His dark eyes full of panic and fear.

I couldn't get his anguished screams out of my mind.

The strong man I knew changed into something else. He was just another human living a painful moment.

He was actually scared.

I've never seen Alessio scared before.

He was so broken. Tears poured down his angelic face and I felt his hands tremble as he held me.

Everything had happened so fast. I didn't expect the pain to come on so strongly.

I was just grateful for the dark that followed.

His eyes gave me comfort though. Despite the pain that was evident, it felt peaceful staring up at his pitch black eyes and feeling the warmth of his hands on me.

It felt like I was home for the last time.

I could feel myself drifting but I had been fighting to stay with him. I wanted to hang on for him.

Every part of me wanted to tell him it was okay and I loved him. I just couldn't seem to hold on any longer.

My timing had not been what I expected. I knew what was going on in that room but I wanted to help him.

I just wanted to see him and know he was okay. I didn't want our last kiss to really be a goodbye.

Yet...I was wrong.

It was my last night with him. I felt his lips for the final time. His warm fingers and soft skin. Heard his heartbeat and saw his beautiful, sculpted face before everything disappeared.

As I drifted away, I felt okay.

I didn't really feel scared to die anymore. It was time to accept it and I was just ready to let the pain go.

I would die in the arms of the man I loved.

I know I had felt as if I should've never pursued Alessio, but now I'm so grateful I did.

Seeing him that day in English had sealed our fate. I took the leap and I'm so glad that I did.

Alessio never really knew what love was supposed to be. He was subjected to such violence and darkness for years. He never had someone really love him.

I got to be that person.

He was only brought into this world to be a mold of Adolfo Romano. A man so sick in the head he was ready to kill all of his children.

A man who hunted down children to avenge his own pain.

In the end, he got what he wanted. He was the one to bring me down.

But... he didn't get what he wanted from Alessio.

Because he isn't just chaos and destruction. He's more than anyone could ever truly know.

Alessio always put his family first. He's gentle and kind. He has a great sense of humor and he lights up any room.

And I fell madly in love with him.

My time with him may have been cut short but I'm glad I had him while I did.

I just wish I wasn't trapped in my damn mind.

If this is death, it's already so fucking boring. What am I supposed to do forever?

Talk to myself.

I thought there would've been some kind of grand entrance to heaven. Everyone always talks about seeing some kind of white light.

There was nothing though. No bright light. No personal heaven.

One where I was with my parents again.

Giovanni would be there with Anna and Beto. Kimberly would be there...and Alessio would be waiting for me.

I'm going to miss them.

I wish I could've told my parents I loved them one more time. I wanted to let my dad know I forgave him for hiding his past.

I just wanted them to know I didn't do this to hurt them.

Then there's my best friend. Kimberly Simmons.

The loud-mouthed girl from down the road who took me under her wing immediately and showed me a whole new Olivia.

She showed me that I'm actually a really fun person. I like to party...so metimes too much.

She pushed me to find my confidence. She helped me accomplish things I would've never done alone.

Without her, my Senior year would've been a nightmare. I would've been so lost.

Maybe I would've distanced myself completely. I would've kept my head in the books the entire time and kept focused on Art school.

I would've probably had a mediocre life and maybe that would've been okay.

My life could've just been boring.

Yet, I'm not that kind of person at all. I crave excitement and adventure.

And a little danger.

Being part of Alessio's life was terrifying but it meant being close to him.

I lived as much as I could while I had the time.

"Olivia."

Woah! Maybe I won't be alone forever.

"Olivia..."

Who the hell is this?

"Please..."

Now this is getting weird...

"Wake up."

Aren't I dead?

"Her eyes moved." The voice says.

"Olivia...if you can hear me, follow my voice. I need you, baby."

Alessio? He's here?

Did he die?

"She looks so pale dude. Like a corpse."

"Giovanni! Seriously?"

What the hell...?

"My bad! I was just saying."

"Olivia...if you can hear me, it's mom. I love you so much, sweetie. Please wake up. Come back to us."

My mom's voice rings out.

"Bitch, if you make me raise this baby without you! Wake your dramatic ass up."

"F-fuck you, Kim..."

"There's my bitch!"

My eyelids flutter a little and I see a light overhead start to come into view. The ceiling above me is tall and the entire room looks to be white and blank.

"There she is!"

I try to move towards the voice and feel a wave of nausea rush over me.

Someone grabs onto me and helps hold me over a trash can as I puke my guts out into it. Giovanni's groans of disgust mirror my own retching.

"It's the medicine."

I nod a little and look up to find mom's face. Her blue eyes are gentle as she looks me over.

"W-what's wrong?" I struggle out. My throat feels dry and constricted.

"Do you remember what happened, baby?"

I think back to the horrific scene.

All the dead bodies in the room. Adolfo's gun aimed at Alessio.

The searing pain and the sounds of him screaming as I hit the ground. I could feel the warmth of my own blood as it seeped onto my shirt.

"Yes."

"You're okay,"She promises and reaches out to stroke my cheek. "The doctor's have been wonderful."

I peer around the room again and notice the massive windows on the left side next to us looking over a city.

"Where am I?" I ask and glance at the balloons and flowers at my bedside.

"San Diego Medical," Alessio interjects and steps closer. "I didn't want you in the clinic."

His voice comes out rough and he looks exhausted. There's dark circles under his black eyes and his hair is untamed.

As always, he's beautiful.

Even in his distressed state everything about him is as perfect as ever.

He studies my face for a moment and moves to sit at the edge of my bed. His muscular arms straining against his white tee.

"How are you?" He asks quietly.

"I'm not sure..."

His head bows, "I'm so fucking sorry, Olivia."

"Alessio..."I start and try to push myself up into a sitting position. "Please don't say that."

I continue on, "I was the one who made the choice to run in there."

He lifts his head a little. "I should've been quicker."

I sigh a little and lean back in the bed. I get a full view of everyone before us and feel my heart squeeze.

Giovanni, Anna, and Beto are all huddled together on the opposite end of the room. Kim and Joe even made it up here.

I spot my dad next to my mom and realize they are actually holding hands for the first time in a long time.

"You guys are...all okay?"

Giovanni laughs loudly. "Nothing takes us down."

"So...who is going to really fill me in here?"

I know my parents had been unfortunately thrown into the mafia drama, but Kim and Joe were completely clueless.

I wasn't entirely sure what they knew.

"Can I talk to Olivia?" Alessio asks them. "I'd also appreciate it if someone can let the nurse know she needs more medicine soon."

"Of course! We'll be back in a few hours," Mom says and reaches over to kiss my cheek. "I'm so glad you are up."

I smile back at her and look up to find my dad looking down at me.

"Liv..."He whispers and leans to rest his head to mine. "I know you have a lot of questions, I promise we'll talk."

"I know,"I squeeze him tight. "Just spend time with mom."

He stands back up and pulls her close to him. He kisses her firmly on the mouth and her cheeks redden quickly.

"I can't leave this one! Go find another." I tease them and he chuckles.

"We'll see you soon, hun."

I watch them exit and look back over at Kim and Joe.

"You have to stop this shit, Liv!" Kim gushes and tears pour down her cheeks. "Why are you getting involved with such crazy shit?"

"I-I don't know," I start and look at Alessio. He just shakes his head at me. "I'm sorry."

"Well, be careful! I need you through this pregnancy."

I eye Joe behind her. "She told you?"

He nods and a bright smile lights his face. "I can't wait to be a dad."

"You'll be great parents."

"You two are next," Kim winks.

"Stop!" I playfully bat at her and hear Alessio chuckle.

She wraps her arms around me and holds me close. "I was so scared, Olivia. I really am so glad you're okay."

"I know," I stroke her back. "We'll catch up and hang soon when I'm out."

She pulls back and holds my hands. "Love you, sweetie. We'll see you soon."

"Bye, Liv!" Joe calls out as they leave together.

Beto, Giovanni, and Anna decide to seize the moment and all three come hurrying over to the side of my bed.

I notice Anna first and realize her lip is busted up and she has a bit of a bruise.

"I'm so glad you all are okay."

Anna smiles down at me. "You were so brave."

I reach out and pull her in for a hug. Tears threatening to spill. " I'm so sorry for what happened."

"Don't be!" She laughs and looks at Giovanni. "Like he said, nothing takes us down."

He nods proudly and flexes his muscles for everyone to see.

"I'm glad you're okay," He knocks my shoulder gently. "I think I underestimated you."

"I'm full of surprises." I snort and look over at Beto.

For once, he doesn't have his dorky grin and sunglasses attached to him. He actually looks timid.

I don't think I've ever seen this side of him before. He looked so young and normal.

"Hey you."

I smile at him. "Sorry for all the trouble.

"You trouble?" He snickers. "A piece of cake."

"Alright," Alessio interjects and wraps his arm around me. "She needs to rest."

They all three lean in to give me a quick hug before turning to leave. I watch after them as they exit the room before realizing I'm finally alone with Alessio.

I lean back a little in the hospital bed and nervously look at my hands.

I could feel shame washing over me and I didn't know what to say.

"Talk to me."He says after a moment. "Not knowing what you are thinking is driving me insane."

"I'm sorry."

He says nothing, instead he pulls me to him and crushes his mouth with mine. His hands cup my face in them and I feel his thumb trace my lower lip.

I kiss him back just as hard and for a moment it feels like the first time. Electricity is running through me and my hands can't stop touching him.

I trace the curves of his biceps and feel his fingers run carefully along the edge of my waist.

My head swims from our embrace and I feel myself floating.

"Okay,"He pulls away a little. "I know you have questions for me."

"What even happened? After...after I was sho-"

He kisses me again. "Don't say it."

"Okay,"I say against him. "What happened to Adolfo?"

He sighs and looks out towards the sun setting through the window. The long shadows casting against his high cheekbones.

"He's dead."

I stare at him. "Did you kill him?"

"No."He looks back at me with his voice free of any emotion. " Michele did it."

"He did?"

"Yes, he was behind you with Robin. As soon as you went down Adolfo was distracted so Michele shot him in the chest. I was too focused on trying to keep you awake."

I reach for his hand. "I'm sorry, Alessio. I should've thought before I ran in there."

"You're alive, Olivia. That's all I care about." He squeezes my fingers.

"What about everything else? What all really happened?"

"Kim and Joe know nothing about the mafia, but they do think you got involved in a drunken altercation between myself and Tobias. I told them he had some problems and tried to attack us."

"He's dead too?"

"Yes,"He nods. "I killed him right away. They're both gone, Olivia, I won't ever let anyone hurt you again."

"It isn't your fault for what happened. I just didn't know my dad was involved."

He holds my face in his hands. "I have no hate towards you or your family."

"You have every right, Alessio." I cross my arms around my knees. "I'll never understand why you picked me. Apparently, I'm just cursed."

"No you're not!" He argues. "I'm offended you'd even say that."

"Whatever!" I tease and playfully bat at his chest. He grabs onto my hands and holds them there.

"What?"

He continues to stare down at me and his eyes roam over my face. A little smile playing on the corners of his lips.

"Are you going to say anything?" I roll my eyes.

His grip tightens around me and he pulls me close. His lips tickle the edge of my jaw.

"I love you so much, Olivia."

I melt into him and smile. "I love you too, Alessio."

"Listen," He pulls back and strokes my cheek. "I want to turn this day into a happy one."

"What do you mean?"

He doesn't respond, instead he stands up from the bed and fishes something from his pocket. He holds the tiny black box in his hand and looks down at me nervously.

"What are you doing?" I glare at him.

He knows I hate surprises.

"Stand up."

I look stupidly down at the floor. "Why?"

"Just do it." He laughs and helps me to my feet.

I push up from the bed and stumble a little. I almost felt like a toddler learning how to walk with how weird my legs felt.

Alessio notices my expression.

"It's just the medicine." He reassures me. "You've been out for a few days so it'll take time."

"Did you just say a few days?" I gasp.

"About six actually. You were in a medically induced coma to help you heal love."

"Oh my god." I breathe out and look at the room. "I can't believe I was out for almost a week."

"It's fine, baby. Focus on me." He says and pulls me to him. "How much do you love me?"

"Obviously a lot."

"How much is a lot?" He teases.

"A LOT," I snort and kiss him. "Why are you asking? You should know."

"I want to ask you something." He starts and pulls my hand to his cheek. "I want you to stay open-minded and listen. I'm nervous as hell right now."

I stare up at him terrified. "W-what?"

He wastes no more time and lowers down onto one knee. He holds the box in front of him and keeps my hand in his.

"I know I move fast and I know I've scared you with this before." He takes a deep breath. "I've never been so sure about something, Olivia. I love you more than you can imagine and I never want to lose you."

My breath catches in my throat. "I-I..."

"I want you to marry me more than anything. Will you please do me the honor of being my wife? Will you marry me, Olivia Moore?"

He smiles up at me and waits. I can feel his fingers shaking in my hand but can't focus on anything other than my own heart pounding in my chest.

"I need to sit."

"Of course," He stands and leads me to the bed. "Do you want some water?"

"Please." I gasp and rest my hands on my knees.

He grabs the water bottle from the table next to us and hands it over. I gulp it down quickly and feel my throat relax a little from the liquid.

"Sorry...I just needed a moment." I apologize and put it down.

"Take your time."

"Okay." I smile at him. "Continue."

He pulls my face towards him and kisses me softly. "Do you want to marry me, Olivia Moore?"

I stare up into his dark eyes and feel myself being sucked in. I want him more than anything.

He has me forever.

I'm his.

"Yes."

He blinks and stares at me confused.

"Excuse me?"

"What?" I frown at him. "I said, yes!"

"You'll marry me?"

"I'd love to be your wife, Alessio. Yes, I'll marry you."

Before any more time passes by he scoops me up in his arms and presses his lips to me in our heated embrace. Time seems to slow down as we hold one another.

Everything felt so surreal. I wasn't sure if this was reality anymore.

"To our future," Alessio begins and slides a massive diamond rock onto my finger. "My soon-to-be bride."

Our hands fold to one another and I kiss him once more.

I felt everything in that kiss.

Pain, love, desire, and loss.

Nothing can change how I feel about Alessio.

I found all odds and in the end...

I won.

www.ingramcontent.com/pod-product-compliance
Lightning Source LLC
Chambersburg PA
CBHW070426170726
48291CB00002B/383